Hidden Wings

ANA RAINE

Published by
DREAMSPINNER PRESS

5032 Capital Circle SW, Suite 2, PMB# 279, Tallahassee, FL 32305-7886 USA
www.dreamspinnerpress.com

This is a work of fiction. Names, characters, places, and incidents either are the product of author imagination or are used fictitiously, and any resemblance to actual persons, living or dead, business establishments, events, or locales is entirely coincidental.

Hidden Wings
© 2016 Ana Raine.

Cover Art
© 2016 Anne Cain.
annecain.art@gmail.com
Cover content is for illustrative purposes only and any person depicted on the cover is a model.

ISBN: 978-1-63476-750-7
Digital ISBN: 978-1-63476-751-4
Library of Congress Control Number: 2015950527
Published January 2016
v. 1.0

Printed in the United States of America
∞

This paper meets the requirements of
ANSI/NISO Z39.48-1992 (Permanence of Paper).

To Thomas, for always letting me talk through my story ideas, even when we both get headaches. And to everyone at Dreamspinner Press for giving me a chance to work with them.

CHAPTER ONE

I COULD smell the excitement reeking from their pores, and it made me sick with fear. Was this the time I wouldn't get to the trees in time? Joel and Zain were on the patrol schedule with me, and in the thirteen years we had served as guards to the Dryma fairies, our masters, we had yet to slip up.

The same could not be said for all of our kind, because there had been plenty of mess-ups due to a simple case of negligence. The dreary cold Canadian wilderness did nothing to boost our strength because by nature, swans were meant to be in warmer climates.

A familiar ache formed between my shoulder blades, and I longed to feel the pressure of wings bursting from my bones. To hear the incessant flapping against my back and to feel my feet lift from the stale ground. What I wouldn't give to feel the flight my relatives spoke about as if they were reliving a dream.

I could scarcely remember what my life was like with wings before they'd retreated back into the marrow of my bone. Before my kind had become servants to the Dryma.

The flapping of wings above me diverted my attention as the birds taunted me with their continued flight.

Zain, where are you? I asked.

My friend of twenty-six years could not initiate a telepathic conversation, much to his dismay. Only a few Kuro swans had retained the trait.

There was a knot forming at the base of my neck, like he was trying to split my skull open. *By the north border. Where the fuck is Joel?*

I pulled my hat down over my ears to keep the chill from dulling my hearing. According to the humans, the weather was relatively tepid, and on my way to the nature reserve, I had even spotted humans sporting shorts and spring jackets. But the weather was never going to be warm enough for me.

You're telling me. This weather is ridiculous. Can't we just close the park down or something until it gets warmer?

I hadn't realized my thoughts were still channeling to his. *Don't I wish.*

As if the Dryma would ever allow such foolishness. I imagined death himself would show more kindness to his victims than the Dryma fairies showed us. Before I knew it, I was racing through the forest, motivated by my fear of the Dryma.

I rounded the bend, my foot catching on a protruding stone and making me stumble. Just before falling to the ground, I caught myself and, despite the burning pain in the sole of my foot, continued to run. Even though I'd been protecting the trees of the Pasky Nature Reserve since I was fourteen, my lungs and legs had never become accustomed to the constant running. Most of us were tall and very slender, just as swans should be. Sometimes I wished I could have some more muscle so I could get through the woods in one piece.

My gun clacked against my hip, reminding me of the wildlife threat. I did a quick look around before diving into the woods. The lake was behind me, the water beckoning me to forget my duty and come swimming into its depths.

I could hear Joel's similar longing.

Stay focused, I ordered.

Yes, Kanji.

Joel was as optimistic and obedient as Zain was pessimistic and defiant, but I wouldn't have traded their friendship for anything. I wasn't sure how long I'd been running from the south border, but I saw the sign signaling mile marker nine. Whoever these kids were, they'd certainly deviated from the suggested beginner trail. It was going to take everything in me to not rip their heads off.

I caught the scent of alcohol and heard a high-pitched giggle before I broke into the clearing. Joel wasn't there yet, but he was close. I could hear the beat of his heart.

Clearing my throat, I slowed my steps and took a moment to brush my shoulder-length hair back into a ponytail so I looked less frightening. With pitch-black hair and pale skin, I often frightened the tourists enjoying the park. I figured my height probably had something to do with that too.

"Can I help you?" I asked, regaining my voice as I assessed the scene. All of the Kuro swans that were old enough to be on protection duty had specific trees, which they knew they had to guard, but unfortunately the trees were scattered into different groups amongst the nine miles of wilderness.

There were three teenagers on the ground circled around a fire that was nowhere near up to code. One of the teens had his hair cropped short and so much ink I wasn't sure what the tats were even supposed to be. The other two teens, a boy and girl, were encircled together. The beer cans were scattered about the ground, and the girl was naked save for a pair of underwear.

But none of that mattered because to humans, I was nothing more than a ranger, someone they didn't need to fear. Despite my very human title, I needed to protect the tree they were encroaching.

The girl covered her mouth and giggled violently as she tried to stand up. The other teenage guy who wasn't her boyfriend took hold of her hand and tried to help her, but she kept stumbling. Judging by her flushed face and her swaying body, she was flat-out drunk.

After running nearly three miles in fifteen minutes because of the threat I felt to the tree, I had only encountered this?

There had to be something I was missing….

Carved into the tree near the base of the trunk were words, names I presumed belonged to the teenagers. The offending weapon was a cheap hunting knife sticking out of the dirt. I crossed the space between us and grasped the knife so I could pull it from the earth.

The guy with the tattoos stared at me open-mouthed and I thought he was trying to form words, but I just heard babbling sounds. I ran my thumb along the blade before shutting the knife and pocketing it. I would need to keep the weapon as proof I wasn't too late in case the Dryma fairies pitched a fit.

"You do know it is illegal to harm any of the trees here?" I asked, struggling to keep my voice even.

They had a half-cocked tent, and through the trees, I could see their jeep. They were obviously not native to the land, which meant their offense could've been all that much worse. The Dryma were not forgiving when we failed in our duty to protect, as evidenced by the scars on my back.

"What's the problem, man?" the teenager still on the ground slurred. His shirt was unbuttoned, revealing tanned skin. If anything made me hate him more, it was seeing he obviously came from somewhere warm.

A chill ran down my spine as a particularly nasty bout of wind whistled through the trees right before Joel and Zain joined me.

"The problem, man," Zain sneered, "is that this isn't the designated zone for fires. And these trees are protected."

Zain had short dark hair he was constantly dying vibrant colors. For the past couple weeks, he had light blue and purple streaked through his hair. Joel was more conservative with his light brown hair parted neatly on the side and well kept. Both of them wore the same pale green and brown ranger uniforms we were required to have.

Beneath our gloves was the mark the Dryma fairies had placed on our wrists, a seal we would take to our graves.

"Sorry guys," the teenage guy with the short hair said as he stood up and brushed off his khaki pants. Out of the three of them, he seemed the one most likely to come to his senses. Extending his hand, he fumbled to help the girl to her feet. "We'll just head back now."

"Why do we have to leave?" the girl whimpered as she leaned on her boyfriend for support, her head lolling back.

"Because we're not supposed to be here."

The guy with the tattoos looked like he was going to put up a fight and said, "I don't want to leave. There's no sign or anything."

His friend seemed to have all the sense. "Billy, let's just get out of here. There's three of them, and I have to help Katy keep standing."

I noticed Billy's knuckles were bruised, so he was clearly prone to getting into fights.

"Probably a good idea to follow your friend's advice, Billy," I agreed, straightening to my full height.

He backed away, grabbing their equipment as they went until there were only the beer cans left over.

The sober friend luckily got behind the wheel, and then they peeled away from the scene, leaving a trail of dust in their wake.

"Well that was shitty of them," Zain coughed as he kicked a beer can before sighing and deciding to pick it up. "Where the hell is Micky anyway?"

Joel kneeled down next to the tree and ran his fingers over the words etched into its flesh. "Probably sleeping somewhere. Poor kid never does at home."

Leave it to Joel to think the best of people.

To be honest, part of the reason I always tried to help cover Micky's shifts was because he had just turned fifteen and I remembered how unfair I thought life was back when I started. The last thing I wanted to do was become tied to some tree because Dryma fairies told me I had to.

"I'm here."

I spun around and saw Micky take a step out of the cover of the woods, guilt on his face. He had one of those faces that made you want to bend over backward to help him, and god only knew how much of a heartbreaker he'd be when he grew up.

If he grew up, I amended.

"Where were you?" Zain growled as he played with a strand of blue hair until I thought he was going to pull it straight out of his head. He was only twenty-seven, just a year older than me, but he'd taken on a lot of responsibility and as a result, he looked older.

Not that we aged like humans did. In ten years, I'd probably only look a year older, so I could easily pass for being twenty, which was kind of creepy at times.

"I got lost," Micky admitted as he kicked a pebble with the toe of his scuffed boot. He was rather short, so the uniform was ill fitting on him. If it weren't for the gun at his belt, the humans would've thought he was a kid impersonating his father.

"Sure you did."

"Just leave him alone," Joel whispered as he stood back up and began to collect beer cans. "Help me out, Micky, so we can go home for the day. Night shift starts soon."

Micky crouched unmoving on his perch by the clearing, looking like he was ready to run if need be.

"The tree is fine," I remarked, giving it a once-over. "They won't punish you."

The kid didn't look convinced, but the promise of food and going home for the day made him jump down so he could collect the cans with Joel. We checked the perimeters while we waited for our patrol to be relieved and then made our way back to the nature center where our car was.

Because of our dark hair and dark eyes, the Kuro swans passed as Native Canadians. So the fact we lived clustered together like a tribe didn't put us on the radar with the humans and made it easier for us to serve. The problem was in order to get to our ramshackle houses on the highway, we had to pass the several gated communities nestled in the woods where the fairies lived.

Zain climbed into the driver's seat of his yellow truck while I gathered the schoolbooks from the passenger's seat and went to pass them back to Micky, but saw he wasn't in the car yet.   "Where's Micky?" I asked Joel, who pointed out the window.

There were small ponds scattered throughout the wilderness, some dangerously close to the road. Standing beside a small splash of water that could hardly be called a pond was Micky. He had his hands in his pockets and was staring at a white swan. Its feathers had been matted and dirtied to the point where it was more brown than white.

"What's he doing?" Zain grumbled.

I quickly scanned his thoughts and wondered whether or not I should voice them. When Zain grumbled in discontent, I quickly explained. "He's wondering what it would be like to be able to transform into a swan again."

Joel shuffled nervously in his seat. His voice was small. "Kanji, if we ever got our wings back, would transforming completely even be possible? Our magic has been kept from us for so long…"

"I don't know."

If Micky hadn't turned around and shuffled to the car, I would've retrieved him just so I could stop seeing the forlorn look on his face.

"Take these." I handed Micky the books after he'd climbed into the jeep.

"What's the point?" Zain asked as he jacked up the heat. Shivering, I dug in the glove box for a packet of hand warmers and basked in the small offering of heat. The summers were bearable, although nowhere near as warm as we wanted it to be, but the cool September weather was killer.

"Don't listen to him," Joel said as he dug through a well-worn copy of a romance novel with a girl standing beside an ocean on the cover. "One day you'll be able to go to college."

Zain started to refute the claim, but I shot him a look. The words died on his tongue, and he muttered something incoherent. Eventually, Micky thumbed through the schoolbooks. He'd be homeschooled and get his GED, but then he'd be a protector until he was old enough to retire.

"What do you think they're doing?" Micky said excitedly as he pressed his hands against the glass and stared enviously at the bright decorative lights above the fairy mansions.

"Beats me," Zain commented, fiddling with the heat and pulling off his gloves.

"They've got to be doing something," Micky persisted. "Look at all those lights."

The fairies lived in their mansions, and some of them even worked alongside humans as CEOs, bankers, and investors. Before coming to the human world, they had lived in a parallel world that I'd been told was beautiful beyond imagination. They'd only come to this world seeking freedom and expansion, but because they needed nature to survive, they had only succeeded in becoming prisoners in another world.

And now they could never leave.

Because they needed to be so close to their trees, the majority of the Dryma Fairies lived within their gated communities and only left to go to the woods when they held events and festivals.

Or when they wanted to fly.

The bitter reminder came back to my shoulder blades and made my head feel heavy. "They're having a ball," I told him.

"How do you know that?" Micky asked.

"What do you mean?" Joel scoffed. "He's our prince—"

"Don't." I cut him off, the ache in my neck decreasing slightly. "Not anymore I'm not. Just let it go."

"Never," Zain gripped the steering wheel so tightly his knuckles turned white.

I gave him a pat on the shoulder and resumed looking at the mansions. I would never admit it, but I always wondered what the insides were like. Because of my bloodline as former prince of the Kuro swans, the fairy guard always seemed to seek me out. When someone needed to be punished, they'd find me. When they needed extra protection or servants, they'd find me. And when they were angry, they'd definitely find me.

It was exhausting as hell.

So the idea of living in a private little world with indoor swimming pools sounded pretty damn good.

"A ball for what?" Micky asked as the last of the lights disappeared from sight and we neared our town.

"One of the princes is having a birthday or something," I muttered. "There's seven of them, so I can't keep them straight, but I think it's the youngest."

"Have you ever seen them?"

"The royals? No way," Joel exclaimed. "The guards come here when they need us."

"But Max said when they go to the woods…."

"Max needs to never repeat that," Zain warned him, a dangerous edge clinging to his voice. "Got it?"

Micky nodded, and then there was only the sound of turning pages until we reached our community. To call what we lived in houses was an insult to the name because most of them were more like glorified mobile homes. As the former prince, I had an actual house, but my aunt and uncle lived with me. After retiring, a Kuro swan wasn't allowed to guard the trees anymore, but they couldn't leave either. So without having any income or job, the elders tended to die quickly from lack of purpose.

At least my aunt and uncle continued to fight after my parents gave up. Zain parked next to my dusty blue sedan. "See you guys later."

Joel and Micky argued about who got to sit in the front while Zain asked, "Are you coming later?"

"Yes, I'll be there," I promised, swinging my heavy workbag over my shoulder. I had left it in the car during my shift, but it contained spare clothes and an extra coat if the weather deemed it necessary.

"Be where? What's going on?" Micky stopped fighting, and Joel took advantage of the moment to jump into my abandoned seat.

"Never you mind," Zain snapped as he waved to me. "Later."

I could still hear Micky and Zain arguing as the car left a trail of dust behind. The house smelled like arrowroot pasta and vegetables, which made my stomach constrict with hunger. I hadn't eaten anything for hours because there simply hadn't been time.

"Kanji, there you are. You're late."

"There was an incident as we were leaving." I shoved my coat and bag into the too small closet. "Nothing to worry about."

My aunt leaned in the doorframe between the kitchen and the hallway. In her hand, she absently spun a wooden spoon while she tapped her foot against the hardwood. My aunt Catarina was the kind of Kuro swan men would've flocked to in the hopes she would look back at them, but years of warmth deprivation and captivity had dulled her features so much that when I looked at younger pictures of her and my mother, I hardly recognized her.

Still, even though her hair was much shorter than she had kept it before, it was a rich black. Her prolonged life made her wrinkles less severe than they would've been otherwise, and human women would've killed to look like her at eighty.

"Your uncle is downstairs resting." She spoke with a smile, but I saw the worry on her face. When Kuro swans mated, they mated for life, and just knowing her mate wasn't faring well made her sick. It was part of the reason I didn't actively seek out a mate.

Male and female Kuro flocked to my house often, sensing my leadership in their blood. But their efforts didn't matter; the truth was I had yet to find my mate.

"Mari called and wants to come over later," she said as she adjusted her sweater so her wrists were completely covered. "I went ahead and told her it was fine."

"Why?" I stacked my shoes by the door and headed toward the stairs. I'd told them they could have the upstairs room and bathroom, but they'd insisted I have it. "I'll be going out later."

My aunt called up to me, "And where will you be going? Don't tell me you have to go back on patrol?"

"No." I paused at the top of the stairs just long enough to finish my sentence. "I have a meeting."

She made an annoyed groan but knew better than to ask. The few times she had, the answers she'd received were far from what she wanted to hear. When there was talk of peace and freedom, then she might be willing to listen.

I shut my door with a click and tried to ignore the nagging suspicion telling me I should go see my uncle. Usually, I would have before even taking my shoes off, but today was different.

Between the extreme chill that had come out of nowhere and the stupid kids defiling the tree, I was at my limit. I felt like complete shit, and the "meeting" loomed ahead of me like the disfigured trees they made us protect.

But all those things I could deal with. Hadn't I come to terms with my fate years ago when I'd tried to escape and had been dragged back by a faceless Dryma wielding a whip? I could still feel the sting between my shoulder blades where I thought he was trying to dig the remnants of my wings from my bones.

No... what I felt wasn't the anguish for myself. It was for Micky and the other youth like him. I peeled my shirt from my sticky skin, turned the space heater on full blast, and collapsed onto my bed. Having seen Micky's startled face when he saw a tree with carved words, something no ordinary human would bother caring about, scared me more than I liked to admit. The fear had been raw and wild in his eyes, the same look I'd stopped seeing in my own eyes shortly after my seventeenth birthday. Two years... that was how long it took me to come to acceptance.

My aunt rattled her spoon on the handrail to signal dinner was done. I hunted through my drawers for a warm sweater and pulled it over my head, but the chill was still there. If I could help it, I would never mate. I would never willingly put another Kuro swan through the same hell I felt.

THERE WAS nothing wrong with Mari and as far as Kuro females went; she was considerate and had empathy extending far past the norm. The Dryma fairies at least allowed our females to stay at home, but my guess was they only did so because they thought the females would be useless.

I had no doubt Mari could've held her own in the woods if she were given the chance. I knew her eyes perfectly because shortly after I'd started protection duty, I'd tried to mate with her. I stared at the blues and purples and greens of her eyes for so long, my eyes felt like they were going to pop out of my head. Nothing came of my staring except for the fact that she was convinced we were mates.

"Must you go already?" my aunt asked as she wiped her hands on her paper napkin before crumpling it into a ball and setting it beside her still full bowl. She'd taken a bowl of food down to my uncle but had come up shortly after, food in hand.

"Where do you have to go?" Mari inquired, curling strands of her hair around her pinkie finger. I could tell Mari had been into town because I could smell the scent of human males clinging to her skin. With her large eyes and beautiful dark hair cascading like waves to her waist, there was no denying she was stunning. Male Kuro swans and humans gathered around her, and I was sure if a Dryma saw her, he would've been smitten.

"They're going to be there at eight," I told my aunt as I rinsed my plate in the sink before shoving my phone into my pocket and retrieving my coat.

"Be careful," my aunt warned me in the same flat, dead tone she'd been using for years.

I had just finished lacing my boots when Mari met me in the hallway, her own coat pulled over her shoulders. "I'm going with you."

I squinted at her. "Why would you want to come? What makes you think they would even let you?"

She shook out her hair and gave me an indifferent look. "Makes no difference to me what they think. Just let me come with you."

"I can't," I said firmly as I slid a pair of gloves into my pockets and marched to the front door. I heard her at my heels.

"Tell them I'm your mate," she said, her voice hollow with longing. "Then they'll be okay with it."

I groaned inwardly. "But you're not and they would know."

Mari placed her soft hands on my shoulder and spun me around so she could look up into my face. I realized I had been seeing her but not really looking. Her cheeks were sunken, and there were thick dark circles underneath her eyes. Her ever-luscious hair was thick and long but lacked the bright sheen I was accustomed to seeing.

"We're dying," she said flatly, tightening her grip on my upper arm. Despite being taller, I was more slender than her and unable to shake free. "Tell them we need to be around the sun and maybe they'll let us."

I laughed. "You think we can plead with them and they'll let us go down south for a vacation?"

"We don't have to go all at once. There are more than enough of us who can stay and guard the trees while the other half goes. Then we could...."

Gently, I detached her hand from my shoulder and placed her arm at her side. "We're tied to the earth just as surely as they are, so there's no feasible way we could leave. And you're right about there being more than enough of us, and that's what the Dryma are counting on. If we actually all started to die they might care, but until then...."

Her voice was dead. "Until then nothing will change." The wind whipped my hair around my face and pierced my skin through my clothes. Standing on her toes, she pressed her lips to my cheek, the action demanding. "How long have we known each other?"

"Forever," I answered automatically.

"Then why do you refuse me? I could be everything you need in a mate."

"We've been through this," I pointed out. "I don't feel the pull."

"Then how can I?" she countered, her voice vicious.

I knew the action would appear heartless, but all the same, I shrugged. "I don't know why you feel it, but I don't."

"There is no one else for you to mate to," she snapped, crossing her arms over her chest. "Unless you happen to find a human lover."

"Many of us have yet to find our mates."

Mari gave me an evil smile. "Which could mean only females are feeling the pull."

If Zain hadn't pulled up behind us honking the horn like a deranged murderer, Mari might've tried to kiss me. She was right about there being a lack of mating rituals taking place, but maybe that was for the best. Did I really want to bring a child into this sick world where they would never know the feel of wind through their wings?

"I have to go," I replied, my throat dry. "Go back inside and stay warm."

Dragging my eyes from her face, I made my way to Zain's car and refused to look back. I knew the only thing I would see in her eyes was a pile of accusations at how weak I was. After slamming the door, I fastened my seatbelt. Zain gave me a quizzical look.

"Everything okay?"

"Yep, just drive. We're going to be late."

Joel made a noise from the back to signal he agreed, and then we were plowing our way down the road and away from Mari.

"What was she doing at your house?"

"Same old, same old," I replied, smoothing my hair down and trying to get it to stay on one side. Above all else, Dryma prided themselves on beauty and grace, so we had to do our best to meet their expectations.

"Why won't you just mate with her, man?" Zain asked, flicking his fingers through his blue hair. "She's pretty."

"And kind," Joel volunteered.

"And not my mate," I threw back. "Guys, how many times do we have to go over this?" Without meaning to, I sent my thoughts to them about what she'd said. A wave of silence filled the car before Zain broke it.

"Well, shit, I never thought about that. If only females can choose mates now, who's to say ours isn't freezing to death in one of those shacks right now?"

I turned up the heat. "We have to focus and worry about mates later."

To respect their privacy, I made an effort to stay out of their heads, but I was also afraid to hear what they really thought of me. The same things Mari had been telling me with her eyes could easily be how they felt.

Christophe Olen was the captain of the Dryma guard, but he was also the owner of the Crystal Cove Dance Club. Whenever I walked inside, it was easy to forget the place wasn't just for Dryma fairies because the walls and doors were decorated like something right out of a castle. With glittering double doors leading into the club, a full dance room complete with mirrors, and then an upper floor for private parties, the Crystal Cove was never empty.

Zain muttered under his breath because we had to park far away and brave the cold to get into the club. "Why can't we use valet parking?" He slammed his door and wrapped his coat more tightly around himself.

Joel and I exchanged a glance but were too cold and nervous to speak. I knew that once we got into the club and were led upstairs into the private room, most of my efforts would be spent making sure Zain didn't say anything that would lead to him being punished.

Still, there was no one else I would've rather had by my side.

We sidestepped a few human girls clustered together in miniskirts and leather jackets. I saw a blonde appraising Zain, her eyes settling on his blue-and-purple-streaked black hair. I wasn't surprised she would focus on him, not when his broad shoulders and defined arms gave him the appearance of being both strong and caring.

Zain noticed the girl and gave a half nod. "Hey, how ya doing?"

That was all it ever took for a human girl to be smitten by him. I didn't blame him for clinging to whatever he could of his heritage, even if that something was extreme sex appeal. Sometimes I wondered if mine was broken because I never noticed people looking at me the way they gazed at Zain.

"Later," I reminded Zain patiently as we pushed past the girls waiting outside and made our way to the front.

"Why did he choose a Saturday night to meet?" Joel asked nervously as we continued to push past the throng of people to the bouncer at the front. The air was brutal and whizzed through my clothes, chilling me to the bone. "He never summons us on the weekend."

Probably the prince's birthday needs extra protection or something, I channeled to them. *Let's just get this over with.*

Although the Crystal Cove was mainly a club for humans, sometimes there were fairies within the glittering walls. I could never figure out why Christophe had bothered with the club because I knew all Dryma had more than their fair share of money. I got the impression he tired of the sedentary lifestyle most of the Dryma experienced locked behind their fancy gates, which made sense considering he was the most violent fairy I'd ever met.

The space between my shoulders ached in reminder of how miserable he could make me if he wanted to.

When we finally made our way to the front, the bouncer completely ignored us so he could browse through his tablet. I cleared my throat and looked into the eyes of a new Dryma fairy I hadn't seen working there before.

"Can I help you?" he asked, a bored tone in his voice. Determining age was practically impossible because like us, Dryma fairies tended to not age past what a human would gauge as thirty. He had his blond hair pulled back into a ponytail, and his glittering blue eyes gazed at me intensely.

He took a deep breath, inhaling my scent, and a wave of realization washed over him as he recognized what we were. His eyes flitted from me to Zain and then finally to Joel. In the club, he could pretend his shimmery skin was just due to the light, but I knew better. The same healthy glow that we were supposed to have was clear as day on his skin.

Contrary to popular belief about fairies, they were not a bunch of twinks with delicate wings. As evidenced by the tall, redheaded man heading toward us. A hush swept across the floor and the new bouncer nervously checked his tie. Female Dryma stared at him appreciatively, but looked away before he could call them out on their staring.

Christophe's neck was corded with muscle, his broad chest demanding the attention of everyone in the room and his accusing eyes keeping every human at a distance.

He was wearing a tight button-down shirt with the sleeves rolled up past his elbow and a pair of dark jeans that hugged his legs. In spite of my hatred for the Dryma in front of me, I was also disgusted with myself for thinking he was beautiful.

Absolutely not.

"Don't worry, Marvin, I'll take them upstairs."

The newbie, Marvin, nodded in agreement and then turned back to his tablet before signaling a group of guys lazing beside the bathroom door.

"You're earlier than expected," Christophe said with distaste dripping from his voice. He raised his hand to alert his favorite two guards, Ivan and Seth. They were both fairly similar to Christophe's build, but they had their hair cut short so it barely made it to their ears. At their hips was a slight bulge where I knew they kept their whips.

I shuddered at the thought and urged Joel up the narrow staircase before following. The music was loud and drifted up into the private room, but was muted enough for us to be able to hear.

Ivan locked the door behind us before he and Seth settled into plush chairs at the front of the room. Christophe lifted a pitcher of something from the table and poured himself a glass as he stared out the large bay window offering the glittering view of trees and the night sky.

I could feel Zain's irritation beside me because he wanted to sit down too, and he wanted some of that alcohol Christophe was drinking with relish. Of course, we weren't offered any.

When he'd downed his second glass, I took a hesitant step forward and ran my hand through my hair in an attempt to tame it. "Is there something in particular that you would like us to tell you about?"

Ivan raised his eyebrows at my boldness but didn't say anything. He crossed his legs and leaned back on the couch. Out of the Dryma guards, I liked Seth the best because of his quiet, reserved nature. Protecting the trees was crucial to the fairies' survival, so naturally they were tense about the forest at all times. But more than once, Seth was known to take it easy on the younger Kuro swans who slipped up.

Seth was also one of the more beautiful fairies I'd seen, although he didn't drip with sex appeal the way Christophe did. Today he seemed on edge as he kept checking his phone and then straightening his shirt with the open collar, exposing his creamy throat.

"Prince Tristan's birthday is quickly approaching," Christophe started, not bothering to turn around. Faintly, I could see his face in the dark glass. "I expect you to have doubled protection in the forest."

"Done."

"There is more," Christophe said, stopping me in my tracks. "The party is a week from today, on a Saturday."

"We know what day it—"

Roughly, I nudged Zain in the ribs to shut him up. I felt the anger dripping from his body, but he smartly didn't say anything else.

Christophe finally turned to face us, his expression wary. I wasn't used to seeing him nervous, so I was instantly on alert. "There will be… visitors attending this party. The Prince of the Sidhee and a small guard of his choosing will be coming from their world to visit us."

I thought Joel's eyes were going to bulge from his skull, and I could feel the same anxiety tearing holes through Zain. I struggled to keep my voice even. "The Prince of the Sidhee?"

Although the ones keeping our wings held captive were the Dryma Fairies, we could never forget or forgive the Sidhee for tricking us. When we had offered our wings, we'd been afraid of the Sidhee and had only met them in our swan forms. But they had coaxed us into shifting into our human form, and with magic I didn't quite understand, they had bound our wings and given us to the Dryma.

"Yes," Christophe said tiredly. "They will be leaving their world and as expected, they must be presented with a soul before leaving or they will be barred from reentering."

Kuro swans had once been friends with the Sidhee and had offered their wings in service when the soul stealers needed to come to the human world. I tried to make sense of what Christophe was saying and stuttered a response. "Y-you, I mean, you can't expect us to steal a soul for them."

Christophe played with the buttons of his immaculately tidy shirt. "No, I do not. I simply expect you to deliver this." He reached into his pocket and produced a white envelope sprinkled with colorful flowers. "They will be arriving the night before the party on the south side of the forest. You will meet them there and present them with this. Afterwards, you will escort them to the Castle De Mar. The envelope contains instructions so should they have questions, they will know who to consult with."

I swallowed, my lungs dying from a lack of oxygen. "May I ask why you are not meeting them yourselves?"

Christophe stared at me for so long I thought he was going to tell me to go to hell and reach for the whip looped through his belt. To my surprise, he said, "Ivan, Seth, why don't you go downstairs and see if Nicolai needs some help. I'm sure Kanji won't mind speaking to me... alone."

Zain tensed beside me, but I gave him a nod. Sensing they didn't have much of a choice, Joel and Zain followed the two guards from the room, the door swinging shut with a soft click.

The music floated up the stairs, and the scent of fried food wafted through the floorboards. I rubbed my sweaty hands on my pants and waited for the assault to begin, just like it always did.

"Did you know the Dryma fairies have a long history of deception and trickery?"

My jaw clenched. "I can imagine so."

"So naturally, we would decide to host a masked ball to celebrate one of our great prince's birth."

"I suppose it does seem fitting."

"Your kind are not the only ones averse to forming an alliance with the Sidhee. The Sidhee knew what would happen to us when we came to the human world, but did nothing to stop us. They then gave us your lives in exchange for letting them have as many souls as they like when they come to the human world. It is a degrading, humiliating life.

"Having a masked ball where my kind can congregate without fear is the perfect way to introduce the Prince of the Sidhee into our community without opposition." Christophe paused to pour himself another drink from the crystal pitcher before taking a step toward me. He took a swig of the drink and then set it down on the table. As he circled me, I could smell his cologne mixed with the alcohol on his breath. "Sidhee can be ruthless and tend to regard all life as little more than rungs of a ladder."

"So why unite with them?"

Christophe parted my hair with his hand so my neck was exposed, my silky strands falling just above my shoulder. He trailed his hands down my back, resting on my shoulder blades and gently manipulating the muscle so a forced relief washed through me. "Kanji, you should know what it can take to survive."

I flinched as he snaked one of his hands around my stomach and pushed his cool fingers up underneath my shirt and jacket so he could touch my skin. "So you need the Sidhee now?"

"Everything is changing," Christophe whispered in my ear. "Your lives are tied to the trees just as surely as ours are. So why not stop pretending? I can feel your power in every breath you take. With every movement you make, you are trying to maintain control."

"That's not true."

"You were born to be a prince," he said softly, stroking my abdomen and working his way up to my chest. "Your father was tricked by the Sidhee, and yet you bear the burden for him. You don't even know what occurred."

"I don't need to," I spat. "The fact they betrayed us is enough."

Christophe made an indifferent noise before wrapping his other hand around my neck and tangling my hair in his fingers so I was trapped. "What do I have to do to get you to give in? I can provide for you, give you things that would make even Dryma fairies jealous. All you have to do is become mine."

"Become your slave, you mean," I said coldly, bumping my shoulder upward in an effort to disentangle myself. His fingers tightened in response, and my fragile bones dared to crack if he pressed much harder. "What about the others? My friends? My family?"

"Relationships are empty," he said, suddenly releasing me. I dragged air into my lungs and readjusted my shirt over my pants so he couldn't see my bare skin. "In time, you'll come to see your kind is done for and when they realize that, every one of your friends will want a Dryma for protection."

"You need us to guard your trees." I narrowed my eyes.

Christophe waved his hand dismissively. "For now."

Mari's words haunted me. "We need warmth."

Christophe paused in drinking and stared at me. "Warmth?"

"Yes, we're slowly dying from this cold."

"Cold? You've gotta to be joking." He pointed at his light shirt and outside. "The weather has been better than it has for days."

"All the same." I took a step toward him, my heart thundering in my chest. "Perhaps we could work something out where half of us could go down south and then when they get back—"

Christophe's laughter shook the room. "Let me get this straight. You want a group of Dryma guards to accompany you down south so you can be a little warmer?"

I flinched at his words. "We need to migrate. This weather is killing us."

"You've lived, what, twenty-three years like this? I think you can survive."

How could I tell him the coloring of our skin was wrong? When I looked at Micky, I could see signs of aging that weren't supposed to be there.

"Get on your knees."

I was sure I misheard him. "Pardon?"

Christophe gestured to the floor as he leaned against the table. "Get on your knees and tell me you'll be mine. Then roll over and let me take you."

I felt sick. It was a small blessing I hadn't vomited everywhere. "Never."

"Take the envelope and go collect your friends."

I shoved it into my pocket and was halfway to the door when he called my name. Reluctantly, I turned to face him.

"Just for the record, you're already my slave. But I don't want to take you until you're willing."

"That will never happen," I promised.

"I won't give up."

"Honestly, what do you even see in me?" I hated him, but I was confused why he was so persistent in claiming me. I figured he would say it was because I was a prince and he would gain status, but he remained silent.

He just nodded before flitting his hand in my direction like I was little more than an annoying fly. Anger seeped through my body and made my joints stiff, but I turned from him and didn't look back.

"How did it go?" Joel asked as he saw me coming and hopped from a barstool.

"Did he do anything to you?" Zain asked as he studied my face, turning away from the human women he'd been speaking to. Whatever he saw in my expression clearly riled him.

"Let's just go."

It wasn't until we were outside that I permitted myself a backward glance. Standing at the window with a full glass in his hand was Christophe looking down at me like he had for most of my life. Sickened, I stumbled into the backseat of the car, ignoring Zain and Joel's pleas that I should sit in the front, and nestled into the window.

CHAPTER TWO

AS WAS expected of me, I safeguarded the envelope. Despite my aunt's increased interest in what business I had conducted with the Captain of the Dryma fairies, I stuck to my story that he only wanted an update on protection duty.

Joel and Zain were not as inclined to turn a blind eye, and when Tuesday rolled around, we were on twelve-hour protection duty.

The forest was mostly quiet, but just to make certain, we'd patrolled the area where the Castle De Mar was concealed with magic and overgrowth. Zain chewed on a sunflower seed, spitting the shell on the ground before kicking a patch of dirt over it. In the last few days, he'd given up on the purple and blue hair and had changed to a dull red.

"Why do they even call it Castle De Mar? It's under a freaking lake," Zain scoffed.

"A sea is more powerful than a lake, which is exactly how the Dryma see themselves."

Zain stuffed another handful of seeds into his mouth. "I don't see why we have to go see the Sidhee."

Joel leaned against one of the normal trees and let his arms hang loosely at his sides. If there was anyone else who could've come without being exhausted, I would've enlisted the help of a different Kuro swan because Joel looked close to fainting. His normally parted hair was askew, and he had forgotten to put a shirt on underneath his heavy ranger coat.

"Rough weekend?" I asked, taking a sip of my black coffee and offering the thermos. Gratefully, he took the steaming liquid and swished it in his mouth for a moment before swallowing and passing the container to Zain.

"Yes." He winced in pain. "Chiaki is still sick, go figure. He kept the others up most of the night."

"And you too," I noted.

"If Micky or Calvin are getting too cramped at your house, they can stay in my room."

Zain choked on his sunflower seeds. "No way are those brats going to be allowed to bother you. They can come to my house if necessary."

Before I could speak, Joel nodded in agreement.

Once, I'd told Micky if he needed a place to sleep, he could crash in my room and he'd looked at me like I asked him to be my boyfriend. For a kid, he was strangely devoted to a monarchy that crumbled before he'd existed.

"Well, what did it say?" Zain asked, directing my attention back to the question at hand.

"The note? I didn't open it." I tightened the cap on my thermos and then slid my black gloves over my numb fingers, but there was a hole and my index finger poked out. "Christophe's seal was on it."

They stared at me, the only sound Zain's crunchy sunflower seeds.

I realized what I'd said. "Guys, I've always called him Christophe."

"Did he do something to you?" Zain demanded, spitting out his sunflower seeds at his feet, some of them unshelled.

"No." I cursed myself for saying the Dryma captain's name.

"What did he do to you?" Zain's face was flushed as he stood up and crossed the space between us. He was tall and covered in slender muscles, but I knew he'd die before stooping to hurt me.

"Just felt me up a bit. Let it go."

"Fuck," Zain cried, kicking a rock and watching it spiral into the lake. "Why is that guy so—"

"Pompous," Joel offered, his own anger a quiet mask on his face.

"I was thinking something worse, but we'll go with pompous. I knew we shouldn't have left the room."

I took a breath and forced a cool relief through their bodies. "Thanks for worrying, but he has been after me for years now. If I cried every time, I'd never be okay."

"You're right." Zain calmed down, but I wasn't sure if it was because of my words or the relieving emotion I'd sent through his body. "But I still hate him for thinking he can touch you."

"I wish we didn't have to see the Sidhee, especially the prince," Joel murmured, bringing the main problem back to our attention. "What do they want?"

"An alliance between the Sidhee and the Dryma."

Joel's jaw dropped. "What? So we'd be free?"

Zain chewed his lower lip anxiously.

"No," I replied bitterly. "We would just serve two masters. No way will they release our wings."

"Why?"

"Because we'd kill them," Zain snapped. "At least I would."

I bit the inside of my cheek to keep myself from commenting. The injustice of it all hovered between us as thick as smoke clouds, but there was little we could do about it.

"Why can't they just release us?" Joel pondered as he stared up at the cloudy sky. Anyone who didn't know him would've thought we were simply talking about the weather, but the gray pallor of his skin and the dulling of his hair told me everything he wasn't saying. We were dying... slowly.

Guilt ate away at my insides, turning my stomach violently. Focusing on my boots, I sent the conversation between Christophe and me to them so they could see what I'd asked.

Instead of being amused, they both looked murderous, even Joel.

"Never, do you hear me, Kanji? Never will he touch you."

"Not even for your freedom?" I asked softly. My pride was my worst sin, and at the time, I had vowed never to lower myself to be Christophe's pet, but if it meant warmth for my kind....

"It would only be temporary, but he would use that as an excuse to keep you forever."

"Zain's right," Joel added, covering his yawn with the back of his hand. "Forget about it. We can survive, like we have been."

There was nothing left to say, so I instead fiddled with the radio at my belt and focused on the different breathing patterns of the forest. There were some bears scratching the trees and endless birds wrapped in the branches, but no humans in the protected area as far as I could tell.

I stared up into the trees for a distraction and noticed how old and strong they appeared to be. When a Dryma was born, their soul went into a tree that befit their personality. The softer, fragile trees were the Dryma who were the weakest.

The anger had just about subsided when I realized we needed to break away and do our rounds of the forest, just in case we'd missed something. I was about to take off along the water trail when a shuffling from behind me made us freeze in place.

I knew it was Micky even before he shot through the woods.

"What are you doing here?" Zain demanded.

Micky doubled over, his hands pressed to his knees as he gulped for air. His body trembled with overexertion, and sweat poured from his forehead. "I needed to come find you, Kanji."

"Why, what's wrong?" I took a step toward him, my arm outstretched. Even though I could force my kind to reveal their thoughts, I only did so with permission.

Micky wasn't scheduled for protection duty until later this evening, and he wasn't wearing the ranger getup. Instead, he had a heavy wool coat pulled over a long-sleeved shirt and jeans with holes in the knees.

Without another word, he straightened and pressed his hand to mine so his thoughts could channel.

I saw distorted images of him at my house, preparing to drop something off, and then Mari's worried face beside my aunt. My uncle's face was ashy, and his eyes were clouded over like he'd spilled too much milk into them.

"My uncle," I breathed, more for Joel and Zain's benefit than my own.

Micky had stopped panting and shoved his hands into his pockets. "I'll stay here and cover your shift. Mari is waiting for you."

So that explained how he got here. "I'll come back later," I told him.

"Take your time," Micky replied dutifully.

"Call me if anything changes," Zain said, his face a neutral mask. Over the years, he'd gotten good at hiding his emotions, probably because he and Joel no longer had older family members.

"I will. Thanks."

Stumbling from the clearing, I was halfway out of sight when Micky's blue fingers came to mind. Rushing back to the clearing, I tore off my gloves and shoved them onto his hands.

He called my name to stop me, but I was already gone. My heart thumped in my chest, and I never thought I would be so happy to see Mari sitting in my blue sedan. A rush of heat slapped against my face as I opened the door and slid inside.

I knew she'd left in a hurry because she was wearing only a long-sleeved dress and sweater.

"Here, take my coat," I offered as I started to slide my arms out.

"No." Mari shook her head so hard it looked separate from her body. "I don't want you to freeze. We need you."

Her words nearly undid me because I was nothing. There was nothing I'd been able to do for the Kuro swans, but I didn't dare tell her my fears because I knew she was clinging to my status with everything she had left. Shattering her fantasy would've broken her.

We drove in silence, Mari forcing the old car to careen down the highway as quickly as it could without overheating. Each time we went over a bump, my heart slid into my throat and hitched my breathing.

"What happened?" I finally asked when I could see our mobile homes stretching out on the horizon.

Mari took a shuddering breath before flipping her dark hair over her slender shoulder. "Your aunt went to give him lunch and found him on the floor. He had... he...."

"It's okay," I whispered. This was the part where I was supposed to wrap my arms around her and pull her to me. I could smell the longing in her scent, the desire to fully submit and do whatever necessary to placate and please me. But I couldn't, and it made me feel like a heartless monster.

"He tried to kill himself with a pair of sewing scissors. He needs healing medicine."

Human medicine was advanced, but not enough to heal our wounds. The thought made me sick, but if I had to, I could go to Christophe. On a Tuesday evening, he would be at the Crystal Cove, swarmed by beautiful humans tantalized by the Dryma pheromones.

I didn't feel the tears slipping down my cheeks until Mari grasped my hand so tightly, I could feel the pressure in my bones.

My house was already filled with a whirlwind of people. Lyon, the oldest of Joel's wards, was standing in the kitchen, telling his adopted brothers and sisters what to do. I saw Chiaki in the dining room, lighting candles with his mate, Aiden. They were only sixteen, and yet they'd somehow found ancient love that those years older were cheated of. It was hard to contain my jealousy when they were around. They had their heads bent together, their blond locks entwining to give off the impression they were connected as they hovered over the candles and chanted soft words.

But their young mating wasn't the only thing that made them rare. Having light hair was even more uncommon amongst Kuro.

I saw the markings of illness on Chiaki's thin arms and crisscrossing up his neck and into his face. The scarlet rash usually caused Chiaki unbelievable pain, and a sting of guilt slammed into my gut when I saw what he was doing for my uncle. Instead of helping me, he should've been resting.

A path was made for me to go downstairs where the only other swan besides my uncle was Aunt Catarina.

She knew I was there but didn't tear her eyes away from the sickly pale man lying on the bed. He had thrown off the covers, the blankets and pillows lying in a heap beside the bed. His eyelids were heavy, his lips moving without sound coming out.

In his day, my Uncle Wallace had been something of a legend. He claimed he was the most sought after Kuro swan, right after my father. From pictures I'd seen, he had the same long curly hair and startling blue eyes as my father, the former Kuro king. His arms and neck were corded with muscles, and his wings could never be contained for long.

But this was what we were now; sickly thin, tall creatures devoid of vibrant color.

With a single nod from my uncle, my aunt rose from her precarious perch beside his sickbed and shuffled up the stairs wordlessly.

My uncle rarely looked at me because I reminded him of his brother, of the days when he was second in line to a great and powerful throne. For him to send his mate away meant there was something of great importance he felt the need to tell me.

"How are you feeling?" I tried to not look at his patched up arms.

"Tired," he groaned.

"I can go and get you medicine," I offered awkwardly.

In this small basement, I felt too tall and lanky. Like I was a doll that didn't quite fit into its box.

My uncle waved his hand dismissively. "I want to fly again."

I bit back my tears.

"I've always thought you were a disappointment," he croaked between a fit of coughing. "But that's not true."

"What do you mean?"

"I thought you were weak because you don't fight"—another fit—"but the truth is that is what makes you strong."

I felt like shit. "You're wrong. I am weak."

"There are things I've seen. Things that will come to pass."

He was an elder, a Kuro in possession of sight, yet over the last twenty-three years, he had rarely spoken of his ability.

"What do you see?" I raised my hand to touch him, but he shrank away. His wrinkled skin hung on his bones, his once alert eyes now devoid of light.

"Tell me, have you met your mate?"

"Mari is interested in me...."

My uncle raised his thin eyebrows and surprised me by saying, "But is she your mate?"

"No," I admitted. "She is not."

"You need an heir, true, but an heir is worthless if they are not the child of your mate."

"What does my mate have to do with our future?" I asked tiredly, annoyed with myself for thinking he was actually speaking of visions when he was just delirious.

"Everything. They are the key to saving our kind." He sighed before convulsing violently on the bed.

I screamed for my aunt, and she came tearing down the stairs so fast I wondered if she'd stood by the door and waited for my call. As she wiped his forehead with a damp cloth and stroked his lackluster hair, I made up my mind.

"I'll be back."

"Where are you going?" Her eyes were wide as she stared at her decaying mate.

"To get medicine."

My aunt Catarina loved me, but her mate was dying and he made everything else pale in comparison. Without a word, I raced up the stairs to my room and threw on the nearest shirt and jacket I had before going to my car. Mari came reeling out of the house after me, but she was little more than a speck of dust in my rearview mirror.

I drove to the Crystal Cove in a daze. It wasn't until I'd parked that I realized I hadn't taken the time to focus on my feelings, so how was I supposed to articulate anything to Christophe? I could already see his smug expression as he pointed to the floor. He would expect me to get onto my knees and beg for the healing medicine required to save my uncle. There was no way I could be sure he'd give it to me or that once I had the medicine, it would save my uncle's life. But the longer I debated outside the club, the more life drained from his veins.

Raking in oxygen, I felt my heart constricting and thought I would pass out. Without warning, my hands started to shake and my legs were knocking against each other violently. A cold sweat broke out on the back of my neck, and there was an empty feeling deep in the pit of my stomach that no amount of rationalization could push away. What was wrong with me?

Kuro swans were known for their inability to forgive death, but my uncle wasn't my mate. If anything, the reasons why I wanted to save him were selfish when I should've been considering my aunt.

No, this distortion was completely different.

Unable to handle the heat of my car, I shoved the door open and spilled out into the cool air. My blood pumped in my ears, and the aching intensified. Pressing my hand to my forehead, I thought I might be running a fever.

The birds were oblivious to my searing pain and chirped mercilessly. I could hear the voices of the humans entering the club, a cataclysm of annoying sounds and tones. Then there was a moment in which everything was silent among the chaos, and I realized what was wrong.

My mate was nearby. The fever, the profuse sweating, the painful ache like I would never be whole again were all symptoms of being near my mate.

But I couldn't, not now. I closed my eyes and inhaled sharply, but the only scents I caught were that of cheap perfume and the Dryma. If there were any Kuro swans nearby, they were masked by the scents of humans and fairies.

I was in no state to go traipsing into the Crystal Cove to beg for help from Christophe, but time was running out.

Everything in me warned me to run, to pretend I hadn't felt the tug of my mate and forget. This couldn't happen to me; isn't that what I'd already decided?

"Are you all right?"

His voice broke through the fog clouding my senses, demanding all of my attention forever be on him. I was kneeling on the ground, dirt and rubble plastered against my knees and hands.

Closing my eyes, I nodded once and made a gagging sound so he would think I was vomiting. *Please just go away*, I pleaded.

But he didn't hear my pleas because he wasn't a Kuro swan.

To my surprise, he moved forward and dropped to one knee beside me. "Don't," I pleaded, my voice a hoarse whisper. "I don't want to get you dirty."

His laugh was hollow as he rested a hand on my upper arm and helped me to my feet. I refused to look at him, but when I was fully standing, his fingers grazing my shoulder, I had no choice but to thank him.

The Dryma fairy standing before me was what I imagined humans thought of when they read fairy tales involving gorgeous creatures. His hair was bright blond—the color of gold as it gleams in the sunlight—and his skin was the perfect shade of bronze. I would've envied his coloring because it meant he was able to enjoy the sun, but all hate dissipated when I stared into his bright green eyes outlined in gold. As I peered closer, I could see the coloring of his eyes was similar to a precious stone.

Christophe was the only other fairy I'd met who towered over me and sent my hormones kicking into overdrive. But the fairy standing in front of me was easily the most beautiful male I'd ever seen, completely overshadowing Christophe. He was tall, and even under his bulky coat, I could tell his body was tapered in muscle. I longed to touch his slender body, outlining each of his muscles until he pushed me away.

"Thanks for your help," I hinted, trying to get him to realize I didn't need his assistance. Okay, so if my racing heart wasn't enough to prove he was my mate, the fact I was ready to drop to my knees and serve him certainly was. Not happening.

He stared at me curiously before glancing at the Crystal Cove. Did he really not know what I was?

"What are you doing here?" he inquired, his eyes flickering back to mine.

"I'm here to see… Captain Christophe," I finished lamely, stepping away so his hand fell back to his side. My body threatened to crumple from the lack of his touch.

"Oh." His eyes clouded over in recognition and flickered to my wrist. "I'm also here to see him."

It was on the tip of my tongue to ask him why, but I caught myself. "I'm sorry to detain you. Please forgive me." The pleasantries were like acid on my tongue because all I really wanted was to know his name.

Never before had I felt so sick with my actions. If the Dryma standing before me had been human or a Kuro swan, my next course of action would be simple. I would've told him I'd mated to him and then claimed him for myself.

My palms itched at my sides, urging me to lift them up and touch his skin. Even pressing his hand to my lips would've been enough contact to placate me.

The lashes on my back were a reminder of what would happen if I acted insolently, but I found myself uncaring of Christophe or his goons. All that mattered was connecting with the Dryma fairy. The thought made me physically ill because he was nothing, could never be anything to me.

I was a slave to his kind, so I refused to gaze at the handsome face, better suited to a gilded painting than in a parking lot.

"Look at me," he ordered, his voice soft and yet full of strength and possession.

My eyes flickered to his, and although I expected a pompous stare, he was simply looking at me with bemusement. Then to my surprise, he murmured, "Captain Christophe tends to be intimidating."

"So he's not just like that around us?" Being so close to my mate was clouding my judgment, and I needed to be careful or I'd be sorry.

His eyes twinkled and he shook his head. "No, definitely not."

I cursed my body for being so lanky and tall. I hid my hands in my pockets so he wouldn't see the pale, sunlight-deprived skin.

"Are you cold?"

For the first time in years, I wasn't. I was beyond confused, torn between my resentment for his kind and wanting to become closer to him. If he knew my thoughts were solely centered on him, his beautiful features would've been marred in disgust. And worse, the pain of rejection would've been like a knife sliding through my heart.

I cleared my throat and tried to look away from his face, but his stare was imposing and demanded my attention.

Clearly, he was exceptionally well-off, but that didn't surprise me. His strong muscular legs were covered in tight jeans, and I could smell the faint scent of an iron on his jacket. He had an air about him that made me think he could wear tattered rags and still come across as being elegant.

"A little bit, yes. Are you?" My concern for him startled me.

"No," he sighed and looked at the Crystal Cove. "What did...?" He stopped midsentence, and a flash of concern crossed over his face. The tan creamy skin at his throat tightened as he swallowed and leaned in. "Is that blood? Are you hurt?"

If I hadn't been so overwhelmed by his distress, I would've burst into laughter at the irony. I touched the wetness pooling at my neck and stared at the scarlet blood staining my fingers. My uncle needed me, and I'd allowed myself to become sidetracked.

"It isn't mine," I said quickly, stepping back.

I couldn't be sure if it was my imagination, but I thought I saw him relax. "Whose blood, then?"

"My uncle's."

Why was he still standing there, speaking with me as if we could be friends?

"Why are you here?"

"To ask the captain for medicine." My reply was automatic. My mental filter had been completely disintegrated. "Stupid idea, right?"

I laughed, the cool air charging down my throat and filling my lungs.

"No," he whispered.

Instantly, I was silenced. He reached into his pocket and withdrew a small bottle, the kind you put shampoo or conditioner in when you go on a vacation. The liquid was clear, but when he raised the bottle, a prism of light formed inside.

"Beautiful, but what is it?"

"Do you know why our medicine is so powerful?" He twirled the bottle around in his slender fingers.

I shook my head, my tongue thick in my mouth.

"Humans often cry, but it's rare for a fairy to. The emotions built up inside a Dryma over time make the tears appear like liquid diamonds."

"I never knew."

"Yours." He presented the bottle to me, a small tube in the palm of his hand.

"I couldn't possibly take—"

"But you were willing to ask Christophe?" His eyes narrowed, and I knew I was imagining his jealousy. The Dryma didn't condone rape, and that was the only reason I was free from Christophe's desires. But relationships between Dryma and Kuro swans were forbidden.

"What do you want from me?"

Without answering, he took the bottle and slid the plastic into my jean pocket. His hand grazed the flesh of my hip, sending shivers down my spine.

He pressed his finger to his lips and gave me a look that made me feel like I was going to die. "Tell me your name."

My knees knocked together, and the medicine felt heavy. My uncle was wrong about my mate being the key to saving our tribe because as the Prince of the Kuro swans, my mate was supposed to be mine. Looking at the Dryma fairy in front of me, I knew I would do anything to have him claim me.

Knowing full well he was going to be the undoing of me, I whispered my name.

"Can you say it again?"

"Kanji," I said louder. "Thank you for the medicine."

Before he could stop me, I'd lunged into my car and was hightailing it back to my house. I was a fool for not lying and giving him a false name. But I knew why I had. Even if I was only a fleeting moment to him, at least I'd willingly given him part of myself.

I could've laughed myself hoarse. He'd given me the medicine, and for that I owed him more than just my name.

When I could no longer see him in the rearview mirror, a paralyzing cold swept through my body. I realized that not knowing about my mate could not compare to the devastation I felt at having to renounce him.

CHAPTER THREE

MY HOUSE transformed into a kind of psychic reading shop filled with so many essential oils and candles that distinguishing between the scents was impossible. Slumping onto my hardwood floor, I rested my elbows on my knees and raked in air.

The noises below had become little more than murmurs, but even through the floorboards, I could hear the heaving sobs of my aunt as she mourned her mate. In a daze, I'd wandered into my house and had only to hear the cries of despair from the basement to know what had happened in my absence. Mari had reached for my arm, but I slid away and disappeared up the stairs like the pathetic prince I was.

A knock on the door startled me from my thoughts. I didn't speak, but the doorknob turned all the same, and I saw Zain's tall figure in my doorway.

"Can I come in, man?"

I shrugged.

He started to take off his boots, still wet from the Pasky Nature Reserve, and his ranger uniform, which clung to him like paint plastered onto brick.

"Don't bother." I pointed at the dirt I'd dragged into my room from my own boots still laced tightly on my feet. I had managed to shake off my jacket but was still wearing my sweater and jeans with the plastic bottle of tears cradled in my pocket.

Zain rolled his eyes and pulled his boots off before venturing farther into my bedroom. "It wasn't your fault," he told me softly as his socked feet padded over the floor before he sank down next to me. I could smell the damp air clinging to his hair and the dirt caked on his hands.

"You weren't here," I reminded him. If Zain was here, then his shift had ended. "How long have I been up here?"

"Couple hours." He sniffed. "Your aunt wasn't able to speak, so Mari told me...."

Of course she wasn't. This was what I wanted to avoid, the aching pain of losing your mate. Unfortunately, even though I'd found mine, he was too far out of reach.

"Do you ever want to find your mate?" I asked, stretching my legs, the joints protesting.

Zain squinted and looked at my ceiling. "Yes, why?"

"Don't you worry this will happen?" I waved my hand around the room. "I don't ever want to feel the way my aunt does."

"But she loved him."

"Yes."

"And he loved her."

"Yes."

"Kuro swans mate for life. Knowing that happiness for however long is worth the pain at the end, I think." Zain twirled a red strand in between his grubby fingers, clearly frustrated. Of course he'd want a mate. The young blond Dryma assaulted my mind, and all I could see were his green eyes staring as though he already owned me.

"I went to get medicine," I admitted, knowing the truth would come out eventually.

Zain stiffened beside me, grasping my shoulder and shaking me so hard my teeth rattled. "What the fuck were you thinking? Don't tell me you went to the captain."

"I was going to, but I didn't."

"Good."

"I should've been able to save my uncle."

He grimaced. "Their medicine isn't guaranteed to work on us, and it doesn't matter. Like I said, it's not your fault. As soon as you left, he passed away. You would've been too late no matter how fast you got back here."

I felt the little obtrusive bottle in my pants pressing against my thigh. I wanted to hate the blond Dryma so badly; I could feel the anger bubbling in my veins because I couldn't.

"Zain," I whispered. "They can't keep getting away with this."

He grunted beside me.

"My uncle, he died because of what those fairies did. Because he couldn't fly anymore…."

"What can we do about it?" Zain waved his hand around violently, exposing the branding mark on his wrist. "They own us. If we fight, they'll just line us up and beat the shit out of us. All the stores around here will be fresh out of bandages because we'll need them all."

I could hear the rage in his voice. "We can find out where they are keeping our wings."

My old friend looked at me in disbelief, "Well, if it's only that easy."

"I'm serious," I pressed. "There has to be a way of getting to them." For the briefest of moments, I considered telling him about the Dryma fairy with the shining skin and beautiful hair, but stopped. More than anything, I wanted to free my friends. But I couldn't betray or use my mate to get what I needed. "We can think of something."

"Like...." Zain clicked his tongue against the roof of his mouth. "Just give the word and I'll be right behind you to storm the castle. But you should probably take some time to rest, you know?"

But I wasn't listening to him anymore. "Storm the castle?"

"Figure of speech. Hey, where are you going?"

I rummaged through my papers on my desk and lifted my old computer keyboard to find the sealed letter Christophe had given me for the Sidhee prince.

"Wait, hold on, Kanji," Zain warned as he jumped up and held his hand out for the letter. "I'm all for a revolution, but come on. We have no idea what that letter says."

"Exactly." I needed to stop and think. Needed to remember what I was doing affected others, but I couldn't stop my finger from sliding underneath the brittle flower paper and breaking the seal. "If the Dryma fairies are planning on creating an alliance with the Sidhee, we should know. They are dangerous alone, but together.... I don't even want to think about what that means for us."

"I don't either, but you want to go against Christophe about something this important?"

I showed him the torn envelope, a heaving sigh raking from his lungs at the finality of what I'd done. Nestled between the sheets of the letter was a fake fabric flower dyed red.

Christophe's handwriting was just like him; neat, precise, and unrelenting. I scanned the words once and then again just to make sure I'd read correctly.

"Well?" Zain demanded, his hands shoved deep inside his pockets. He may have hidden his hands, but I could feel the anxiety rolling off of him in waves.

"Read." I offered him the letter, and after surveying the room like he thought Christophe might dart out of my old wardrobe, he took the letter between his fingers and read the words. His eyes widened and his breathing hitched before he carefully refolded the letter.

"Well, damn."

I twirled the delicate flower in my fingers, closing and opening my palm around the soft petals. "Christophe mentioned the ball as an excuse to 'integrate' the Sidhee into their world, but I never imagined something like this."

The floor looked less than inviting, so I crumpled onto my bed. Zain glanced at my bed nervously like he was going to follow suit, but didn't.

"How long have we been friends?" I murmured.

"Since we were like two."

"Then you should know you can sit on my bed."

He rubbed his jaw with his pale hand and muttered an inaudible curse word as he sat down beside me.

"So the plan is to give the youngest Dryma prince to the Prince of the Sidhee? How desperate are they?"

I shook my head. "Christophe was… off. But I never imagined they would sink so low as to offer up one of their own."

"That flower is the only way to distinguish who the Prince of the Sidhee is?"

"According to the letter," I noted, tucking the flower back within its protected envelope. "But I don't understand why they would need a flower. Surely the fairies could sense the difference between their own kind and a demonic monster. Unless they use a bunch of scents at the ball so everyone smells the same."

Zain grunted, clearly lost in his thoughts. "Why a ball anyway? Why not just take the bastard back to his world?"

"Fairies don't take kindly to having their royal members stolen, nor having to become part of another clan. Christophe must be one of the few who knows this plan. It's ingenious really." If I didn't hate the Dryma and Sidhee to the point of my vision blurring red, I would've given them credit. "At the end of the ball, the Prince of the Dryma can tell his people he's fallen in love with the fairy wearing the red flower."

Zain nodded. "Surprise, it's the Prince of the Sidhee."

"Exactly."

"We have to stop them," Zain said quickly.

"What made you change your mind?" Truthfully, I was relieved my friend was on my side because alone I wouldn't manage to succeed in even the most thought-out plan.

"If they have to whore out one of their own, then something's wrong, and I don't want to be there when the shit hits the fan."

"Have a plan?" I coughed, wiping my mouth with the back of my hand. I caught the scent of the blond fairy's cologne on my sleeve where he'd touched me. I ached with need, my neglected member throbbing inside my pants.

"You okay?"

"What? Yeah."

Zain squinted at me but continued as he jumped from my bed and headed to the door. "I'll think of something. In the meantime, you should rest. You look like shit."

I tried to smile, but I was exhausted and the best I managed was a cock-eyed grin I was sure didn't do anything to convince Zain I was okay. "What about Joel? Tomas?"

"Joel is going to have a heart attack, but I'll tell him. Why not Mari?"

I raised my eyebrow but was too tired to fight him. "Any plan we come up with will invariably end up with me selling myself to Christophe—"

"Never."

"But if that's our last resort," I continued evenly, forcing his gaze to stay on me, "then I can't have Mari standing in my way."

His lanky frame swayed in my doorway like he was going to be sick, but he nodded curtly before disappearing down the stairs. I longed to tell him how deplorable the idea sounded to me now I'd found my mate, but I had to stop and remind myself I hadn't been accepted. I would never, could never love Mari the way she wanted me to. And the best Christophe was going to get was my malnourished, uninterested body.

I dug in my pocket for the flower and stared at the stained petals. Would the blond fairy be at the Castle De Mar? I doubted he would miss a grand celebration of his kin. My pulse quickened at the thought of his defined jaw and tanned skin.

The little fabric flower was so delicate and petite. I unwrapped my hand and smoothed down the edges, thinking of how it would feel to have my wings fluttering at my back. As a slave, I was nothing. But if Zain and I could formulate a plan that would lead to our wings, then I could face the blond fairy on equal terms.

But the question that dug through my spine was whether or not he'd want me or if I was just chasing what I'd never reach.

THE SERVICE was quiet and colorless, not at all what I thought my uncle would want. My aunt and other Kuro females bundled themselves up in heavy dark skirts and shapeless tops, accentuating the paleness of their skin. I wore a simple dark shirt and dress pants, the best I had.

The sound of crying and sniffling rang out through the hall as stories about my uncle were shared. I saw Chiaki and Aiden shift uncomfortably a few seats behind me because they could not empathize with what my uncle had lost.

The idea of flying sounded foreign in their ears, to the point where they were little more than human.

Our entire clan huddled into the large meeting hall like starved fair-haired dolls, and I knew there wasn't enough room, but not even the youngest spoke out. There was a quiet reverence in seeing my uncle's dead body, in knowing there was only one royal member left of the Kuro swans.

No one said anything about what they expected from me, but they didn't have to. Joel and Zain initially resisted when I tried to get them to take the empty seats beside me because they wanted me to have my given space. Finally, Mari broke the distance and wrapped her strong fingers around my bony arm.

I couldn't be sure if the tears I shed were for my uncle's corpse or for my clan's unrelenting loyalty.

After the ceremony, I signaled to Zain to gather Joel and Tomas.

"Where are you going?" Mari asked, her voice strong over the howl of the wind. My aunt clung to her like a frightened child, her eyes empty and somber.

"I have to speak with Zain," I told her. "Please take my aunt on ahead, and I will meet you there." My words sounded foreign, and she recoiled like I'd been replaced with a machine, but I didn't have time to care.

Luckily, Aiden called for Mari to start the car so Chiaki's fit of coughing would cease, and she left with my aunt.

Joel trembled the way a newborn lamb does when it tries to stand. But he masked his discomfort with a heavy scarf wrapped around his neck and face and a cap pulled low on his forehead. I hadn't had time to speak with him or Tomas after my uncle's death, apart from the words of comfort they'd offered up prior to his service.

"So you heard?" I said point blank as I crossed the precarious stones meant to resemble a path. There was a bench covered in moss and a cluster of trees surrounding the area to give off the illusion of privacy.

Joel nodded and Tomas reached into his pocket to pull out a pack of cigarettes. They were cheap and smelled terrible, but that wasn't why I snapped.

"Why are you still smoking?"

Tomas covered the butt with his hand so he could light it. "Comforts me."

"Smoking is going to deteriorate your lungs."

Tomas shrugged, but when he saw Zain and Joel eyeing him, he stamped the cigarette out with the tip of his boot. "It's not like we're ever going to fly again."

"We will," Joel protested.

"Which is why we're here right now," Zain said gruffly, stepping up so he was standing beside me. I'd never noticed before, but my friend really was quite stunning when he tried to be.

His hair was bobby pinned back, but the rebel strands tickled his defined jaw and wrapped around his neck.

"So what's the plan?" Tomas asked.

I wiped my face with my sleeve, but instantly regretted it. The scent of death and candles had overtaken the fabric with no hope of escape. "We're going to infiltrate the masked ball."

Tomas bent over with laughter as he clung to his sides. Out of the four of us, Tomas was the shortest but also the broadest. Instead of accepting our fate, he pretended we were never anything more than human. His natural dark hair had been bleached white, and now he looked like the human albino from *The Da Vinci Code*.

"How do you plan to do that?" Joel interjected, his eyes narrowing as he darted them around the trees.

Nearby, an animal was pawing at the ground, the scratching of its nails incessant.

"Don't laugh at the prince." Zain's voice was dangerous.

Tomas instantly straightened and wiped his eyes. "Sorry, I didn't mean to disrespect you."

And that was exactly why I'd chosen Tomas to be made aware of our plan. Even though going to the masked ball was a ridiculous notion, there was true sincerity in his voice when he spoke to me.

"No time for pleasantries," I told him, before gazing at my other two friends. "If we get caught, we have to be willing to make sacrifices...."

Zain growled and looked away before I could reproach him.

"If we get caught, I plan on taking full responsibility. As long as we can all agree on that, then we can move forward."

"Why would you—" Joel started.

"'Cause he's the prince. They won't kill him," Tomas finished, and even though his bleached hair was driving me crazy, I saw the flicker of doubt in his features.

"If we can get into the ball, then the goal is to persuade the Dryma prince to believe we are the Prince of the Sidhee and his companions," I continued. "Therefore, we can gain access to the castle and hopefully convince the prince to divulge where our wings are."

"And the Prince of the Sidhee?" Joel asked fearfully. "I doubt he's just going to agree to our plan. And there's no way we can overcome him."

Zain smiled, twirling a strand of natural dark hair around his pale pinkie, the contrast striking. "And that is what we still have to figure out."

MY AUNT retreated within herself, and even though I wanted to help her, the only thing I could offer were cheap words of comfort she accepted even though she knew they were lies. Mari became a constant presence in my house, bombarding me with requests to watch movies and talk about the books lining my shelves.

I couldn't blame Mari for wanting to grasp on to anything she could because I knew how desperately she'd loved my uncle, but I knew the truth in her mind. She wanted to be a princess, the queen of our clan.

"Tonight, let's go see that movie that just came out."

"Which one?" I asked distractedly as I pulled my dark jacket over my T-shirt. "Maybe we can see it tomorrow."

Mari uncrossed and recrossed her legs where she was sitting on my bed. I couldn't deny I'd relished in her comfort the past week, but now I needed to think. The envelope was neatly in my bag, nestled between the pages of my favorite book. I hadn't heard anything further from Christophe, so as far as he knew, the plan was continuing.

There was still time to back down, to prevent any possible pain.

Mari scoffed behind me, "Why can't we go tonight?"

"Look, it's not like I don't like hanging out with you, but I have to meet Chr—Captain Christophe today."

Her eyes widened like saucers in her skull. I could hear her thoughts pounding inside her mind and was reminded of Zain. *Pervert. Jerk. Self-absorbed....*

I chuckled. *All of those things are true, but all the same, I have to go.*

Mari gave a startled jolt at hearing my voice echoing inside her head, but then she looked away, her heavy lashes resting on her cheeks. "You could tell him you've found your mate."

The envelope was stiff as I grazed my fingers over the seal to make sure I'd packed it away. I was too tired and distracted to fight her, so instead I said, "What do you see in me?"

The metal springs of my bed squealed as she stood up and crossed the floor to retrieve her discarded coat and purse. "A lot more than you see in yourself. Be careful."

With a fleeting scent of her perfume, she was gone. I heard her muffled voice as she spoke to my aunt, and then there was nothing. It was better this way because if she knew what I was planning, she would've demanded to come.

Joel and Tomas were on protection duty, so Zain picked me up, and we headed toward the Nature Reserve so we could swing by and pick them up. They could've met up with us in Joel's car, but we didn't want to arrive separately and give the Sidhee reason to think we were conspiring. Pretending we came from the same place was the best idea.

"Mari was at your house again," Zain remarked as he flipped through the radio stations. He stopped on a popular song with too much bass and screaming.

"Yes."

"Damn, she's persistent. Wish I had someone chasing me."

The only one I wanted chasing me was the blond fairy. For him I wouldn't have thought twice before divulging my plan. I had to ensure I stayed away from him if I saw him at the castle.

"Do you think it's possible to mate to a guy?" I adjusted the buttons of my jacket so it lay straight over my flat stomach.

Zain shrugged. "Guess so, but I don't see what the appeal would be. Aiden and Chiaki did, but Chiaki is so pretty he looks like a girl anyway. And I mean, you can't have kids or anything."

"Maybe that's a good thing."

"Are you trying to tell me something?" He blasted the heat, but my cheeks were already enflamed. I held my breath as I waited for him to continue. "Should've known you had a thing for me all this time." He grinned and lifted his toned arm so he could flex for my benefit.

"Yeah, right. You're not my type."

"What's wrong with me?"

I punched him in the arm and turned back to the empty forest racing beside us. The car became so quiet, I started to think Zain was lost in deep thought, but then he whispered, "Joel is gay."

I turned on him so fast I thought my neck would snap. "What are you talking about?"

"Come on, all those romance novels and the tea every night? He's gay."

"Guys can like tea."

Zain rolled his eyes. "Forget the tea. He's def gay. Read his mind and you'll see...."

"Whatever." I tried to maintain privacy and not read minds, but I felt the strongest urge to reach into Joel's and grasp at every memory and thought he'd had concerning being gay. I was sure it would be informative, but when I thought of Joel's good-natured temper and the quiet, reserved way he fought for me without being aggressive, I knew I could never do it.

"If you're gay, it won't change anything," Zain said abruptly, nearly jolting me from my seat. "I will fight for you, forever."

Words wouldn't form in my dry mouth so I nodded, and then there was an unspoken agreement to not say anything more.

I'd dressed the dutiful part of a Kuro slave, complete with brushing my hair. It was long enough to put into a ponytail if I had enough bobby pins to secure the shorter strands. My heart was pumping too much blood into my body, and I felt dizzy at the thought of Christophe showing up.

My fingers clutched at my throat, zipping my jacket fully so I could conceal as much as of my skin as possible. Bribing Christophe with my body was something I would do if I had to, but I found I wasn't nearly as prepared as I needed to be. I felt sickened when I thought of someone other than the blond fairy touching me.

"Damn, turn up the heat," Tomas grumbled as he slid into the back seat, pulling his duffel bag between his legs and consequently ramming into Zain's seat with his knees. I hadn't even realized that we had stopped the car because my thoughts were so consumed with the blond fairy.

"Can you watch it already?" Zain cried as he spun around in the driver's seat to glare at Tomas.

"You're the one with the tiny car," Tomas argued as he rubbed his hands together like he was trying to start a fire.

"Guys, please." Joel closed his eyes, his lashes caressing his cheeks. "I'm nervous too."

Zain and I were the only ones adequately dressed to meet the Sidhee so they unzipped their bags and undressed in the narrow space. Police rarely went through here, so I knew we wouldn't get caught for indecent exposure, but I was ashamed we'd been reduced to this.

Mud and dank water clung to their pants, the scent lingering on their cold skin even after they'd fully changed.

"Last chance to leave," I warned them as Zain navigated his jeep down a narrow, abandoned path. Our plan was to park and then head into the trails. Humans wouldn't have bothered with the dense thicket, but I knew that after a quarter mile, the forest thinned enough to form a slight meadow.

"I'm not going anywhere," Joel said as he unfolded his knit cap and pulled it low over his light brown hair.

"Me neither." Tomas tugged on his lip ring, and I feared he was going to pull it out. "Let's get this over with."

"Kanji is the one who talks. Agreed?"

Closing my eyes, I focused on their individual minds melding and folding until I could hear them all at once. A chorus of agreement flooded my mind, and only when I was satisfied I couldn't change their minds did I open the door and admit the chilly air.

"Who is on protection duty tonight?" I asked as we started up the small hill of fallen trees and debris.

"Micky, Lyon, Shinji," Joel rattled off, his breathing labored from the incline. "I have to go back in the morning, and I'll do the rounds."

"Tomorrow they'll be there again?" I asked. Tomorrow was the masked ball, and if we managed to clear this stage of our plan, we would find ourselves outrageously dressed and waiting for admittance into the Castle De Mar.

"All of them will be there, though Micky threw a fit."

Zain raised his eyebrow. "He's got a problem doing more protection duty?"

Joel shook his head. "He wanted to know what's going on."

"That kid is crazy perceptive," Tomas commented. It was one of the rare times I'd heard genuine respect in his voice. "But he's going to get into trouble if he doesn't get it out of his system."

"At least the forest will be guarded," I told them. "Christophe's orders were to double the guard, so we'll have everyone available working the forest."

Our plan had sounded so foolproof, and now I was wondering if it was actually going to work. If the other Kuro swans needed me, I'd be unable to answer their call. I would just have to issue orders to not look for me because I'd be part of the detailed protection order.

The blond fairy infiltrated my senses once again, and the longing to know his name was so severe, I stumbled over the smallest of rocks.

"You okay, Kanji? Your face is all red," Zain pointed out as he carefully trod toward me. We had spread out so we wouldn't get clustered up in the trees, so his pace toward me was hesitant and slow going.

"I'm fine. Just concentrating."

He stared at me for another moment before decidedly believing me and continuing along his small trail.

By the time we burst into the meadow, I was exhausted and could feel beads of sweat dripping down my neck and clinging to my forehead. My hair felt plastered to my skin, and in an effort to regain some of my dignity, I swept it back and fluffed the strands with my fingers.

"They're not even here," Tomas panted, his hands on his knees.

Tomas and Joel had been working all day, and I felt guilty I was so tired when I'd spent the day reading.

"Course not," Zain retorted as he leaned against a tree and crossed his arms over his chest. "They'll show up when they feel like it."

Tomas's jaw tightened, but he shrugged and pulled out his phone. Joel was already reading a book, so I was left alone with my thoughts of the blond fairy.

The way his hair fell over his face was ridiculously alluring. The bright green eyes were like a dragon's, and his tanned skin shimmered like gold. I found my thoughts drifting downward, and I wondered what it would be like to taste his skin.

A shuffle nearby brought me back to the present. The sun had all but set, emitting an eerie glow between the trees. We had our flashlights in case they arrived later, but hopefully our business would be conducted quickly.

The first thing I noticed was the Sidhee Prince's build. I'd grown accustomed to looking at the tall, sinewy bodies of my kind and the muscular, beautiful bodies of the Dryma. But the Prince of the Sidhee was different in stature. I knew him at once because of the way he commanded the attention of his guards. They marched silently beside him, their eyes darting like scurrying rats over our bodies.

He made no effort to conceal his inhuman nature because although there was little sunlight and the wind brutally ripped through the forest, he wore a dark short-sleeve shirt and a pair of loose jeans. In an attempt to fit in, he at least could've worn a jacket in the event wandering hikers spotted us.

"You were sent by Captain Christophe?"

It was impossible to tell their age because out of Dryma, Sidhee, and Kuro, they tended to have the longest lives. Their skin was chalk white and papery, like there wasn't enough skin to stretch over their bones. A Sidhee who looked about my age was standing erect beside the prince, his question lingering in the air.

"Yes, I am Kanji," I told them. My boys surrounded me, prepared to step in.

"This is Prince Calhoun," the one my age said, indicating the tall brooding man facing me with an uninterested gaze. Now that he was closer to me, I could see that although we were about the same height, his body was stocky and built. He could've passed for a pro-wrestler in the human world. Out of the others, his skin was the least papery, but the bright red eyes looked stressed, like what was left of the sun was blinding.

"Thank you for coming," I said awkwardly, not sure what I was expected to say.

"I believe you have something for me." When he spoke, an instant chill raced down my spine, and my insides stiffened.

Sidhee were not known for their patience or their kindness. My uncle had told me how the King of the Sidhee had betrayed my father, and despite knowing better, anger crawled over my skin like a contagion.

"You seem familiar somehow," Prince Calhoun stated in a deep booming voice as he took a step toward me. "Your eyes and your hair… there's something in you I remember."

I cleared my throat and held my ground. "My father, Akai, had once served your father."

His face cleared and he looked startled, but he recovered quickly. "Ah… so you're the fallen prince?"

His words were meant to hurt, but I didn't rise to the bait. "We serve the Dryma," I said matter-of-factly. "There is no longer a Kuro prince."

Prince Calhoun nodded once, but his eyes were clouded in something I couldn't quite discern. Doubt, maybe? "I think we are more similar than you think."

"Our similarities don't extend past our dark hair and pale skin," I told him. He clenched his jaw and I knew I'd pressed him too far, but there was something dark eating away at my insides.

If the prince had wanted to integrate himself into human life, he would've needed more than makeup and new clothes. There was something distinctly dark hovering about him, and when he shuffled his weight from foot to foot, I saw the tally of symbols on his arm I didn't recognize.

The prince grinned ruthlessly, revealing a set of jagged teeth that could've torn through rock. His height rivaled our own, and I wondered how we'd ever been able to support them with only our wings. "The symbols detail how many souls we've carried back with us to the underworld."

But they didn't serve death himself. They were simply demonic monsters who stole souls not slated for death so they could return to their dark, secretive world. The Sidhee were known for tricking humans to come back with them to their world, but because they could not fly, their visits to the human world were few and far between. I knew there would be several human lives lost tonight and felt a tug of pity in my soul.

"I hope you will refrain from taking any of our souls," I said bitterly. The gun I had in my pocket suddenly felt much heavier, and my fingers goaded me toward retrieving the weapon.

But Sidhee couldn't be killed with any human weapon. They had to be cut down by a sword created from materials found in their world.

Prince Calhoun flicked a speck of dust from his shoulder absently and then brushed his hair from his eyes. "I wouldn't dream of it."

There was still time to change my course of action, but acting on autopilot, I slid my hand into my jacket pocket and pulled out the letter. Christophe's seal gleamed like a blood oath from the clasp of the envelope.

The split second when the envelope was taken from my fingers and slid into his was the longest of my life. I had weighed the consequences for days, and this was the only action I could accept. So why did it feel so wrong to betray Christophe when he was little more to me than a pervert?

I knew the answer was because jerk or not, Christophe was in the same world as my mate.

"What is this?" Prince Calhoun asked, his voice low and murderous. "Explain yourselves."

Prince Calhoun reminded me of a cornered bear ready to lash out at even the smallest intrusion. I took a breath. "I was only in charge of delivering the envelope."

"What's wrong, Calhoun?" It was a different guard who spoke, and I was surprised when he removed his hood, revealing soft dark brown hair and startling eyes. He had the same tired look about him, but there was a strength glittering in his eyes and movements. Here was a guy who knew what he needed to do to get what he wanted. He looked like Christophe's right-hand man, Seth.

Beside me, Joel's breathing hitched, but before I could delve into his mind, my attention was snapped back to Prince Calhoun.

"The captain has said the offer was revoked. The Dryma no longer wish to form an alliance with us."

"And their prince?" the eager, handsome man at his side pressed.

"Revoked," Prince Calhoun said flatly as he crushed the envelope in his fist. "This news will not be received lightly."

I could see the anger boiling off him and feared for my friends, but the prince was in more control than he seemed to be. "I am sorry the news is not what you expected."

"Surely, they could've told us before we arrived and saved us the trouble?" the Sidhee guard said. "Selfish, self-important...."

To my astonishment, Prince Calhoun stood still, his anger seeming to mold and transform into something much more deadly. "I will have their prince," he promised, "One way or another, I will ensure I have their prince as my slave if not my lover."

I fidgeted uncomfortably. "Is there a message you would like me to send to them?" I offered.

Prince Calhoun had forgotten I was there or simply didn't care because he tossed the letter at my feet and briskly started back in the direction he'd come from.

Before the trees swallowed their massive bodies, he looked back and spoke. "When the Dryma fall, so will your kind. There is no place in this world for you."

His passive-aggressive warning was more shocking than if he would've swatted at me with his meaty fists.

For several moments after they'd gone, we stood in the clearing with sweaty palms and sweatier foreheads.

"Well that went better than expected," Tomas pointed out.

Zain instantly glared at him. "Don't talk yet. Wait until we get to the car."

In response, Tomas shot him a patronized look, but luckily neither felt up to arguing, and slowly we made our way back to the jeep. I could hear Joel wheezing as he tried to keep up, but there was something different in the way he walked. In the way he smelled.

"What's wrong?" I hung back so only Joel could hear my words.

"Just tired," he sighed. He knew I could read his mind, and yet he'd lied to me, which meant whatever thoughts he had he desperately wanted to keep private.

I jogged through the thicket to catch up to Zain who was trying to wake up the whole forest with his thrashing about. "Do you think he bought it?" Zain asked.

"Definitely," I said nervously. "But I'm worried about what he said. Christophe said he needed them and for the Dryma to give their beloved prince to someone like that.... Something must be wrong."

Zain nodded as he bit his lower lip. "But what could be so pressing? And a guy at that! What do the Sidhee want with a prince?"

I shook my head. "No idea."

"Maybe the prince is a great catch," Tomas teased as he caught up to us. And because I knew they all needed an emotional reprieve, I let them laugh although there was nothing comical about our positions.

"What if the Sidhee prince contacts the captain?" Joel pointed out. "Did we plan for that?"

"We might have the most advanced gadgets here." Zain patted his data phone for emphasis. "But the Sidhee are still living in the stone ages. If they don't go to Captain Christophe right now, it could take weeks for them to contact him."

"Too late for them."

Another round of laughs, but this time, I didn't join in. Prince Calhoun had been calm, too calm, and his composure didn't sit well with me. There was something he and Christophe knew that threatened to shatter our lives, but I couldn't begin to guess what.

By the time we got to the car, I couldn't feel my fingers or toes. All I wanted was a blanket to pull over my head, but there were still preparations to be made for tomorrow.

CHAPTER FOUR

WHY I had thought this would work, I couldn't decide for the life of me. I stood in Zain's tiny bathroom, turning from side to side in an expensive costume that was oversized and made me look like a twig wearing a pile of leaves.

"Impossible," I muttered.

Zain rattled on the door, appearing in a maroon suit tailored to his body. We had come to the conclusion Prince Calhoun was the type who wouldn't want to be outshined, so Zain, Joel, and Tomas all wore the same costume. He held a hideous demon mask loosely in his hands, the dark feathers poking out like fluff from a pillow.

"What do you mean?" Zain asked, but I knew he saw the problem.

"I'm way too thin to pull this off. Did you see that guy? He was colossal."

Zain gnawed on his lower lip as he stared at my appearance. "I admit you're slight, but the costume looks great."

I turned back to the mirror and gazed at the irony that was my costume. Christophe was expecting a Sidhee prince, so I was banking on the fact he would think the swan costume was meant to insinuate their power over us.

My suit was a glittering black, so I had that going for me at least. My sleeves were too long and the heavy feather-decorated coat limited my movement.

I felt an ache between my shoulder blades and wished desperately that my wings would burst through my bone.

"Wow, you look good," Joel complimented quietly as he maneuvered his way into the doorway. The maroon suit actually looked decent on him.

I smiled humorlessly. "I feel like Big Bird."

Zain shook his head. "You don't look anything like him. The jacket looked silly on the hanger, but you pull it off. Don't worry, they aren't going to notice you're smaller than that jerk."

Sighing, I reached for the plastic case teetering on the soapy ledge of his sink. "Don't forget your contacts." I looked at my blue eyes before covering them with a dark shade of red.

IT WAS unreasonable of me to schedule every available Kuro for protection duty and not be present at the Reserve, but that was exactly what I had to do. I told myself the plan would succeed and when I came back, there would no longer be a reason to serve the Dryma, and my people would be free.

But the section of my brain concerned for the welfare of my newfound mate told me I couldn't run without him.

To humans, the trees were shapeless and blended into the background at night. As we drove through the Reserve trails, through the area that didn't need to be protected, I noticed characteristics about the trees I hadn't before. Even in the dark, we could see well, which meant I could see the twisted branches jutting out from the massive trunk like they were trying to escape. The littered leaves were mostly green, but there were brown cracks running the length of them like an inseam.

As looming as they were, the clustered trees were also frail and delicate. Once they were torn down, that was the end of their lives. Startled by my increased empathy, I readjusted my dark suit until the fabric lay flat against me like a second skin.

"Stop here," I whispered.

If Zain hadn't been expecting my command, I doubted he would've heard me. The jeep came to a shuddering stop, the headlights casting a cluster of small trees in an unnatural glow.

My kind needed to think I was there with them so I needed to go through with my announcement, but the guilt was eating me alive.

The Dryma fairies are meeting at the Castle De Mar for a ball they are holding. Our efforts to preserve and protect the trees have proved to be efficient. Although I know this is not what you'd like to do, I thank you for your service and will be in touch with you should the need arise.

Projecting my thoughts to others was the easy part. When I allowed foreign thoughts into my head, I got a searing headache. All at once, individual voices forced their way into my mind. Some were thought-out responses about obeying and not minding the protection duty. Others were blunt words they never would've allowed past their lips. I took a breath and felt a hand tapping my arm.

Startled, I snapped my eyes open and saw Zain staring at me with concern. The car was still in park, the lights creating jagged shadows on the stiff trunks of the imposing trees.

"You okay?" he asked, raising an eyebrow. Up close, I could see the contact lens clinging to his eyes, but just as soon as I noticed, Zain blinked and backed away.

"Fine," I sighed, leaning back as much as the seat would allow.

Obviously, we couldn't simply pull up to the castle and demand entry, so we would park deeper in the woods and walk the rest of the way. The bright red flower was pinned to my chest like a scarlet letter, and even in the darkness, the color was stark.

The drive to our designated spot was far too short and as much as I wanted to take everything back, I knew we had to go forward with our plan. The night air chilled me to the bone, my costume doing little to contain my heat. Joel and Tomas stumbled from the back of the car, tripping over their suits.

"This costume cost me half my paycheck," Tomas complained as we crossed through the woods, working our ways toward the path leading directly to the castle.

According to the letter Captain Christophe had given me, the Prince of the Sidhee and his company were supposed to act completely like fairies and go through the front door.

"Shut up," Zain snapped as he grasped my arm in an attempt to make sure I didn't trip on anything with my ridiculous costume. I wanted to tell him I was touched by the gesture, but my throat completely closed up and I was afraid I'd choke on air.

Tomas grumbled something behind us, but I didn't take the time to figure out what.

The glittering lights of the castle stuck out against the night sky, dazzling like thousands of diamonds and precious stones. Much of the prominent structure was comprised of rare metals, and even though I'd never been, I had always imagined the inside was as elaborately decorated.

I had to hand it to the Dryma; they were able to create a beautiful castle as large and grand as any palace in England or Russia and had successfully managed to hide their Castle De Mar from prying human eyes.

More than once, I'd ventured through this part of the woods so I could behold the castle. The others believed Joel, Tomas, Zain, and I were guarding this elite part of the forest. With so many Dryma gathered in one place, I knew the others would be too frightened to seek me out and risk Christophe's wrath.

There was a space that looked like a cluster of trees crowded in front of a small pond, but only to human eyes. I led my group through the trees, securing my mask as I went in case there were other Dryma who had yet to make the journey through the woods. I felt my feet gliding on the smooth stones to the island where the castle was. If humans had been more perceptive, they may have noticed the dazzling castle, but the Dryma would've just adapted by using another form of deceptive magic.

Behind the castle was a modern-day parking garage where shiny, impressive cars gleamed like status symbols. There were floating lanterns illuminating the parking garage, and I heard Tomas curse as he bumped his arm into one of them. The papery lantern barely registered the jolting movement and continued to sway like a remote-control airplane.

"Beautiful," Joel stuttered, his voice muffled through the mask. Mine was a half mask so I could speak without interruption, but we couldn't all risk having our faces exposed.

"It's okay." Zain tried to sound bored, but I could hear how impressed he was.

Truthfully, it was hard not to be. The castle towered into the sky, complete with brick turrets and a steep set of stairs leading to a set of glass double doors outlined in crystals. I imagined this was what humans thought of when picturing a fairy castle.

The garden was immaculately well kept, lotus flowers floating in the ponds and koi darting around the fallen petals. There were stone steps guiding guests through the park and ornate golden benches where I saw Dryma talking.

"Why don't they just live here?" Joel whispered, keeping close to me. "There has to be a hundred rooms at least."

I had my invitation in my hand so I could quickly show the imposing guards and get inside. I glanced around to make sure there were no Dryma within earshot and whispered back, "Because it's impractical."

"Right." I could imagine Zain rolling his eyes. "Because they just have so much to do in the human world."

Really, I couldn't imagine why anyone wouldn't want to live here all the time. The closer we got, the smaller I felt; a difficult feat considering how tall I was. My heart raced as I clambered up the steps, feeling every bit the monster I was impersonating.

What if Prince Calhoun had decided to contact Christophe directly and was waiting inside to capture me? The humiliation of having to beg for mercy wouldn't kill me, but that was if he even let me get that far.

My blood thumped in my ears, the sound like crashing waves against rocks. I saw Marvin, the Dryma who had been acting as the bouncer at Crystal Cove, and wasn't surprised to see he was the one checking invitations.

We'd managed to douse ourselves in cologne to help mask the scent of what we were, but the hope was that the guard wouldn't be able to distinguish us from the Dryma because of our close proximity.

I held my breath, waiting behind a male and female Dryma dressed as vampires. Of course, there were slits in their costumes running down their shoulder blades so they could fly if they chose to. It took every ounce of willpower I had to keep from vomiting right then and there.

"Invitation please," Marvin drawled in a bored voice as he held out his hand for the invite. His light hair was pulled back with bobby pins, exposing his face. I wasn't sure what he was supposed to be because he had his half mask hanging loosely from a rope connected to the same belt loop holding his whip.

Shuddering, I presented the invite and straightened until I thought my spine might snap. Marvin barely grazed the invite slip before snapping his head to attention and raking his eyes over the bright red flower pinned to my chest.

When he spoke, his voice was uneven and on edge. He gave a single nod to the other guard who was chatting with a group of young Dryma not much older than Micky before leaning in. "Welcome, Your Highness. Prince Tristan will be sure to find you, so please enjoy our hospitality until then."

If Zain hadn't spoken up, then my nervousness would've given us away. "My prince does not intend to wait long. Make sure your prince attends to us at once."

Marvin blinked in confusion, and there was a fire behind his eyes he struggled to conceal. "Of course." He bowed ever so slightly. "Your prince will not want for anything while he is visiting."

"Good save," I whispered to Zain as I stopped inside a small landing where we could remove and hang up coats. I reached underneath my mask to wipe sweat away from my brow. "I thought we were done for."

Tomas reached up to undo the ribbons holding the fluttering curtain open, and we were hidden from view. I could hear the soft sounds of music from a room nearby and then the intense fluttering of wings.

The landing we were in consisted of an elaborately carved wooden bench, a coatrack, and a tall coffee table with a crystal pitcher full of water.

The four of us were crowded inside the landing, but it gave me a moment to breathe.

"The Prince of the Sidhee is proud," I started, "but he is also cautious. If you guys follow me all night, then the other fairies will become suspicious. If you don't at all, Christophe will know something is wrong. Make sure you can always see me, and if I take off my flower, then it's time to leave. Understand?"

Joel's chest was heaving, and I poured him a glass of water and forced it into his hands before he passed out.

"You can still turn back," I told him gently.

Joel shook his head, lifted his mask, and downed the water. "No, I'm staying."

"Then we're agreed. The prince will find Kanji, and he'll move forward with the plan."

A round of nods went around the room, but I couldn't keep my fears under wraps. If my mate was here, and honestly how could he not be, the entire plan was going to be a disaster.

Taking a deep breath, I secured my mask and looked around at my friends. They were as ready as they were ever going to be, so I nodded. Tomas drew the curtain and admitted us entry into the core of the castle.

The castle had circular stairs leading upward, but the majority of the party seemed to be occurring in the large ballroom we had just stepped into. The first thing I noticed was how pale everything was. White lacey chandeliers, creamy fabrics for curtains and tablecloths, and sheer crystal cups, plates, and silverware. It was like stepping into an expensive home catalog where everything has a perfect place.

The veranda doors had been thrown open, emitting a cool air that didn't reach me. There were fairies seated and talking, but most of the Dryma were on the dance floor. There wasn't a modern DJ, but a group of Dryma at the front playing flutes, violins, and instruments I didn't recognize.

"Oh my god," Joel gasped.

I followed his gaze and nearly lost my breath at what he was seeing. Flying above us, like tiny dolls plucked from fairy tale dream houses, were Dryma fluttering in a dance I could only dream of knowing. The beating of the wings should've drowned everything else out, but they harmonized perfectly with the music drifting across the floor.

Each costume was ornate and expensive, so I was glad we had spent the extra money to buy ours. At least we wouldn't stand out due to our macabre colors because most of the costumes were dark, a perfect contrast to the pale background.

In spite of myself, I found my eyes wandering the floor for any sign of him. It was impossible to tell who was who because of the flourish of masks and fluttering wings, but I would've known him anywhere. Most of the Dryma were blond, but their hair was lackluster in comparison to his golden curls.

The guard was easy to spot because like my friends, they all wore the same crimson red suit complete with a dark half mask that looked like a goblin. Swinging at their hips were their whips, and some of them even carried guns with ivory handles.

Inwardly, I cringed, but I managed to compose myself enough so they wouldn't see how uncomfortable I was beneath my mask. I surveyed the room and questioned how the prince would be able to seek me out with how many Dryma were present. But even though all of the Dryma seemed to be in attendance, the ballroom was open, and there was plenty of space.

The floors were made of marble, and there were candles locked in large glass orbs positioned at various heights along the wall.

"Look at all that food," Tomas exclaimed, and I was sure I could've heard his stomach grumbling if it wasn't so loud.

I smiled ever so slightly. "Go for it. Just make sure to keep me in sight."

He nodded curtly. "Of course. Do you want anything?"

There were several tables pressed against one of the walls with intricately woven pastries, giant multi-tiered cakes, and roasting meat, but I didn't trust my stomach enough to keep food down.

"Maybe later," I said, my throat dry. "Go ahead and mingle so we don't look suspicious."

Joel and Zain broke away together, heading toward the wall where several Dryma were huddled, sipping from delicate flute glasses.

For the slightest moment, there was absolutely nothing but the sound of the bells clinking and the strings of the violins being plucked. But the moment was short-lived, and before I knew it, my anger bubbled from my stomach and made me taste bile.

The Dryma were so carefree in their notable costumes and finery, while my kind suffered and could hardly afford to keep their heat on. In the moment, it was easy to be swept up into the glamour that was the ball. How many days had I wasted wanting this life for myself? The guilt climbed through my body, and before I could wallow in my own self-pity, I tweaked the flower so it stood out more.

I'd met a few of the princes, but it was hard to keep track of them because there were seven. I noticed the way a few Dryma held their heads higher than the rest and kept to the front of the room where two Dryma dressed in riches and silk sat upon golden thrones. The only distinguishing mark the princes had was the way they carried themselves, but it was enough. I tried to make eye contact so they would search for me, but none of them made a move toward me.

I had the red contacts so the guard would think I was Sidhee and the fairies must've assumed they were part of my costume, so what more could I do to get him to notice me?

Without warning, my senses were assaulted by my mate's presence. My blood burned in my veins, and my thoughts reeled. The desire to rip my clothes from my body and kneel on the ground before him was maddening. I fought the desire to seek him out, but I couldn't escape.

My mate stood before me, his hands clasped neatly behind him so I couldn't see the strong, tanned fingers. In the lighting, his skin had a light shimmer as though he had just put lotion on. I thought I was going to go blind from his costume because the irony combined with my longing was too much.

"Seems like we were thinking along the same lines, Prince Calhoun," he laughed, his eyes sliding over my body. I hated how he sounded so nervous, but he thought I was the evil Prince Calhoun here to claim him.

I cleared my throat. "Seems so."

Instead of an oversized feather jacket like what I was wearing, he had a tailored white suit made of feathers and a swan mask complete with a beak. He was also wearing a half mask so I could see his lips and strong jaw.

"Are you part of the guard?" I asked, desperately wanting him to introduce himself to me.

His lips spread into a sad smile. "Of course you don't remember me. It's been so long. I am Prince Tristan."

My world spiraled into madness. Dear god no. My mouth was hanging open, but I made no attempt to close it.

He was Prince Tristan… the Dryma meant to be given to the Sidhee to unite their clans? How could these pathetic excuses for life give such a beautiful creature to the evil soul-stealing demons? I clutched at my chest to keep from fainting.

"Are you all right?" Tristan asked, his gemstone green eyes glittering from behind his mask.

I needed to find Zain….

"Would you like me to get you a refreshment?"

And tell him that it was off….

"Or is there something else you would like?"

Because I couldn't do this to my mate….

"Prince Calhoun?"

"Sorry," I said suddenly, lowering my voice. "I am just not quite used to all this noise."

"Of course. How careless of me. Would you care to follow me outside where it is quieter?"

I nodded and followed him through the throng of Dryma to the open doors. It wasn't until we were outside and alone in a gazebo overlooking the lights of the castle that I could breathe.

"Forgive me for being so bold," he started, leaning against a column of the gazebo.

"Say whatever you'd like."

That definitely surprised him. "But you are not anything like what I expected."

I bit my lower lip and turned my back on him so I was facing the sculpture garden farther out. I heard him come up behind me, my cock jerking to life at the sheer scent of him.

"I heard my brothers propositioned you, but you would only accept me…. I am honored."

The Prince of the Sidhee had wanted him that badly?

"I will do what I can to be a good mate for you."

"Enough." My voice cut through the air, and I felt him stiffen behind me. Tristan was so tall and built, but he had instantly stopped at my command. He hadn't flinched or cowered, just held his ground. He was more than a handsome face; he was tactful and intelligent. I could tell by the guided way he moved and spoke. "You are being sold. Don't you care at all?"

His resigned voice surprised me. "I am not in a position to feel entitled."

There was agony in his words, locked deep within his heart. I was more willing to gouge my eyes out than continue on this way. I looked around for Zain and the others, but they must've lost me in the crowd because we were completely alone in the garden.

Before I could divulge my true identity, he stepped so close to me I could hear his heart thumping against my back. He seemed to tower over me, but I knew that was because of his muscular frame and chiseled features. A few inches of height seemed to make all the difference.

He had me pinned, trapped, and even though he could've called for the guard or forced me to answer, a strange calming sensation drifted through my body. It was a knee-jerk reaction to him being my mate, and I knew that, but couldn't bring myself to pull away.

"I'm not Prince Calhoun," I whispered as I gripped the railing until my knuckles turned white.

Tristan ghosted his fingers over my arm until he had his hand wrapped around my wrist. The gesture was gentle and unthreatening but sent jolts of pleasure into my body.

"I know." His voice was husky. "Prince Calhoun couldn't be bothered to come here himself so he sent you."

"What?" The word had slipped from my lips before I realized what he'd been insinuating. Yes, I'd admitted I wasn't the prince, but not that

I wasn't a Sidhee. I inhaled and tried to take a step away to get some distance from Tristan, but his body acted as a wall keeping me where he wanted me.

"Your name?" he inquired, turning my wrist so I had no choice but to detach myself from the railing. Before I could stop him, he was spinning me around to face him.

To me he embodied everything I'd ever wanted, and the realization I could lose him made my stomach slide up into my throat and words escaped me.

"Mason." There had to be a Mason serving Calhoun, right? It was a pretty popular name after all.

"Mason." Tristan's teeth were bright white and perfectly complimented his golden skin. The word sounded foreign on his tongue, and I found I hated him saying someone else's name.

"I thought he would come himself," Tristan continued. "What was his intention? To have me think you were him and then when I divulge who I was interested in, I would announce Calhoun?"

Seemed like something the Sidhee prince would think of. "I believe so."

"He failed miserably, then."

"How so?"

"There is no way I could mistake you for him."

"Why?" The bars of the gazebo were pressing into my lower back and legs, daring to break me in half if I kept trying to scoot away.

Tristan snaked his hand around the back of my neck, his fingers threading underneath the strings of my half mask. For a moment, I completely froze and waited for him to reveal my face, but he didn't. Instead, he wound his fingers through my long hair and pulled me into a kiss that seared the flesh from my lips.

His mouth tasted of cherry wine as he explored the inside of my mouth. With a strong arm around my waist, he lifted me from my feet. His mouth locked onto mine possessively, like he'd never let go. A soft moan escaped my lips as he broke away and traced the outline of my lips with his finger.

"You asked me why. Do you still want to know?" Tristan's green eyes flashed.

"Yes."

"Because there's no way someone like him could be my mate."

"Your mate?" My words betrayed me. "How do you know I'm your mate?" Had I accidentally given him some sign? Then I realized my mistake.

To the other Dryma, my scent had been masked due to the sheer amount of us crowded into the castle. But in the privacy of the garden, there were no barriers I could put between us to mask who I was.

"I didn't know I could mate to a Sidhee," he confessed, pressing his nose to my neck so he could inhale my scent. "I thought such a thing would be impossible."

He should've known I was a Kuro, just like I'd known he was a Dryma from the moment I saw him. When I thought back, I'd identified Tristan as a Dryma based on his looks, not his scent. Finding a mate meant only recognizing them as your other half, not distinguishing between what they were.

"I didn't think it was possible either," I told him.

My head ached, and I needed to run from him, but I felt like I was drowning. This was a chaotic nightmare I needed to escape from before everything blew up in my face.

"I'm not your mate. You're going to marry my prince." Denying my mate with my half-hearted lie made me physically ill.

Tristan narrowed his eyes. "Yes, I am. I have no choice... but you already know that."

A pit formed in my stomach. I couldn't let Tristan see my face or realize who I was because then he would know everything was a lie. Despite knowing I'd changed his life, I didn't regret turning Calhoun away. Tristan deserved better.

"So tell me why I'm your mate?" I asked bitterly.

In the moment he was caught off guard, I wrenched my arm upward and out of his grasp. I had half a mind to run down the gazebo steps and tear the flower from my chest to signal the others, but my feet were glued to the ground.

"I understand your loyalty to Calhoun."

He had no idea. "I have to go back," I told him, stepping away before he could take my hand again. "I am sorry for tricking you."

Tristan cleared his throat, and the small sound made me stop and slowly turn back to face him. He was standing with his arms at his sides and his face angled upward so he could stare at the sky through the golden panels of the gazebo.

"You came all this way on behalf of the prince, and my guard will think it strange if you leave me now," Tristan murmured as he went to a panel of the gazebo and pushed a button. Above us, in the oval panel of the gazebo, lights came on and beautiful music played. I saw there was a crystal oval that broke apart and twirled while the music played. "So dance with me."

"I'm not your mate." But all my conviction was gone.

He sauntered over to me like a cat stalking his prey and wrapped a strong arm around my waist. "You have already accepted me as your mate or else I would not be able to sense you were my mate."

I blinked. "What are you talking about?"

Tristan captured me in a waltz, and I was afraid I'd step on his feet. "Mating happens between two people, but it's like a chemical reaction. There is a primary person who mates first and then there is a secondary who realizes the mating and reacts."

I narrowed my eyes, the music thumping in my ears. "So how do you know I'm primary?"

Tristan grinned, the lights from the music box above us casting a sparkle show on his white costume. "Because fairies rarely are so observant."

I tried to not laugh, but failed. "That's quite a thing to say, considering you're a fairy and all."

Tristan pressed his lips to mine. In the gazebo where the only sounds were of the music box and our shuffled dancing, I let myself imagine this was what my life could be.

Dancing with him, kissing him, telling him my hopes….

They were all things my mind was telling me I needed to do in order to become his true mate, but I couldn't. If he knew I was Kuro, a slave, he might not be as harsh as Christophe, but the captain would find out and the only thing awaiting me was punishment.

"You're a good dancer," I told him for something to say.

"Practice." He flashed his white teeth. "These balls are rather common, but we don't usually host them here."

"Why not? It's beautiful."

"You like it?" he asked softly. "It is… stunning, but it's too large for my taste."

"Castles are meant to be big, though."

He chuckled, ducking his head down so he could bury his face into my hair. If the feathers and string of the mask were uncomfortable to him, he didn't make it known. "Why did this happen? After all these years of wanting to have a true mate, I finally gave up and resigned myself to Calhoun. Why do I have to find you now that it's too late?" He sounded frustrated, like he couldn't quite say all that was on his mind.

It was as if he was reading my mind.

"Why do you have to be with him?" I asked.

Tristan stiffened, and I held my breath to see if I'd betrayed myself. "Of course you wouldn't know. Calhoun is a private demon after all."

He stroked my lower back, easing his hand up my jacket so he could touch my bare skin. The feel of fingers on my flesh sent a fire raging through my body. "He doesn't tell his inferiors much."

Tristan paused our dancing and looked at me. "You're not inferior," he stated boldly. "But to Calhoun I suppose you are."

We resumed our dancing, but I knew time was running out. The musical orb above us was starting to reform, the music dulling. "No matter what I want, I have to do what's best for my people," Tristan said quietly. "As much as I loathe having to give you up."

My stomach bubbled. Unlike the last time we'd met, I knew there would be finality in our good-bye. I couldn't reveal myself to him and maintain the hope he would still want me.

And he was right… a prince had a duty to his people.

The song ended, and he released me but was close enough for me to smell the wine on his breath.

"The prince mentioned the Kuro swans as being part of this plan." I took a step back so I could breathe.

Instantly, he closed the gap and touched my cheek. He couldn't keep his hands off me, and I wasn't in a place to complain. The more he wanted to touch me, the more I wanted him.

"What about them?" he asked pleasantly, as if discussing the weather.

I hated the anger that boiled inside me, but it was too late to stop. "They are your slaves."

"They serve us, yes." Tristan ran his hand through his golden curls before reaching for the top button of his jacket and undoing it. I thought he was trying to seduce me, but when I looked at him, he didn't seem to notice the lust I felt reddening my cheeks and ears.

"What happens to them in this agreement?"

Tristan smiled. "Why do you care?"

I shook my head. "Curious. They used to serve us, after all."

"We need them," Tristan said, and his words were so sincere, I almost felt guilty at what I was going to say next.

"You're keeping their wings, right?"

Tristan nodded curtly, but a dark shadow crossed his features and even under the mask, I could see his discomfort. "We are, yes."

"How?"

"Your kind used to ride the Kuro swans between this world and yours. In order for the Sidhee to harness the Kuro ability to fly, a certain allotment of their powers was transferred to your kind. When the Kuro were betrayed, that section of power the Sidhee owned was given to the Dryma in the form of flight. Christophe is the only one who knows how it is contained. Make sense?"

Before my uncle had fallen ill, he had spoken of the relationship between the Sidhee and the Kuro, but not how the Sidhee were able to take away everything. My father had been the one to be betrayed, but the details I'd been given were from my uncle.

Christophe had insinuated I was betrayed and didn't know what had happened. Was he right?

A crushing pain gripped my chest, grinding my muscle and bones into powder. Everything we had done for our plan, all those we'd betrayed and tricked were for nothing. Christophe was the one who had my answers all along, but I had thought I could get to our wings through the prince.

This was a disaster.

"You're concerned for them? You must be very kind." Tristan circled me, stopping when my back was to him. "Can I touch you?"

My lips trembled.

Tristan slid one of his arms around my waist while his other hand went to the hem of my jacket and slipped underneath. But he was patient, and his hand hovered inches from my skin while he waited for my reply. "Please?"

I swallowed. "Yes."

Then he was all over me as he gently pulled me from the gazebo to a small garden shed. He shut and locked the door before reaching above us to turn on one of the crystal orbs hovering in the room.

Even the shed was fit for royalty. There were no windows except for a small slit at the top of the door. There were rows of instruments and gardening tools along the walls, but what caught my eye was the pile of silk blankets and pillows piled in a corner of the room.

"Is this where you bring your lovers?" I asked nervously, desperate to find a sense of normalcy.

Tristan stepped away from the door, no longer barring me from leaving. "No, I come here to be alone."

"This can't amount to anything," I whispered. "You said so yourself."

His resolved expression faltered. "I know, but does that mean you don't even want tonight?"

Amongst my kind, there was no such thing as only liking one sex or the other; it was all about who was your mate. And although there had been both male and female Kuro I had found attractive, never had I been so hard my pants threatened to burst at the seam.

If I gave myself to him, that was the end. "I want you."

He crossed the room slowly, walking past me to the blankets and pillows and arranging them quietly. I watched his back as he moved, noticing how the fabric creased around his muscles as he bent. The folds of his suit were cut into slits so he could have the use of his wings if he wanted to. But like Kuro, Dryma were able to conceal their wings within their bodies until they had a need for flight.

When he straightened, he tore the mask from his face, revealing his carved features and delicate eyelashes. I wanted him more than I'd ever wanted anything.

"I need to leave my mask on," I told him as he undid the buttons of his jacket and let the material fall to the floor. He was bare-chested beneath the creamy fabric, his sculpted abdominal muscles on display.

"Why?" He cocked his head to the side and crossed the room.

"Safer for me...." My voice was muffled against his chest.

He didn't object, just pressed kisses into my hair. "I want you," he whispered. "Right now, I can't even think because of how badly I want to make you mine."

"Are you sure this is what you want?"

Tristan cupped my face between his large hands, making me feel fragile, safe, and wanted all at the same time. "Are you?"

"I need you."

Then he was on me, undoing the black buttons of my ridiculous coat and chucking it to the floor. His hands were on my pants, undoing the buttons and pulling them and my briefs down so I was exposed before him. Gently, he pushed me to the floor while he worked on his zipper. He positioned me on my hands and knees, but the blankets were so soft I didn't feel the hardwood floors beneath.

Luckily I'd worn cover-up on my wrist where the Dryma had marked me so unless he was looking for the seal, he wouldn't find it.

"What happened to your back?" he asked quietly.

Shit. I had forgotten about the scars on my back from where Christophe had punished me and fumbled for an excuse. "An accident."

I held my breath. But if he didn't believe me, he didn't say so.

"I don't want to hurt you," he told me as I heard the tearing of foil I assumed belonged to a condom. Even now, in the heat of our one night affair, he was cautious.

"I don't have anything," I told him. When was the last time I'd been with someone?

"I believe you," he said simply. "I don't either, but I don't have any lubricant handy."

As simple as that, we believed each other. If only I hadn't betrayed his trust by pretending to be someone I wasn't. Tristan's fingers were at my entrance as he pushed past my inner ring of muscle with a newfound need. The lube from the condom was on his fingers so he entered my slick entrance without problem.

I sighed deeply as I felt his fingers entwining within me, his attempt to make me wholly his. Even though his words pushed me away, his actions showed what he truly wanted. And that was to unequivocally make me his.

His hand slid from me, and he gripped my hips so he could keep my body still. Before he could enter me, I stole a backward glance and nearly lost my breath. His uncut, thick erection was standing proudly at attention. I was leaking with need at the sight of my mate's parted lips and the blush coloring his cheeks. He was completely naked, which made me feel foolish for still wearing my mask, but he barely seemed to notice.

"I don't want to, but I won't take away your options." He struggled to keep his voice even. "So I'll stop if you want me to."

"I'm afraid," I admitted as I turned to face him.

"Of me?" His eyes darkened and he backed away slightly.

"No, of...."

He closed in on me and lifted me so I was straddling his hips, my legs instinctively wrapped around his. "I won't harm you."

Neither one of us pointed out we were talking about my heart and not my body. There was no place in our heated embrace for technicalities.

Tristan slid his hands up and down my sides, tracing each of my ribs and tickling the space between. The moments ticked by, but the fervor with which he'd started slowed just enough for me to see the changes in his expressions.

Something in my face must've given me away, because without giving me warning, he lifted me easily and impaled me on his long, beautiful cock. I cried out, arching my spine and almost falling back. If his hands weren't so strong, I would've been useless on top of him.

The pain was immense as he stretched my tight ring of muscle, but he didn't give me time to adjust. He eased out of me and then slammed back in so fiercely I saw stars. My heart pounded in my head, and I never wanted him to stop.

"So tight," he whispered. "I feel like you're trying to swallow me up."

If I could, I would have.

When he was able to easily slip in and out of me, he lifted me off his lap and spun me so I was on my hands and knees. I fisted the silky blankets carpeting the floor and screamed as he entered me again.

"I want to be kind," he rasped as he continued to thrust, the pain turning into pleasure. "But I can't. I want you to remember this. Am I hurting you?"

"No, just keep going," I cried. Only my mate could bring me so close to begging.

His hand wrapped around my shaft, and he rubbed the precum leaking from my slit. With firm, sure movements, he fisted my cock until I thought I'd pass out.

Tristan's cries were frustrated.

"Tristan," I breathed, nearing my orgasm. "Give me a second."

He paused balls deep inside of me and helped me so I was fully supported on my knees. One strong, tanned arm took hold of my midsection while his other hand continued to milk me. He slammed into my body with such force he lifted me from the ground, and I could feel him in my stomach.

My head lolled back on his shoulder, and I could feel his pulse racing. Just hearing his life thumping from him was enough to drive me crazy, and I wondered how anyone could resist him.

"I'm close," I warned him, expecting him to ease his grip so I could finish myself. He only tightened his hand in response, raking his fingers up and down my shaft until my inner thighs tightened and heat pooled in my stomach.

Struggling to find something to hold onto, I settled for Tristan's forearm. Within moments, I was a quivering wreck as he coaxed my orgasm from within me, forcing me to ride through the aftershocks.

I silently screamed, but the rush of the wind against the wooden walls of the shed and Tristan's heavy breathing masked my voice. His grip tightened, and as he panted in my ear, I could feel him tremble inside of me as he found his own release.

Tristan was unlike any partner I'd ever had. His face was flushed but instead of seeking air, he took possession of my lips. The raw pleasure of his hand still on my cock and knowing he was orgasming was enough to send me into another fit of intense pleasure.

As my breathing stabilized, I gave one final moan into his mouth. I expected him to turn away in disgust as the heat dissipated between us, but he startled me by pulling me closer. Really, I shouldn't have been surprised because I didn't think he was one to run away.

The wind chortled outside, violently slapping the walls and making the tiny window shudder in its frame. I had no idea how long we'd been gone, but I knew Zain and the others were probably going out of their minds looking for me.

Furrowing my brow, I tried to clear my mind long enough to tell them I was okay, but Tristan's hand rubbing my lower back made all other thoughts impossible.

"I'm sorry," he told me, his voice hoarse from exertion.

I gathered my jacket from the floor before putting it back on. "Why?"

"This was wrong of me."

"We both knew this was all there was going to be," I said coldly, trying to mask my hurt. The thought of being torn from Tristan was unbearable, and now that I'd let myself be claimed by him, how long did I have until I turned into an empty shell?

I would've suffered less if he just killed me.

"Mason, I—"

I flinched at the sound of that name on his tongue. Fastening my pants, I turned around to face him, taking in his appearance. He'd managed to pull on his slacks, but the top button remained undone and revealed the blond curls just below his belly button. Even when he was half-naked, he managed to appear regal.

"Please," I whispered. "Don't make this harder than it has to be."

"I won't let you go."

"Huh?" It was a less than dignified response, but I was certain I'd heard him wrong.

"I've always wanted my mate," he confessed quietly. "And now I finally have you."

"What about Prince Calhoun?" I reminded him, quickly pulling the rest of my clothes on so I could escape the confines of the shed. If I didn't get out of there now, I didn't stand a chance.

"I thought I would be satisfied with just this, but not having you will drive me crazy." Tristan closed the gap and suddenly the shed felt like a shoebox.

"If you don't let me go, you're going to regret this."

"I need you."

"What about your kind?"

He inhaled sharply, and I knew reasoning had won.

"Look," I said softly. I raked my eyes over every inch of him, committing his long lashes and golden hair to memory. "We can't choose who our mates are, and it's confusing you. But you know I'm right. You can't betray the Dryma, and having me as your mate would do exactly that."

"Is that what you want?" Tristan's eyes bore into mine like freshly polished stones. "To pretend none of this ever happened?"

I closed my eyes and prayed he wouldn't see through my lie. "Yes."

Time ticked by, my heart a frozen bomb of fear that he had believed me and when he told me to go, I wouldn't be able to. Leaning in close, I could feel his breath on my cheek as he gently parted my hair. For a second, I thought he might try to remove my mask and reveal my identity, but he didn't.

"I don't believe you."

My lower lip quivered, and I felt bitter resentment toward this gorgeous fairy. How could he reduce me to such a state where I felt like a child? And yet, trying to stay angry with him was downright impossible.

Before I could open my mouth to let another lie pass my lips about not wanting him, there was a shrill scream that could've reduced the tiny shack to little more than plywood and screws.

Tristan stood absolutely still, and I wondered if he had heard the scream or if it had come from one of my kind. Quickly, I turned from him and let my mind go blank so I could run through the thoughts of the other Kuro swans. The ones on protection duty had monotonous thoughts about when they could sleep and what was for dinner.

But Zain, Joel, and Tomas's urgent pleas to find me derailed my thoughts.

Man, we have to go, right now. It was Zain calling for me, his sight a blur of images as he searched the masked faces for me.

Kanji, where are you? Please, we have to go? Joel sounded frantic, his fear less concealed than Zain's.

I tried to make sense of the images blurring my vision, but the Dryma fairies were twirling together and forming a kaleidoscope image I couldn't piece together.

What's wrong? I demanded quickly, knowing I had a few seconds at most before they would see what I had done. In my weakened state, the barrier I had keeping them from my thoughts was fragile. *I'm coming right now. Meet me at the car.*

No, Zain growled as the air assaulted him. I noticed the other two were with him, along with a teenager. Through the hazy images, I realized Zain and the others were shielding Micky. *I'm not leaving without you.*

I could barely control my anger and fear for my friends. Why was Micky here? How could he be so foolish? *Did they find out?*

No. Zain paused for a moment before the screaming continued. I flinched in spite of myself. *A Dryma has been killed.*

His five words challenged everything I'd ever known. Before I could continue to speak with him, Tristan's hand was roughly on my shoulder, and he was dragging me from the shack.

I let him lead me but was confused at the direction we were heading.

"Why aren't we going back to the castle?"

Even in haste, Tristan stood tall and had his broad shoulders prepared for an outside attack, his blond hair whipping around his neck and the set of his jaw.

When he didn't answer, I found my strength and wrenched my hand from his grip. "What are you doing?"

Tristan slowly turned to face me. He wasn't wearing his mask so I could see the sadness impregnating his eyes, the hollowness of his cheeks as he struggled for words. "Captain Christophe is calling to me," he replied as he indicated a small alcove of sweet smelling flowers we could duck into. The flowers felt dead and limp against my arms, and I was so tall, I had to stoop to conceal myself. "He told me a fairy has died."

My mouth felt dry. "How?"

I saw his resolve falter for the slightest of moments. "His tree was savagely torn down and with it… his life."

How could that be when there was meticulous patrol watching them as we spoke? I had made sure there was an excess of protection duty so we could not be missed and brought into this predicament.

Suddenly, uncontrollable fear seized me. Micky was with Zain and the others, which meant he'd abandoned his post. I had to leave right now.

"I'm sorry," I whispered. I had been thinking of Micky, but Tristan assumed I was talking about the fairy.

"There are many things humans get wrong about fairies," Tristan stated, caressing what he could of my cheek without unmasking me. "But fragility is not among the lies. You need to leave before Christophe realizes that you're not Calhoun."

"And you? Will you seek to punish the Kuro swans?"

"Captain Christophe," he said solemnly, "will do what is necessary."

Any moment, Captain Christophe and his army were going to go rampaging through the forest in search of my kind.

"I'm torn between letting you go," he admitted as he brought my hand to his chest. I could feel his heart pounding fiercely beneath the fabric and flesh. "And escaping with you."

"If you really want me," I promised, "I will come back for you."

"Do you swear?" Tristan's eyes narrowed, his fingers tracing the pale skin of my hand. "Do you swear you will not disappear from my life?"

"I swear."

Pressing his lips against mine, he trapped my mouth in a searing kiss where our tongues fought for dominance. Breaking away, he stared at me with such a raw possessive look, I knew I would never get away. "I will do whatever it takes to be with you again, even if I have to hunt you down."

Looking into his polished emerald eyes, I knew he meant every word.

But by shunning Prince Calhoun, I'd set events into motion that would make coming back to him impossible.

CHAPTER FIVE

WHEN I was absolutely certain Tristan could no longer see me, I ripped the mask from my face and felt the cool sting of air. I darted through the trees quickly, not taking enough time to watch where I was stepping. There was no time.

I could still feel Tristan's kiss sealed on my lips. The farther I got from him, the more I could think, but there was also the undeniable pain of separation.

Realizing I was near the parking lot, I stopped for a moment to catch my breath and clear my thoughts so I could communicate with Zain and the others. His voice stopped me short, and it wasn't inside my head either.

"Where the hell have you been?" Zain burst through the woods into the small clearing I'd sought refuge in. He had removed his mask, the feathers dangling from the plastic in his hand. "I lost sight of you and thought something happened."

Before I could move, he captured me in a crushing embrace. Part of a Kuro's nature was to crave touch when they needed comfort. But even though he was my good friend, his touch could not compare to Tristan's. For the briefest of moments, I thought Zain would be able to catch my changing scent after having been taken by Tristan. But the fear was all encompassing and overtook any other scent clinging to our bodies.

As the others appeared, I had only to look in their gaunt expressions to realize how deep my treachery had gone. Tomas and Joel each had one of Micky's arms, but he looked far too frightened to fight.

"We have to go," I told them, "Before Christophe appears at the woods and sees we aren't there."

"What about the car?" Tomas growled bitterly, tightening his grip on Micky's arm so his knuckles turned white. "You think they won't recognize the jeep as being ours? Or see us in it?"

"Not if we don't use the main path," Zain explained as he released me. "We did park far away for a reason."

"We need to go right now." I nodded once at Tomas who instantly released his grip on Micky. The kid's eyes were wide and frantically darted from me to Zain.

"I'm so sorry, Kanji," he whimpered, his voice cracking. "I just, I knew you were having secret meetings, and I wanted to see if I could help so I followed you."

"Do you know what has happened?" I whispered.

Mutely, he shook his head from side to side like a ragdoll.

"A Dryma died." I let my words hover in the crisp night air. "He died, Micky, and it was because his tree was abandoned."

"It's my fault," he said in realization. Even in the dark, I could see the fear making a home behind his eyes and forever changing him. "What are they going to do to me?"

"Nothing." Joel spoke too soon, but I knew why. He sacrificed everything he earned to take care of our young who had no family. I didn't doubt shy Joel would fight to the death to protect one of his wards.

"What do you mean 'nothing'?" Zain mocked, unbuttoning his jacket. I knew he had to be cold, but he frantically clawed at his costume like he was going to suffocate. "Christophe is going to demand to know who abandoned their post."

"I will figure something out." I didn't want to make a promise I couldn't keep because this went beyond anything I had planned for.

"Kanji, I won't let you take the fall for this." Zain was shirtless, his pale skin gleaming in the dark. Tiny goose bumps painted his chest and arms, but there was relief in his eyes. "This is not your fault. We didn't plan to kill any of them."

"Didn't we?" I whispered. "We planned on destroying their alliance with the Sidhee and consequently tricking the prince into giving us the key to our freedom. But what was the point?"

"What do you mean?" Tomas asked hesitantly. "You didn't manage to get it?"

"The prince said he had no idea where it was," I admitted truthfully, unable to look directly into Tomas's accusing eyes. "We are no closer to our freedom than we were before."

The realization of all our wasted efforts sank like a rock in the air surrounding us. "We need to get back to Pasky," Joel finally said as he pulled Micky close to him.

Zain tugged at a strand of his fire red hair. "Back to the slaughter, you mean?"

"Too bad we can't run away," Tomas said, although I could hear the hope in his voice.

"*We* can't." Zain emphasized the first word before looking at me pointedly.

"No. I'm not leaving you."

"You're our prince."

"Even if I run, I have nowhere to go without my wings," I said. "If we were willing to let go of our wings, we could've escaped years ago."

But the silence of my companions reminded me of what I already knew. They were never going to abandon the wings that made them Kuro swans and that included protecting their failure of a prince.

As we trekked through the woods to the jeep, I came to realize how ill-prepared we were. If I'd managed to get to our wings and freedom, we still would've had to go back and have all the Kuro congregate. With a sinking feeling, I realized I'd never actually thought we'd succeed.

Before I'd met Tristan in the Crystal Cove parking lot, I might've believed in our plan. But I'd allowed my mate to sabotage our efforts at freedom.

Joel was whispering quietly to Micky, but I didn't zone in on his words because I was sure they would just add to the guilt I already felt.

Zain walked quickly, desperate to reach the jeep and his uniform. When the rust-laden jeep came into view, we jogged the last few feet and tore our clothes from our bodies like they were contagious. Our uniforms were piled in a heap in the back so we threw them on hastily before burying our costumes beneath a dirty cotton blanket. Then we took out the contacts and covered them with dirt.

The few moments where my skin was bare was enough time to allow the chill to enter deep into my bones. The fact my ranger uniform was cold only added to the icy feeling seeping in through my skin.

I'd never felt fear like this before and definitely not this confusion. The farther I got from Tristan, the emptier I felt. And knowing I was going to have to beg Christophe was all it took to solidify my hatred.

"Why did you follow us?" I asked Micky quietly as Zain tore through the woods on the thin threads of trail. "Didn't you realize the danger you'd put yourself in?"

Micky was pressed between the glass window and Joel, probably because Tomas looked beyond angry. Now we were inside the car, the heat blasting, Micky gained a little bit of his color back.

Beneath his cheap costume had been his uniform, but the top buttons were undone and his shirt was rumpled.

"I heard your plan when you were talking about it in your room," he admitted quietly. "I wanted to help you."

When formulating our plan, we'd been so careful. But I'd been watching out for obvious threats and older Kuro, like Mari. Somehow, Micky had completely slipped off my radar. "How did you plan on doing that?" I pressed.

Micky was silent, and when I looked around to really face him instead of looking in the mirror, I saw what had become of our youth. His face was gaunt, his skin pale, and there were deep shadows underneath his eyes. But there was also a strength I couldn't help but admire.

When I looked into his eyes, he held my gaze and didn't make excuses although his lower lip trembled. "I'm sorry, Kanji. I just wanted to do anything I could."

"You're a disappointment. If there hadn't been a fairy death, we might've had more time," Zain hissed as he navigated the groaning car through a break in the trees where we were reunited with road. I held my breath and searched the roads behind us for any sight of Christophe, but he wasn't there yet.

If I had said anything to Micky, anything at all, he wouldn't have had such a crushed look on his face. It wasn't his fault we were nowhere nearer to our freedom…. It was mine.

I took out my phone and stared at the screen. "Christophe is going to call me soon and demand to see all of us."

"All of us?" Tomas echoed. "What about the trees?"

"He'll be bringing his whole guard," Zain spat. "They'll guard the trees while they deal with us."

His whole guard? What if he brought others, including Tristan?

"What are they going to do?" Micky asked quietly.

"He'll know who abandoned the tree," I told him because there was no use lying. "We have to keep records of it. But I'll tell him it was my fault."

Zain let out a low sigh, but I could hear the resignation. He knew they wouldn't kill me.

As we entered the reserve, I could sense something was wrong. I slid my hair from the makeshift ponytail I'd had it in and felt my cold strands stick to my neck.

"Do you hear that?" I asked them as I rolled down the window. The air slapped against my cheeks, but I could hear the slow ebbing of pain washing through the branches.

"Hear what?" Tomas's bleach blond hair was all I could make out from the backseat.

I closed my mind and searched through every Kuro mind in the woods. There were jumbles of words, overlaying on top of one another, but finally I could hear the sobbing pleas for help.

"Head to the north side of the lake," I told Zain as I zoomed in on the source of pain. "Someone is hurt."

"Do you know what we didn't even bother asking?" Zain said.

"What?"

"Who it is that destroyed the tree?"

Ice wrapped around my heart like a fist. "The Sidhee?"

"The Sidhee?" Joel cried. "They were here? They attacked the tree. But why?"

"Because they thought the fairies betrayed them," I replied.

"We're here," Zain announced as he cut the engine and we hurried out.

"I'm going to call the others to meet me here," I told them as we hurried toward the water's edge. "In case they ask, we've been here this whole time."

I looked at Micky who guiltily looked at his boots and kicked loose pebbles.

Come to the north meeting point by the water's edge. Can you all get here?

Weak voices mingled with the stronger ones and after a moment, two young Kuro stepped from out of the woods on the south side. They saw us and ran over the bridge to where we were. Others joined us soon after, but they all looked physically fine. Mentally, I could tell they were barely hanging on.

The beach flooded with Kuro swans, some a few years older than me. Staring with dark eyes, they nodded to me once before filing into a broken line in front of the water. They were talking amongst themselves, but quietly. Eventually, there was a small group of about thirty of us—all that remained of our great race.

"What happened?" Lyon, Joel's oldest ward, asked. He was wearing a bright red scarf the color of blood. "Where did the Sidhee come from?"

At the mention of the Sidhee, an uneasy silence went around the group. A few more filed in to the back, but I knew we were missing some.

Joel tapped the back of my hand, his voice frantic. "Chiaki isn't here."

Chiaki possessed the ability to become a healer had we been able to teach him, but he was frail in every other aspect. Even though I had posted him near a warming station shack, he wasn't supposed to be outside. I had wanted to let him stay home, but we had needed every body. I was actually surprised Christophe hadn't demanded I utilize the females of our clan as well.

A divide was made in the group so Chiaki, supported by Aiden, could make his way to us. They were the only two naturally blond Kuro swans, probably because they were the only prospective healers. I met him halfway, Joel taking his other arm and putting it around his neck.

"What were you doing in that section?" I reprimanded Aiden. "You were supposed to be at Mile Five."

He stared at me with unapologetic eyes. "Chiaki's sick. I came to help him." He had his light hair pulled back under a cap and was wearing a ranger uniform that hung loosely from his thin frame.

"Christophe is coming and if he sees this...." Joel started.

Chiaki finally looked up, and I saw why he'd needed help. The tender flesh surrounding his right eye was a deep purplish color, and there was a trickle of blood coming down the side of his face. "I tried to stop the Sidhee," he panted. "But there were too many."

"Was anyone else hurt?" I asked quickly, my phone vibrating.

I didn't have to wait for his response because as the moon drifted over the lake, I saw two other Kuro with dark bruises and cuts. Anger swarmed inside my stomach like poison.

"Why were the Sidhee here?" someone demanded.

Another shout rang out. "Are they at war with us?"

I couldn't tell them about the plan to unite the Dryma and the Sidhee because only Christophe and a select few were supposed to know about it. My lips were sealed.

The notebook detailing who was protecting what section of trees was in my pocket, but I didn't need it to tell me where the Sidhee had attacked. Chiaki had been weak so I'd given him the easier section where there were few trees. But in my haste, I had forgotten the trees were sparse there because they belonged to the royals.

Words swarmed like bees, but I had to take a step away and answer my phone. All Zain had to do was raise his hand into the air and there was silence.

"Hello?"

Christophe's harsh voice greeted me on the other end. "I have my guard positioned within the trees, protecting them. Are you and your kind assembled by the water?"

"Yes," I told him. "I followed the emergency protocol and knew you would be coming. A tree was attacked, and I knew you would find out."

"So you are aware one of our kind died from his tree not being protected?"

"Yes. The Sidhee attacked us."

There was silence and the sound of beating wings. He hung up on me, and I realized they were closer than I'd thought.

"Stay behind me," I ordered, Tomas and Zain falling into step beside me. Micky hovered beside Joel, his arms rigid at his sides.

"Why are we facing the water?" Tomas demanded.

But I didn't have time to answer. The heavy sound of wings drowned out the sounds of life around us; the Kuro behind me instantly silenced. Christophe still wore his costume, a tailored pale suit. His mask wasn't hanging from his belt, but I saw the cords of his whip fastened to his hip.

I had once seen the full power of the Dryma guard, but there were nowhere near as many fairies gathered now. At Christophe's order, they must've dispersed into the woods in an attempt to protect the trees. Lithely, Christophe landed on the soft beach a mere ten feet from where I stood waiting. His red hair was plastered against his forehead, and even though there was nothing amusing about the situation, a part of me was satisfied to see him scramble for control.

All satisfaction I felt was instantly washed away when I saw Marvin, Ivan, and Seth land beside him, their faces a mix of irritation and fear. Joel inhaled sharply behind me, obviously worried about Micky.

Even in the dark, I could see Christophe's golden eyes appraising his slaves in front of him, as if judging their worth.

He straightened his jacket and tie. His wings were obviously the most grand. I'd never touched a Dryma fairy's wings, but I imagined they felt like silk. Unlike a bird's, their wings were large and appeared delicate, but I knew they weren't. Dryma wings were able to rival dragon scales in strength and glittering beauty. Usually, when I saw Christophe, he had his wings concealed within his body, so when I saw just how beautiful they were, I was caught off guard.

"What happened?" Christophe demanded, his voice lingering on the edge of insanity.

I took a step forward, my heart hammering against my ribcage.

Tell me everything, Chiaki.

I heard a soft breath, and then the memories flooded my senses. I started to explain what had happened while Chiaki was still transferring the information. "It is difficult to pinpoint exactly how many Sidhee were here," I explained, focusing on the shiny gold button dangling by a thread from Christophe's jacket. If I looked into his eyes, my connection with Chiaki would be lost.

"I think there were about six," I continued. "They focused solely on the inner ring and attacked my Kuro there."

"And where were you?" Ivan spat, moving toward me. From the way he was shaking, I thought he was going to strike me.

But Christophe placed a muscular arm in front of him, blocking his path. "Why did you not get there in time?"

Chiaki's memories showed absolute chaos. There had been no time to call for help, and by the time word was able to travel through the woods, the only news that had traveled was panic. I hadn't been here when I should have been.

"They are not able to fly," I pointed out sourly. "And they cannot initiate communication with me. Before I could do anything, the Sidhee were already gone. We are accustomed to keeping humans and fires away from the trees, not Sidhee."

"Only one tree was attacked?"

I scoured the woods as quickly as I could, imprinting the shape of the trees, the curve of the trunks. "Yes, only one."

"And who was in charge of this tree?"

"The number assigned to the tree?" I fidgeted uncomfortably before sliding my notebook from my back pocket.

Christophe narrowed his eyes. "Shouldn't you know?"

"As I explained, there was extreme chaos, and in the event of an emergency, I've been told to congregate here." I thumbed through the notebook, but I already knew who was going to be guarding the tree. "Because it is assumed you and your guard will flood the forest and we wouldn't want to get in your way."

The Captain of the Guard flashed me an annoyed look. "Five."

Micky's name was there, but I couldn't speak.

"Is there a problem?" Christophe asked me, his voice dripping with unwanted seduction. "How many of your kind are here watching over the trees on a normal day?"

"Four during the day, five at night."

"Only four to guard the whole of the trees and there has never been a problem."

"We have a system of communication—" I tried to explain, fearing the worst.

"That clearly failed," Christophe said coldly.

"If a tree is threatened, then we usually have time to call for backup, but in this case—"

"Are you telling me this is our fault?"

"I didn't say—"

My friends tensed at my side. I could feel the fight urging them forward, but I knew violence would only succeed in digging us deeper. I had to diffuse the situation as quickly as possible.

"Hand me the notebook."

He pried the paper from my hand, his fingers radiating heat. After reading the name, he stared past me at Chiaki being supported by Joel. "Is this him?"

I noticed he purposely didn't say Micky's name; doing so would've given him an identity. "No, that's Chiaki. He was in the same section."

"So." Christophe shut the notebook and tossed it back to me. "Where is he?"

"Right here...."

Before I could intervene, Micky had broken away from Joel and was now standing beside Zain. I had to admit he had guts. The first time I'd gotten in trouble for being lackluster in my protection duty, I'd hardly been able to look at Christophe. But Micky stared at him as though it were only the two of them standing in the Nature Reserve.

"Why were you unable to protect the tree?" Christophe asked quietly. Ivan and Marvin tensed at the harshness of his voice, but Seth actually winced. There was kindness in Seth's eyes, and I could feel the pain he felt by having to do what was necessary.

I knew what they stood to lose, but I couldn't accept their treatment of us.

"I—"

"He came looking for me," I added quickly, trying to think of a reason. "He thought something was wrong and decided he should inform me so I could provide reinforcement."

"Rather than stand and fight, he abandoned his post."

"I didn't mean to," Micky whimpered, playing along with the lie I'd started.

I couldn't do this. No matter what I said, it wasn't going to be enough for Christophe. A fairy had died, and judging by the somber expressions hanging on the Dryma guards' faces, it had been someone of vast importance. What was the life of a young Kuro in comparison?

"Listen to me." Christophe addressed the Kuro behind me. "Your one job is to protect these trees. So far, your method has proven effective, and so we have let you do what you see fit. That is no longer the case and therefore, I will be putting stringent methods into place so this will not happen again."

"We already told you it was the Sidhee's fault." If I hadn't grabbed Zain's arm at the last minute, I didn't doubt he would've tackled Christophe to the ground. "Not ours."

A murmur of voices behind me only infuriated Christophe more. He was playing a game in which he wanted to keep us subdued and afraid, but we had embarrassed him by lashing out. What upset me more was that it had been Zain who stood up to him rather than me. It was my place as prince to fight for my kind and yet, I couldn't bring myself to do so. Behind Christophe's amber gaze was a deadly intent we couldn't fight without our wings.

"Things will change," Christophe announced. "It appears the Sidhee have initiated a war with us and as our servants, you will be expected to adapt as necessary."

His words struck a chord within my kind. They swayed and staggered just to keep their bodies upright.

"Christophe, please speak with me in private," I petitioned.

Ivan and Marvin had their hands on their belts, as did the other solemn-faced Dryma standing dutifully behind Christophe. The illusion they were always in control of themselves and their situation had been shattered and with it, bits of their pride. They stood in crisp suits, perfectly tailored to them and whips fastened to intricate belts, but for all their glamour, they actually looked afraid.

The fear written on their handsome faces tore a hole through my chest. If they had cause to fear, then what was to say we were any safer? I had betrayed the Sidhee under the guise it was the Dryma who no longer wanted the reunion, but I'd failed to retrieve our wings.

There wasn't a choice really. We had to fight with Christophe in order to preserve our kind.

"Christophe, don't bother," Ivan said urgently. He leaned in so close to Christophe that their heads nearly touched. "He's not worth it."

All I had to do was see the lust in Christophe's gaze to know I'd won. For some reason I couldn't understand, he desperately wanted me to be his.

Before Zain or the others could react, Christophe wrapped his hand around my wrist and pulled me against his body. The force with which he grabbed me pushed the air from my lungs, and after quickly intertwining his arms around my chest securely, he lifted me from the ground.

A Kuro shouted my name, and I thought it was probably Zain, but then there were more shouts.

If I'd ever doubted Christophe's strength, his ability to carry me while flying proved me wrong. The ground turned into bleak spots of muddled brown and black and green. Easily, he could release me, and I could spiral to my death, unable to call up on my own strength. The space between my shoulder blades burned, and I wanted nothing more than to be dropped and see if my wings could become free in order to save my life.

"Why aren't they coming with us?" I expected Ivan or Seth to have spread their jewel-encrusted wings and joined us, but we were alone.

"They have to make sure no one gets any ideas."

"Even if they wanted to find me," I told him, not trusting myself to move even though I wanted to see his face. His manhood pressed into my lower back, and his arms flexed in response to my struggling. "I am sure our conversation will be done before they could find us."

His voice was husky. "Who said anything about talking?"

The wind was wet, slapping against my cheeks. I turned my face into a perfectly still mask so he wouldn't see how uneasy he'd made me. When we finally started to descend, I couldn't decide if I felt safer. On one hand, I would no longer be at his mercy in the sky, but that wasn't the case for the ground.

We had landed inside a playground just outside of Pasky Reserve that had clearly seen better days. There were no lights along the highway, apart from a dimly lit adult entertainment building. The dark tinted windows of the dilapidated building suggested the humans inside wouldn't waste time being bothered by what was outside.

The swings creaked in the wind, the rusty slide threatening to collapse from the stress of having to support itself. Christophe collapsed his wings, the jewels disappearing into the space on either side of his shoulder blades. I scratched the back of my neck where he had pressed his lips close to my skin.

The park wasn't well enclosed, but I doubted anyone going down the highway at this time of night would see us.

My legs were tired, and I barely made it to the swing before they gave out. The chains smelled like iron, so I kept my hands at my sides.

"Do you have any idea who died?" Christophe whispered, crumpling into the swing next to me. I was surprised at his sudden show of weakness.

"No."

"The eldest prince."

My heart lurched forward. "A prince?"

Not only was he next in line to becoming King of the Dryma, but he was also Tristan's older brother. Dryma could be cold and aloof, but when it came to someone they loved dying, they were overcome with sorrow. Just like my kind....

"I swear," I promised, "I did not mean for this to happen."

"We were betrayed," Christophe said quietly, resting his face in his hands. "The Sidhee came to our masked ball, but when Marvin informed me, it was already too late. The prince knew to find me, but he did not."

"What did the youngest prince say?" I didn't trust myself enough to say Tristan's name.

"He said a Sidhee was there at the order of his prince, but did not say his name. By the time Tristan found this to be the case, his brother had already been killed."

I sighed. Even though his brother had died, Tristan had remained loyal to "Mason," a Sidhee who didn't exist. The pain in my gut was like a knife sliding through my body and threatening to separate me into tiny little pieces. I knew I couldn't see him because if I did, I would fall to my knees and beg for forgiveness.

I needed to stay away.

"Kanji." His voice was cold and abrupt. "I need you to tell me what the Sidhee said to you when you delivered my note. I was under the impression they wanted to create an alliance, not start a war."

I took a breath and considered the possibility Seth and Ivan had pulled Zain and Joel aside to ask them the same question. Realizing I had no choice, I told Christophe my rehearsed lie. "They took the note and then left. They did not share their intent with me. If they had, I would've been obligated to tell you."

Christophe's hand came out of nowhere as he grabbed a fistful of my hair and forced me to look into his amber eyes. "You want your freedom," he hissed. "How do I know you didn't create an alliance with them instead?"

I went limp, my body only staying upright because of the rusty chain pressing into my side. "The Sidhee aren't the sort to do something like that."

Satisfied with my answer, Christophe loosened his grip so I only felt a dull sting. "You will never have your wings," he vowed, his eyes burning holes into mine. "And do you know why?"

My throat was dry. He was the Dryma who knew where our wings were, the only one who could possibly help me, but I wanted him dead. "No."

"If the Sidhee really have declared war against us, we will need every one of your kind to fight for us."

"We are not able to fight against them." I thought of all those young faces. Lyon, Micky, Chiaki…. "We are weak." I hated to admit it to him but had no choice if I wanted to keep them from fighting a battle against the fierce, violent Sidhee.

"This is not up for debate. Actually, if you were anyone else, I would've put you into your place by now."

"Please." I slid from the swing, and he released his hold on my hair. The woodchips were hard against my knees. "I will do anything."

Christophe stared at me, and I braced myself for what was to come, but he leaned back and laughed, exposing the skin at the base of his throat. Tiny beads of sweat ran along his hairline as he regained his composure and looked at me. "You already belong to me, Kanji. What could you possibly offer me that I couldn't take?"

My mind raced as I lifted myself from the ground. "You said you wouldn't."

"Not yet," he warned me, reminding me of exactly how tight his hold was. "I have a war to prepare for, and you will do your part as ordered. I will come to see you in a few days with more direct orders. For now, maintain extra protection... double should be sufficient—"

"Double? We are already short on shifts. You saw how many of us there were."

Any pity I felt for Christophe was stripped away when he said, "I suggest you have more children, then."

More children... so they could suffer and die for their masters? Never.

"Kanji."

I pried my eyes away from the darkened bar windows and stared at Christophe. "Yes?"

"At the end of this war, I plan on making you mine. I suggest you remember that because if you help us win this war, we will no longer need your kind's protection."

"But you won't release me?" I asked bitterly.

"Is your life worth more than your kind?"

Tristan's face assaulted my senses. His touch was already fading from my limbs, his smile like a distant feeling I couldn't quite grasp. If he knew my role in his brother's death, he would hate me. In that moment, I resolved to lock up my feelings.

"What do you want me to do?" I pulled my sleeves down so they could cover my frozen hands. "I'll do it if you promise to release my kind when this is over." I knew I couldn't trust him, knew he was going to betray me somehow, but I had to take what I could grasp onto.

"I need you to train your kind to fight," he said casually as if it were the most normal thing to say. "There must be a way to increase the protection of the trees while using the same manpower... I just have yet to locate it. With a war going on, we can't have you all fighting and abandoning our trees."

Of course not.

"I will speak with you again in a few days' time. Should you need me, you know where you can go."

"Wait, you are just going to leave me here?"

He smiled wickedly and spread his wings wide like a fallen angel before lifting himself into the sky. "I trust your friends will retrieve you."

Before I could open my mouth to protest, his feet no longer touched the ground as he rose up into the sky, abandoning me.

Sinking back into the seat of the swing, I felt my phone jabbing my thigh and knew I could call Zain to come and get me. When Christophe returned to where my kind was waiting for their prince, they would panic when they saw I wasn't with him. Would he be kind enough to tell them I was fine, or would he let them assume the worst?

I knew why he'd left me here. In his deranged mind, there was sound logic for causing my kind to feel alarm. It was the same way the Dryma always felt by having their slaves protect their lives. He could've tied me down and beaten me senseless with his whip, but instead he'd emasculated me.

I hated him. I hated the way we were treated. I hated the way we had to live.

But more than that, I hated myself.

If I crawled back to the castle and told Tristan the truth, I would have to see the accusations in his eyes and know he was right to want me dead.

I clung to the icy chains until my fingers went numb and the muscles in my hands cramped. Hours later, Zain and Tomas found me. Silently, they pried my hands away and guided their reject prince to the warmth and safety of the jeep.

CHAPTER SIX

ONE DAY was all I gave myself to come to terms with what I had to do. My fate with Christophe had pretty much been sealed, so all that remained was coming up with a plan to ensure he would give my kind their freedom and finding a way to conceal my mating pheromones from Tristan. In the twenty-six years I'd been alive, I'd never met Tristan before that day at the Crystal Cove. But now there was a war approaching, and I knew I would see him more frequently.

I'd already accepted him inside my heart, and he had accepted me as well.

Even as Kanji, he would know me. What did I have to do so he would be blinded to our mating?

I finally took a shower, reluctant to do so because I didn't want to wash away what lingered of Tristan's scent. When I went back to my room, I saw Mari standing beside my dresser folding clothes.

"What are you doing?" I sighed, too tired to fight with her.

She had her dark hair pulled back into a tight braid that trailed down her back. She was wearing a long skirt and heavy sweater with small pink bows dotting the white fabric. Neatly, she ran her small hands along the fabric of my jeans before placing them in the drawer.

"What does it look like?"

"Folding clothes."

"Exactly."

I snagged a pair of briefs she hadn't managed to put away and slipped them on. "Okay, I get what you're doing. What I meant was why?"

Mari had her back to me as she shrugged. "Someone has to."

"I'm a grown man. I can do my own laundry."

Mari looked over her shoulder. "Kanji, you're not a man and never will be."

Her eyes lingered over my bare chest, trailing the length of my slender body before tossing me a long-sleeved shirt. My skin was still damp, but I couldn't take her eyeballing me anymore.

"It's a figure of speech."

"I know."

She moved gracefully about my room, picking up my discarded articles of clothing and putting them away as if she could tell me where everything went in her sleep.

"What do you really want, Mari?"

"To show you what you're missing." She slammed the drawer with more force than necessary and spun around to face me. Her cheeks were flushed, but I knew better than to think she was embarrassed. "Your hair has gotten really long."

My hair naturally curled slightly at the ends but when wet, it was past my shoulders. "Yeah, it grows fast."

Mari did not trek through the cold and rain to come and talk to me about my hair. "It makes you look way too pretty."

"Great." I brushed past her and retrieved a pair of jeans and heavy woolen socks. "I have to go to Pasky soon, but before that I have somewhere to go."

"I want to know the truth." She stepped in front of me. If I wanted to leave my room, I was going to have to push her out of the way. "About what happened the night of the ball."

"The Sidhee attacked us," I said flatly. "Micky was supposed to be guarding his tree, but wanted to come and warn me. We were ill-prepared for an attack. If someone was passing through the forest and started hacking at them, we would've easily dealt with that."

"What's stopping you from killing them all?" Mari asked as she stepped away from the door.

"They have our freedom," I reminded her.

"And if they died, you don't think we'd be able to find it on our own?"

"They're smarter than that." Christophe was smarter, and now I had a reason to protect the trees as much as he did.

Mari mumbled something as I was zipping up my coat.

"What did you say?" I asked, turning around to look at her.

But what I saw was not the kind Mari I'd grown up with. The same way I hadn't seen Micky and the others develop hollow eyes, I'd missed Mari's hatred. It flooded through her like a storm she was losing control over.

"Maybe later we can watch a movie," I told her, attempting to ease her hate.

She nodded once, but she didn't want to grasp my peace offering. I was going to have to watch her closely for Tristan's sake, because I was sure I had heard her say all Dryma should burn.

"PRINCE KANJI, I didn't expect you. I could've come to your house if you wanted to see me."

Joel lived on the outskirts of our tiny community in one of the supposedly renovated houses. The only reason it was up to code was because the human who had inspected it had been particularly taken with Joel's pleas for needing a home with multiple rooms.

The kitchen and dining room were really one room, and then there was a tiny living room separated by a thin wall. Joel had put up a blanket and claimed the living room as his bedroom so the actual rooms were filled with his wards.

"Where are Joel and the others?" I asked Chiaki, weaving through the many chairs piled close to the wooden kitchen table.

Chiaki had candles he was lighting, but had paused when I'd entered.

"Aiden is sleeping and the others that aren't at Pasky are grocery shopping with Joel."

Chiaki rarely talked about his past, but I knew what had happened to his parents, and it was worse than mine simply giving up. After his dad had shot his mother, he took his own life.

If Chiaki hadn't found Aiden, I was sure he would've fallen apart.

"Am I interrupting you?"

His jaw dropped like he'd never heard something more ridiculous. "No."

"What are you doing?"

The chair creaked under my slight weight as I set my hands on the table, inches from the lit candles.

"Peace candles," he said, lifting an unlit candle from a basket on the chair nearest to him. He handed it to me and smiled. "They are infused with flowers, trees, and water from calm places in the woods. The idea is to select a part of nature where you are most comfortable and then put them into the candle."

"So every time you light it, you can feel peace," I responded.

"Yes." He had small pale hands and long fingers that made him look much younger than fifteen. His pale hair was tucked behind his ear, and I could see the bruise around his eye had faded and was no longer swollen. "These are the ones that we all picked."

I offered the candle back to him, but he shook his head and put his hands up. "That one is yours. I was going to give it to Joel to give to you."

"Thanks."

Around the others, whenever it was silent, I felt like I needed to fill the gaps, but not with Chiaki. "You would be a great healer," I told him, meaning every word.

"You think so?" He fastened a thin ribbon around the base of the candle he was working on, the flame casting shadows across his face. "That sure would be something."

"Maybe it won't be impossible forever," I said, pocketing the candle in my coat. "Chiaki, I have something to ask you."

"Yes?"

"Mating between Kuro swans has come to be rare."

He nodded in understanding.

"And yet you and Aiden have found each other. And you are both male."

He looked uncomfortable so I quickly added, "I'm not here to judge you. I have never thought it strange to see you and Aiden together. In fact… it makes me jealous."

Chiaki's eyes grew wide.

"You knew he was your mate before he did, so you were initially introduced to the mating process?"

"Yes, I knew for over a year before I told him."

I took a gulping breath and wiped my sweaty palms on my jeans. "How did you manage to keep it a secret from him?"

He looked at me in confusion. "If the primary doesn't fully accept his mate into his heart, then he can hide it from the secondary for a while."

"Yes," I pressed, "but it's incredibly hard to keep the pheromones hidden. Aiden would've found out. Did it really take him a year to discover you were his mate?"

Chiaki let his arms fall to his side and glanced at the hallway as if expecting Aiden to walk through the door. His voice grew heavy. "Before my dad died, he was a healer. He taught me about mating and how the stronger one in the relationship has to accept the mating first because that is his way of submitting and showing weakness. Weakness is part of existing after all. But he said that half of the mating process is about perception."

"So if I mated to someone and told them, but hid my pheromones, they would believe me?"

Chiaki nodded. "More than likely. I not only kept my feelings for Aiden a secret, but I also masked my scent."

This was what I needed to know. For the sake of protecting Tristan and advancing my kind, I had to make him forget about me. "How?"

"I found out what he hated the scent of and infused that within my soap." He shrugged nervously as he tugged on a loose thread of his sweater.

"What if I already told my mate and wanted to take it back?"

Chiaki wouldn't meet my gaze. "I take it they didn't see your face?"

"No."

"If they have one perception of you and you give them another, along with the scent change, it might work."

"Chiaki, I'm trusting that you won't tell anyone."

He looked startled. "Of course I won't. Can I say something, though?"

"What?"

"Won't it be lonely denying your mate?"

I forced a smile and abruptly stood, pushing the chair in as far as I could without sending the table toppling. "I'll come back when I have the scent."

"Chiaki, is everything all right in there?" Aiden wiped sleep from his eyes as he appeared in the doorway. He straightened when he saw me. "Oh, Prince Kanji."

"Hello, Aiden," I said pleasantly, waving the candle Chiaki had given me as proof of why I was there. "I was just leaving."

"He was checking up on us." I could see how much effort it took to lie to his mate, but I knew Chiaki would stay true to his word in order to protect my secret. "Are you hungry? We have peanut butter and apples."

"Here, order pizza for yourselves." I reached into my wallet and withdrew my last twenty. When neither Aiden nor Chiaki would take it,

I flattened the bill onto the table and walked from the house before they could recover from the shock and stop me.

Chiaki had the answers I'd come to Joel's house wanting, and yet I felt less than satisfied. After seeing the easy way Chiaki and Aiden interacted, I realized that was what I wanted more than anything.

I touched the back of my neck, the top of my shoulders, all the places where Tristan had touched and claimed me. Before I could stop myself, I was driving toward the gated community where he lived, but I made myself believe I was actually going to Pasky Nature Reserve where Tomas and other Kuro were waiting for me.

A DRYMA funeral was something to behold. I came to realize my kind had adopted the human customs of marriage and death. Historically, funerals had been bright events where we celebrated the long life they'd lived and enjoyed the foods and sounds they had. Imagining my somber uncle enjoying anything was so hard, I gave up and realized that was why his funeral had been such a dreary affair.

The gated community had posted extra guard at various places along the fence, but that was just for show. The actual funeral was taking place in a clearing near the community where they had fashioned an aisle out of strewn flowers and ferns.

Balloons representing flowers and spring were tied to the trunks of trees, swaying almost peacefully. I crept into the woods but made sure to not get close enough I could be spotted.

Every Dryma was cloaked in billowy white clothing, their hair elaborately wound around their head in braids. The females wore flowers in their hair and had them wound into the sleeves of their dresses and the hems of their skirts.

When I imagined how many Dryma lived in the gated community, I had imagined hundreds and maybe even thousands, but I saw now how wrong I was. At least a third of them consisted of the guard, and many of them were older.

To the Dryma, age didn't matter. I resisted the urge to kick the tree nearest to me and cause enough commotion to be taken away.

I saw Christophe at the head of the aisle, guiding an older female Dryma wearing the most ornate tiara I'd ever seen. But my gaze was instantly drawn to the handsome man standing beside the lavish casket resting on top of marble pillars.

I assumed the gorgeous Dryma males beside him were his brothers, but he commanded not only my attention but that of those seated on the stone chairs. He was the youngest of the Dryma princes, and yet he was standing closest to the casket. With a regal posture, he stood in front of his kind with a stoic expression. I could almost feel the pain running rampant through his body and had to race back to my car before I attempted to comfort him.

Besides, my comfort was the last thing he wanted.

CHAPTER SEVEN

THERE WAS no doubt in my mind Christophe was sending his guard to scour the reserve to make sure we had increased our protection duty. Although half of us looked dead on our feet, we maintained double the protection, sometimes having to take short naps in our cars when we were relieved before we could drive home.

Zain insisted I needed to sleep and almost attacked me when I showed up when I wasn't scheduled to.

"Without our prince, we won't have anything." His words had sounded so desperate, I went to the grocery store and bought tea and cookies to drop off at the reserve before going home.

I assumed the reason almost a week had passed without hearing from Christophe was because he was tied up in battle plans. At the funeral, he had looked gaunt and tired. The last person I wanted to have sympathy for was him, especially because I knew when the war was over, I had no choice but to belong to him.

"How is the new system working?" I asked Joel as I shrugged out of my ranger jacket and slid into a warm sweater. "Have there been any problems when you try to communicate with a Kuro in a different section?"

It was Monday, and we were waiting for Zain to finish up his rounds so we could leave. Joel twisted the cap of his water bottle off and emptied an energy packet inside.

"The walkie-talkies have been working, and everyone having the schedule of shifts has helped make sure they don't get confused."

"Good." I eyed his drink that he was still shaking. "I think it's shaken."

"What... oh." He guzzled the drink so quickly I wondered if he even tasted it.

"Let's get out of here," Zain demanded as he stormed through the woods. I saw his coat was unzipped and couldn't see why until he was practically on top of me.

"What the hell happened?"

A crimson streak of blood marred his white undershirt. The line went from just below his right pectoral to his hipbone.

"Nothing."

"That doesn't look like nothing." I moved forward to assist him, but he averted his gaze.

Joel retrieved the white first aid kit box in the trunk and dug through for bandages and gauze. "How deep is it?"

"Shallow," Zain answered gruffly. He pulled on his hair, which had gone from dull red to a tangle of bright purple. "I tripped over myself and fell on some bramble. It's nothing to be worried about."

"Then why won't you let me help you?"

"Because…." He lifted his shirt for Joel, and I saw the blood made the wound look a lot worse than it was. His pale skin was blood-smeared, so I sighed and took a cloth from Joel so I could help clean him off.

I could feel Zain wanting to move away, but once the damp cloth relieved the pain of his wound, he resigned himself to letting me help. I'd thought that the attack by the Sidhee and the consequent approaching war would make my kind frenzied and lose their hierarchal ideology.

Instead, the Kuro swans had increased their loyalty to me. The only reason I tolerated the treatment was because their thoughts told me how much they needed stability.

"Have you heard from the Dryma captain?" Zain removed his coat and shirt so Joel could rub antibiotic cream across the jagged cuts. The cold blasted through the clearing and made my teeth chatter.

"Not yet." I cut the adhesive bandage and handed the strips to Joel so he could apply them onto Zain's skin.

"What the fuck are they waiting for?" Zain's words were interrupted by a fit of shivers. "I want to know what's going on."

"Soon," I assured him. "If I don't hear back within the next few days, I will go to the Crystal Cove and demand to see him."

But I didn't even have to wait a few hours.

AN EXTREMELY flashy Mustang was parked outside my house.

My driveway really was just a patch of gravel with stones on either side forming two makeshift lines. I imagined the only reason the driver had parked in it at all was because parking in the street offered no safety for his car.

I was surprised to see Christophe leaning against the door with his eyes focused on his tablet. When Zain's jeep sputtered into my driveway, Christophe didn't even have the decency to look up.

"I'll see you later," I told them, gathering my bag. "Go home and rest."

"I'm coming with you," Zain said defensively as he cut the engine.

"What are you talking about? You're hurt, go home."

The door opened behind me so Joel could get out, and I realized there wasn't a point in arguing.

"Good evening, Christophe," I called pleasantly. "If you had called, I could've met you at the Crystal Cove."

The Dryma captain was wearing a dark blue T-shirt and khaki slacks, showing how the weather didn't have the slightest effect on him. His fiery red hair and tanned skin made me angry I ever wasted my pity on him.

"I wasn't aware you had a mate."

My heart was seized in fear, a cold sweat dripping down my spine as I contemplated his words. Had he found about Tristan? Was that why Christophe had left me dangling for over a week?

"She wouldn't permit me entry into your house to wait for you."

She? "Mari is not my mate." I could've crumpled to the ground in relief if I hadn't been so nervous.

Christophe slowly lowered his tablet and pushed his hair from his eyes. "Then what is she doing in your home?"

"She's just a friend," I persisted. I had to choke down my pride as I asked, "Do you want to come inside?"

"Yes, as a matter of fact, I do."

"Zain, would you mind taking my aunt and Mari back to your house?"

My friend bristled at the suggestion, but he had come to the same conclusion as me. If Mari had forbidden Christophe from coming into my house, she wasn't thinking about the ramifications. I had to get her as far away from Christophe as possible so I could diffuse the situation.

"I'm not going anywhere." Mari appeared on the front porch, the screen door clacking shut behind her. She was wearing a bright yellow dress with a lace skirt, but she looked anything but cheery and bright. "I want to stand beside you, Kanji."

You're making this worse, I channeled to her. *Christophe is not patient and will not forgive this trespass.*

Her eyebrows rose in defiance. *I am not afraid of what he will do to me.*

I winced. *It isn't you he'll punish.*

Realizing I was the one who'd feel pain, her shoulders slumped and she conceded. Quickly, she darted back into my house and came out with my aunt close at her heels. They were both wearing sweaters that weren't appropriate for the weather, or maybe they were and I couldn't tell because of the chill deep in my bones.

"Come this way, Mrs. Catarina," Joel said helpfully, making sure to not meet Christophe's gaze, not that the captain was looking anywhere but at me. "We'll only be gone for a little while."

My aunt looked like a mannequin that had been hollowed out. She was eating and drinking, mostly because Mari tried to pile food into both of our mouths every chance she got. I watched until they slipped into the backseat and then gestured for Christophe to follow me.

"I don't appreciate having to kick my aunt out of her own house," I told Christophe as I shut and locked the door firmly behind me in case Mari got second thoughts and ran back. "I could've come to you."

"I think by now you've noticed I am also alone," Christophe said as he surveyed my house. Instead of standing beside the door in disgust, he moved to the couch, pushed a blanket to the side, and collapsed. "At the club, there are too many wandering eyes."

I sighed and hovered beside the ratty chair. "I thought I would hear from you much sooner."

Christophe snapped his head up. "I attempted to speak to the Sidhee prince to find out why he rescinded our offer."

"Did he tell you?" I gulped, tightening my hold on the back of the chair.

Laughing, he massaged the space between his eyes. "He refused to speak with me. You know we don't have access to their world, so I spoke to one of his guards and he said Prince Calhoun has no interest in seeing me."

What had seemed like a great plan was falling apart. There were too many factors that could influence the outcome. The only thing that had mattered was our freedom, but now the need to survive overshadowed that.

"What would you like me to do?" I asked.

"My guard is expertly trained in combat, but I have yet to receive a formal war address. Something about the Sidhee attack has been bothering me."

I waited.

"If they no longer wished to keep our agreement, then why did they not kill Prince Tristan? Instead, they killed his eldest brother, our future king. That aim makes sense if they wanted to destroy our society, but I can't imagine why he wouldn't also want the prince."

"Maybe they didn't know which tree was his?" I offered, shuddering at the thought of seeing Tristan's lifeless body.

"No, they would know."

"I don't understand," I admitted.

"Prince Tristan and Prince Calhoun go way back. I'm in disbelief Prince Calhoun would turn away from our offer when he's wanted Prince Tristan for so long."

I remembered the look of hatred that had consumed Prince Calhoun's eyes when I told him the Dryma were no longer interested. I hadn't thought of the ramifications for the Dryma prince until I realized he was also my mate.

"We have to prepare for the worst," Christophe finally said. "Which means I need you to start training your kind in the art of killing the Sidhee. It is ingrained into your blood to know what to do. In addition to that, I have something you alone must do."

"Which is…?"

"Protect Prince Tristan."

My stomach dropped. "His tree, you mean?"

"No, his actual self."

"Why? If they wanted to harm him, wouldn't they just try and attack his tree? Each of you has a life attached to a tree, so if they wanted to attack you, they would attack the forest."

"Like I said before, I believe Calhoun still wants Prince Tristan. I'm not afraid he'll try to kill him."

"You're afraid he'll try to kidnap him or something?" I finished. Over my dead body was Tristan being taken by that gnarly monster. "Why do you want me to protect him when you have an entire guard at your disposal?"

Christophe focused on the corner of the coffee table that was missing a chunk of glass as if he wanted to destroy the offending furniture. "Prince Tristan is the youngest and therefore won't become the next king. But he's a good friend of mine, and I can't constantly guard him when there are five other brothers next in line to the throne."

"So you want me to become his bodyguard?" On one hand, my heart would burst from happiness, but I knew I couldn't keep up a ruse for that long.

"Only during the times I cannot ensure his safety." He withdrew a piece of notebook paper with what I assumed was my new schedule. "It goes without saying that you will continue supervising protection duty within the trees, but do not need to complete a shift yourself."

Just how much time was going to be snatched from me? I stood motionless, trying to grasp my bearings but unable to.

"One more thing." Christophe placed the folded paper neatly on the table before standing up, his height making the ceiling appear low. "There will be two units, should the Sidhee attack. One will be the physical attack on their forces, which would be my guard. The other is the protection of the trees; you and your kind. I suspect you will need someone capable of healing. Do you have a Kuro in mind?"

Chiaki and his lithe hands instantly came to mind. "Yes, but he doesn't have the proper training—"

"Naturally I will provide that."

"Christophe." His name tasted like acid on my tongue. "Is there anything I can do to convince you to give us our wings?"

His jaw locked, but he didn't respond right away.

"With our wings, we will be better equipped to fight," I hinted.

"As long as we are tied to the Earth by those damned trees, then you will be tied to us."

"You want this war. Why?" I took his hand in mine, the first time I had willingly touched him.

"They have what we need to secure our future," he said blankly, looking down at our entwined hands. "I suggest you release me or else I can't be held accountable for my actions."

His threat reverberated through my eardrums, causing me to immediately remove my hand from his.

"Read the schedule. Don't be late. I will be in touch."

Christophe brushed past me as though I were little more than a coatrack. How much time would pass before he decided to contact me again, but what was more, how long could I evade Tristan?

IN MY dreams, Tristan called to me. He begged me to return to his side and protect him with my very life if necessary. I slept fitfully, and finally, when I awoke for the fifth time, I rolled out of bed and refused to try any longer.

My body was ridiculously cold as though I had been repeatedly dunked into an ice bath. My fingers and toes were stiff, my heart aching with more intensity than I'd ever felt. The shock of being pried from my mate was starting to set in the way it had with my aunt, but I couldn't give in.

There was throbbing pain at the base of my neck, and my mouth had a sour taste. The wind made my windows rattle in their frames as if daring to burst open. I glanced at the clock... 5 a.m.

The first day I was supposed to guard Prince Tristan had already started, and even though I still had twelve hours before I had to arrive, I hadn't been able to find out what he hated.

I'd gone over the basic things I knew all Dryma didn't like, but they were all intangible. They didn't like ugly individuals, they didn't like people who fought them, and they didn't like being rooted to the earth. I thought about bringing a piece of tree bark to Chiaki to put into the soap.

Then I remembered the vial of tears he'd given me when I'd first met him. It hadn't occurred to me before now to wonder what he was doing with Dryma tears, but they had to be the essence of sadness and therefore dislike.

I pulled my phone from my pocket and dialed, the bluish glow eerie in my otherwise dark room.

"Hello?" The voice was too strong to be Chiaki's.

"Aiden?"

I heard his sharp intake of breath; clearly he hadn't bothered to see who was calling before answering. "Prince Kanji. Is everything all right?"

"I'm sorry to wake you." I felt a pang of guilt. "I needed to speak with Chiaki."

"Should I wake him up?" Aiden asked warily. I could imagine the turmoil he was facing at having to wake up his weakened mate, but I knew he would if I asked him to.

"No, don't worry about it. Just have him call me as soon as he wakes up." After Christophe had left, I'd immediately called Chiaki and told him there was the prospect of him becoming a healer. He'd sounded so grateful it made me sick he had to learn under these circumstances.

I knew Aiden wanted to ask me what was wrong, but he didn't. "I will."

Chiaki hadn't asked me who my mate was, but I knew he would wonder why I needed to make the soap so quickly. He was intelligent enough to draw conclusions about who I'd mated to, but I got the feeling he'd rather not know.

Just in case, I spent the rest of the few hours before sunrise thinking of excuses I could use in case he decided to pry. Especially because I was going to infuse beautiful crystal tears into soap.

CHIAKI CALLED me a few hours later, sleep etched into his voice. "Hey, Prince Kanji, Aiden told me you wanted to speak with me."

I could hear the commotion of Joel's house in the background, but he said something and the voices were silenced. "Yes, remember what we were talking about? With the soap?"

"Yes, did you find something they dislike?"

"Yes."

"I already have the soap made," he told me softly. "I can drop it off at your house and then you just have to put a small amount of the item into the mixture."

"That's it?" I wasn't a soap connoisseur, but that sounded far too easy.

"I had used a bar, but I made a liquid for you. You just have to soak the item in the liquid and then use the soap when you shower."

"Where are you going?" I suddenly realized he wasn't on patrol duty, so was he going somewhere with Joel?

"I'm going with Aiden to Pasky to help him patrol."

"But I told you that you were going to be trained as a healer and you didn't have to keep up with protection duty anymore."

"I know," Chiaki trailed off guiltily. "But I want to help Aiden while I can."

I couldn't begrudge him for wanting to do everything possible for his mate. I knew exactly how he felt. "Just until your training starts next week."

He made a noise of consent in the back of his throat. "Thank you, Prince Kanji."

"Don't mention it," I muttered before hanging up. The jealousy I felt for Chiaki and Aiden was getting out of control… I really needed to get a grip.

CHAPTER EIGHT

VIGOROUSLY, I'D scrubbed my skin with the soap. Chiaki had hidden his desire for Aiden for a year, but he also hadn't already admitted his feelings to him. Would the soap do its job even though I had already been to bed with Tristan and he'd taken everything from me I could give?

There was no more time to waste because if I didn't show up on time, there would be hell to pay.

On the bottom of the detailed protection schedule Christophe had given me was the code to the gated community. My beat-up car stood out amongst the eccentric cars gleaming in garages bigger than my house. From the outside, the community looked small enough. But once inside, I saw how they'd used trees and water to their advantage so there were actually at least fifty houses, all with large two-car garages and vast yards.

The house in the very center, surrounded by an ivory-white fence, was where the royals lived. I tried to imagine Christophe in one of those big houses and couldn't. He never spoke about his parents, and I wondered if he lived with them or with other members of his guard.

I parked on the street in an attempt to not draw attention to myself, but I failed miserably. A young Dryma male across the street was neatly stacking action figures into a pile. He stopped and stared at me as I headed into the regal garden in front of the estate. His eyes were wide and pale like ice, his clothes sticking to his body like a second skin.

In the back of the house, there was an elaborate garden and a glass structure set to the side so as to not be in the way. Everything in the yard was meticulously placed as though a speck of dirt not contained was unacceptable.

I heard shuffling coming from the greenhouse, the windows open to admit the slightest of breezes. It wasn't the sound of garden tools clinking together that led me to the greenhouse; it was his scent.

Floating across the garden was the scent of flowers and vanilla, overwhelming my senses and threatening to bring me to my knees.

Self-consciously, I checked to make sure my hair was secured into a low ponytail and the loose strands were tame. I was wearing plain dark pants and a long-sleeve shirt with a loose, unzipped sweater. Suddenly, I felt ashamed of my appearance and wished I had thought to wear the new slacks with the tags still on them.

"Hello?" I called, my voice cracking as I peered around the doorframe. I hadn't wanted to disturb him so I didn't enter the greenhouse right away. "I'm Kanji. Christophe said you would know I was coming."

My palms were itchy so I wiped them on my pants, my heart hammering violently in my ribcage. Paralyzed, I waited for Tristan to come to me. He was going to know....

"You can come in, you know?" he said pleasantly as he appeared at the doorway. The greenhouse was as deceptive as the gated community in regard to size. There was a long hallway with rooms jutting off into private sectors where various scents invaded my senses.

"I didn't want to bother you."

Tristan was as handsome as I remembered, his golden hair parted to one side. Despite the fact he was working with dirt, he was wearing a white shirt the color of milky pearls. Without meaning to, I found myself staring at the hollow of his throat.

He blinked, his long lashes caressing the tops of his cheeks as he watched me. "Are you really the prince of the Kuro swans?" I didn't blame him for doubting me.

"We don't really have a prince anymore," I admitted. "We just serve the Dryma now."

Tristan gave me a despondent look. "True, but that doesn't mean you need to give up your heritage."

I shrugged, beyond relieved that he didn't appear to recognize me. The soap must've worked because the last time I'd seen him, he had tried to crawl into my skin. Although happy, I was also devastated I had to pretend to be nothing to him.

"I heard about your brother." I nervously shuffled my feet. "I am very sorry."

"The Sidhee attacks are not your fault. We were betrayed." He gave away a flicker of emotion at those words, but quickly looked away. "I don't know why Christophe sent you to protect me. You are half my size."

I didn't say anything.

"I usually go into the woods to search for herbs and flowers, but I'm not quite ready to leave yet."

"What are you doing?" Curiosity got the better of me, and I realized I had to check myself. I was standing in front of royalty, and without my scent I didn't have the safety that came from being his mate.

Tristan raised his eyebrow. "Didn't Christophe tell you? I'm a healer."

All of the air rushed from my lungs. "You're a healer?"

He beamed. "Yes. And with a potential war, I have to make sure I have enough remedies on hand."

"Hence why you need to go into the woods more." I had thought it was strange Christophe wrote "woods" for many of the locations where I'd be in charge of protecting Tristan.

"Christophe really doesn't need to worry," he said, waving his hand in the air. "If Calhoun really wanted me, he would know where to find me. But I don't intend to give in now."

"Why not?" I held my breath, hoping beyond hope he was talking about our mating.

Tristan gave me a secretive smile and ushered me into the greenhouse. "Let's just say I found something that derailed my plan to go to his world. What he did was unforgivable, but I can't say I'm surprised. Senseless violence is typical of him."

I chuckled nervously, following him into the first room. Piled onto tables were different flowers and greenery, but it was the hanging flowers that caught my attention. They were water lilies that appeared to hover above shallow clay dishes filled with water.

"If you get too hot, there's a fan over there." He pointed at the corner where there was a large circle fan and plastic cooler dripping with condensation.

"I'm never too hot," I told him, and for once I was finally comfortable. The need to migrate was still ingrained into my brain, but at least I wasn't ridiculously cold. "Thanks, though."

The green stems were thick and unlike any I'd ever seen. Drops of dew clung to the fragile white petals, but when I stepped closer, I saw the dark purple spots toward the core of the flower. When I reached my finger out to caress the petal, the flower shrank from me. I stood amazed as I surveyed the flowers and found they were actually hovering. Their stems didn't hold them down and there was nothing connecting them to the ceiling.

"What are these?" I couldn't keep the awe from my voice.

Tristan's arm brushed against mine, causing me to jump in alarm. He didn't seem to notice my jolting reaction to being so close to him. His words were quiet and calm, as if he were talking to an old friend rather than a bunch of flowers. "Do you believe nature has a way of keeping itself balanced?"

"I never thought about it." I hated feeling so incompetent next to him because I found myself wanting to enjoy the things he did. "But I suppose so."

"The trees, our trees, are connected to our inner being." He paused to press a hand against his heart like he was in pain. It wasn't until a smile spread out across his face that I relaxed. "If the trees didn't exist, then neither would we. I started to wonder why we cannot feel their pain when it's extremely cold and the bark peels or when the leaves fall to the ground."

"Would you really want to feel pain as often as they do?"

"No. The point isn't to connect completely to the forest. My goal is to have these flowers hover around our designated trees and regulate them."

"So you wouldn't need us to protect you anymore?" I asked softly. Was he really doing such a thing?

His voice was sad. "As long as we are tied to this Earth, we would need you to keep us safe. But if I could somehow make these flowers form a bond with the trees, then it's reasonable to expect we could divert to protecting the flowers instead. We would then become mobile."

"Bonding to trees." The concept sounded strange to me, but the way Tristan spoke so earnestly made me believe his words. "Do all of the Dryma know about these flowers?"

Tristan shook his head and diverted his attention back to the plant life spread out on the table. "Up until recently, we had a plan with the Sidhee and were going to reveal it to our kind. It was supposed to be a joyous occasion where we would all be free, but then they changed their plan."

In that moment, I truly hated myself. Christophe would never let me go, and I wasn't under any delusions that he would. But what if Tristan had agreed to marry Prince Calhoun and then released my kind?

There was no telling what could've transpired.

"So… I'm impressed you listened to me for so long."

I blinked. "What do you mean?"

Tristan selected a pair of shears and began to trim leaves from a pile of roses. "Technically you are my slave, and I know there are a million other things you'd rather be doing than standing here and listening to me talking about my freedom."

But he was so wrong because I wanted nothing more than to be there. My words died on my tongue, and to distract him, I pulled a pile of chrysanthemums to the edge of the table. "Do you need help with these?"

Slightly taken aback, he reached over and plucked the shears from my hand, instead handing me the pair he'd been using.

"Why did you do that?"

"Those ones were dull, and I don't want you to cut yourself."

I wasn't sure what kind of expression was on my face, but it prompted Tristan to add, "I can't have you bleeding all over my flowers." His dismissive words weren't deceptive at all; he was kind.

Quietly, we worked in the heat of the greenhouse. Separating the stems from the flowers without damaging the petals was difficult. At one point, Tristan turned on the fan, the dull hum of the blades the only sound other than our heavy breathing.

As we worked, I stole sideways glances at Tristan when he was enamored with the curve of a leaf or the scent of a petal. Beads of sweat had gathered at his hairline, the soft golden strands plastered to his head. His eyes moved quickly, and depending on what he was looking at, the color changed in hue.

Everything about Tristan made me want him, and as an hour passed and then another, I came to realize he was much kinder than I'd given him credit for. By now I was convinced he didn't know I was his mate, but he still treated me kindly and with the kind of respect the other Kuro displayed.

When I was thirsty, he already seemed to know and would offer me water. When the sunlight was hitting the greenhouse in such a way that my sight was blinded, he'd shuffle me to another location. His kindness was enough to bring me to my knees.

"I've noticed for a while," Tristan finally said after hours of silence. He abandoned a pile of petals in a ceramic bowl so he could rest on an oak bench pressed against the wall. "But you haven't stopped staring at me."

I threw myself into trimming leaves with more force than necessary. "The heat must be playing tricks on you."

"Hmm, I don't think so."

"If I was, I just wanted to see what you were doing with the flowers."

Tristan sighed and leaned forward so his chin could rest on his entwined hands. "Lying is not your specialty."

Nearly dropping the shears, I set them down before I could cut off a finger and stared at my petal-stained hands. They were the color of the sky when the sun was setting but wasn't quite ready to give up.

"Sorry… I shouldn't be teasing you." He laughed. "I just thought the way you looked at me was rather flattering."

"Don't you have a mate?" I blurted as a distraction. "You've got to."

A sigh parted through his full lips. "Yes, but nothing will come of it."

"Why not?"

"I can't trust someone who lies to me." Tristan abruptly stood up, knocking over a pot at his feet. The dirt cascaded over the ground in spider-like clumps, but neither one of us moved to clean it. "And without trust, love is impossible for me."

"So you'll forget about them?" I choked on my words because his eyes were penetrating the inner chasm that was my soul.

Tristan stared at me for a long moment before looking away, his handsome features marred in despair. "Mating is forever, and I know my senses didn't lie to me. I just have to wait for a more convenient time."

"That must be sad. For you… and for them."

"Perhaps." Tristan wiped his hands on the back of his pants. "I think we've done enough in here, don't you?"

I nodded, unsure if he was talking about our conversation or the plants.

The herbs he needed were just outside the community in the woods so there was no need to climb into our cars and drive there.

"Don't you want to change?" I asked, rolling down my sleeves as the cold air slammed into me.

Tristan looked up at the sky as if assessing the future. "I don't think it's going to get any warmer or colder in the next hour, do you?"

"I meant because you're all sweaty and stuff."

"Oh." Tristan tugged off his shirt, revealing his toned muscles and golden skin. Now I knew he was a healer and spent a lot of time outside, it made sense why his skin was so tanned. "I'm all set. Unless you want to change."

"I doubt anything you have would fit me," I remarked, brushing past him and marching through his garden, desperate to get back to the road. Despite knowing I shouldn't, all I wanted was to glue my eyes to his flesh and rake in every detail.

"Well you're not that much shorter than me." He easily caught up to me, his shirt loosely hanging from a loop in his belt. "You sure are thin, though, and your legs are ridiculously long. Aren't swans normally top-heavy?"

My eye twitched. "In case you haven't noticed, there aren't a lot of swans around here. They've all migrated to the south where it's actually warm."

Tristan held a hand out as though he could grasp the air. "You're telling me you don't think this is great weather?"

I shrugged. "Certainly better than it has been, but it is September. Pretty soon, we're going to wake up and everything is going to be covered in snow."

"You don't like snow?"

"God no."

"I'm not fond of snow either, but not for the same reason. It's harder to create medicine in the winter when we so heavily rely on nature."

"Have you ever thought of just uprooting your trees somehow and transferring them?"

He gave me a sideways glance that made me feel stupid as hell. "Flowers that connect with trees, remember? That's the plan."

"Ah… right." I felt like such an idiot.

When we had finally escaped his family's lavish garden and made it to the road, the stone weights holding me down were lifted. The streets were still relatively empty, but I caught sight of Dryma females gathered in their small park, lifting dishes from a woven picnic basket.

The young male Dryma stopped playing with his toys and hastily stood up when he caught sight of Tristan.

"Hello, Prince Tristan." The boy gave a small nod before digging his hands into his pockets as if searching for precious stones. "How are you today?"

"Perfectly fine, thank you."

"Have a nice day, then." He scampered after his figurines and tucked them into the folds of his jeans before racing off down the street.

The reaction from the female Dryma at the park was no better. Their hands froze on their ceramic dishes and polished silverware. Eyes blinked at us as if assessing whether or not they should speak or act like they were part of a freeze-tag game.

Tristan barely acknowledged them, continuing down the street with a newfound determinacy.

"Sorry about that," I said. "They were probably just shocked to see you slumming with me."

"Not you."

"Pardon?"

Tristan cleared his throat. "They aren't acting that way because you're here. The Dryma are always like that around me. I rarely leave the house except to journey to the castle or into the woods."

The knowledge surprised me. "Why not?"

"I have many older brothers who were all gifted with beauty, intelligence, strength.... I am something of a hermit." The heavy tone in his voice let me know he was done explaining. Gazing at his straight back and broad shoulders, I had a difficult time seeing him as weak or less than any other Dryma.

Just after we'd entered the cover of the trees, Tristan paused and stared back at me. "So I didn't notice before, but aren't you the Kuro I gave the tears to at the Crystal Cove?"

"Yes, thank you for that."

"Did they work?"

I looked away, remembering my uncle's depleting body lying on his basement cot with the raw gashes on his arm. "No."

"I'm sorry." He had said a generic statement everyone is supposed to say when a loved one dies, but the pain in his voice was genuine. "I thought the tears would help."

"It wasn't your fault," I told him quickly. "I got back to my house too late. I'm sure the medicine would've helped if I had gotten there sooner." What I meant was my uncle might've been alive had I not been distracted by Prince Tristan.

Tristan touched the bark of a tree gently before leaning closer as though he could hear soft whispers rushing through the wood. "We used to be immortal, but now our lives are just as fleeting as that of humans. Strange, don't you think?"

I took a step closer to him. "What is?"

"There are so many stories and movies humans have dedicated to fairies and in each of them, they are immortal, beautiful beings. When in reality, we can be killed so easily."

I swallowed my pride for the sake of comforting him. "How old are you? Twenty-five? You have a lot of life left."

Tristan chuckled. "Twenty-four actually."

I had to focus on not letting my jaw drop. This drop-dead gorgeous Dryma was two years younger than me? And yet, he possessed an aura that made me feel years younger in comparison.

"So, what are we doing out here?"

Tristan let his arm drop to his side, losing contact with the colossal tree in the process. "It just rained last night, which means there will be an excess of water in the leaves. The lake is just north of here so if we head over there, we can gather some and I can extract the rain water from inside."

Why did I have to be so slow? "Which leaves are you looking for exactly? Because I've been around leaves my whole life, and other than what clings to the surface, there isn't a whole lot of rain."

"Sorry." He came back to me and before I could blink, took my hand in his. The warmth was an unbelievable current of need and desire traveling through my arm straight to my heart. My breathing hitched, and I could only follow behind him like a dutiful puppy as he named off leaves I had never heard of.

"Why are you holding my hand?" I managed to ask as I interrupted his excited pitch about the difference of aloe leaves from cactus, which really wasn't relevant considering I didn't see any desert plants in the Canadian wilderness.

The water came into view. It was an endless sight lengthwise, cascading in long swaying curtains deep into the woods. The land across from the river was shrouded in the plant life and insects that had yet to die from the cold. I could feel what was left of the sun transmitting its rays directly onto the side of my face, but the only thing I could focus on were Tristan's fingers entwined with my own.

Had the scent of the soap Chiaki had given me worn off?

Tristan released my hand, an empty feeling seeping deep into the flesh of my palm. Like I would never be whole again without his hand there to keep me rooted to the earth. My spidery pale hand seemed ugly without the burning heat of his.

"Habit, I suppose." He shrugged and sank to his knees beside the water. Tristan's large hands were anything but clumsy as he sorted out the various leaves from one another. The way he plucked through the plants was how I imagined a curator would with ancient clay pots. Meticulous and precise. "Also, you looked kind of cold, and cold hands won't be able to feel the weight of the leaves. Come here and see."

Obeying, I dropped to one knee and eyed the lone leaf in the palm of his hand. The contrast of the green against his golden skin was stunning.

"What am I seeing?"

"Touch the leaf."

If it had been anyone but him, I would've stormed back to the road and taken my leave for the day. "Okay, but I don't know what you're expecting me to feel. I touch leaves all freaking day."

And I was right. Other than the extra sliminess from the belly of the leaf, there was nothing out of the ordinary to feel.

Tristan surprised me by smiling and depositing the leaf beside the water's edge. Turning slightly, he took both of my hands in his and vigorously rubbed them together until my palms could've started a fire. Then he retrieved the discarded slug-like leaf and offered it to me again.

Sighing, I pressed my hand over his, cradling the leaf like a sleeping child. I wasn't sure if I could actually feel the life pulsating through the leaf or if it was from being so close to Tristan.

I tore my gaze away from our hands, excitedly preparing to tell him what I'd felt, but stopped short. Tristan was staring at me with a heavy lidded expression, his jaw locked and his precious stone eyes gleaming with desire. "I felt it."

Reluctantly, I wrenched my hand away and dug through the pile in front of us for more of the thick leaves he held.

"Amazing right?"

"I'm going to go ahead and say it was your hands that gave me the ability to feel, though, not warmth."

Tristan howled with laughter. "You're not the first to tell me that. What, do I have magic hands or something?"

I remembered the way they felt on the back of my neck, surging down my spine and into my pants and felt my cock twitch with need. "You mentioned you held my hand out of habit. If you're such a recluse, who did you come here with?"

Half expecting him to tell me to fuck off, I was surprised when he responded. "Christophe. We're old friends."

I watched the dirt snaking up my hands like thick coils tethering me to the ground. "Somehow I...."

"You what?" Tristan prodded, his shoulder bumping mine.

"I don't think I should say it."

"Feel free to say anything you want around me."

"Somehow Christophe doesn't strike me as the kind of Dryma who'd willingly collect leaves or hold hands."

"He was very slow to warm up to me, and I think he only did that because he lost his parents young."

I blinked. "Really?"

"I don't know what happened, not that I'd tell you." He shot me a sideways glance, and it reminded me he was a Dryma, and of course there were things he wouldn't want to share with a Kuro. But somehow, I had the feeling he would've told me had he known because of his kindness, and that only made my stomach slink lower.

"He sent me to protect you because you're a good friend of his," I told him. "At least that's what he said."

"Like I said before, if we're attacked, I think it's me who's going to have to protect you. He probably just sent you here to help me gather herbs for medicine."

"Maybe, but he still really cares for you, or he wouldn't have bothered at all."

"I always got the feeling Christophe thought I reminded him of someone. The person he actually desires."

My throat felt dry, and my hands froze on a sullen flower. Reminded him of someone?

His words were like an ice pick to the back of my eyes. Was the person Tristan talking about Christophe caring for... me? The weight of those words sent a fresh wave of shivers down my spine and made me ill.

Despite the Sidhee attacks, Christophe knew it was Micky who had abandoned the tree that was later destroyed. Our punishment had been extra protection duty, but he could've punished us further. He could've tied me down and lashed me in front of my entire clan, but he hadn't. The marks from where he'd punished me before were still on my back, but that had been years ago. Did Christophe actually have feelings for me?

I shook my head, not wanting to believe in such nonsense.

"We almost drowned," Tristan told me. "When we were younger. Some human guy dove in and pulled us out."

"You almost drowned?" I asked in disbelief. "How?"

"We're fairies." He pointed at the sky. "We fly, not swim. Anyway, the only reason I brought it up is because I think Christophe probably still wants to find that guy."

"Not to be rude, but why are you telling me these things?"

Tristan paused in extracting the leaves from the icy water so he could look at me. "I don't want you to hate us. I just—"

Suddenly, he gripped his head between his dirty hands and closed his eyes tightly. "Are you all right?" I asked, wiping my hands on my jeans so I wouldn't get him dirty. "What's wrong?"

He held up a hand to stop me. "I'm fine. I just get headaches often."

"That doesn't look like just a headache. Your skin is pale, and your eyes are all cloudy."

Tristan forced a pained smile that didn't reach his eyes. "I'll be fine once I get home. Help me up?"

"Of course."

It wasn't as though we had backpacked into the middle of the wilderness, but our slow trek back to the gated community felt like we had. I held tightly to Tristan's waist, refusing to let go even when he stumbled and threatened to take me to the ground with him.

Even in his weakened state, I got the impression he could hold his own if he had to. It was his eyes that scared me. The normal bright green had faded and looked like dull grass about to die.

"Does this happen often?" I inquired, mostly just wanting to hear his voice.

Tristan took a moment to answer, as if weighing the consequences of divulging anything to me. "Not often enough to make me an invalid, but enough to cause discomfort."

"What causes it?" The realization I was willing to do whatever necessary to spare him from pain shot straight through my chest.

"Not entirely sure," he admitted, shifting slightly so he had less weight leaning on my thin arm. Always so considerate. "Dryma usually don't get ill, so it's baffling."

"Have you ever gone to a doctor or something?"

I heard his smirk. "A human doctor, you mean? I wonder what they would say when they drew my blood or felt my wings through my shoulder blades."

"Right, wings would be hard to explain. Maybe they'd just think you were an angel or something?"

"Next thing I know, I'd be on a dissection table. No thanks."

We had entered the community, and I thought knowing we were amongst his kind would make him gain strength in his legs, but the opposite seemed to happen. Our pace transformed into an agonizing slow dance where we were the center of attention.

"Why don't the others offer to help? You are their prince," I muttered angrily.

Tristan burst into laughter.

"What is so funny?"

"You got angry for my sake. I like that."

I stayed silent, mulling over his words and wishing he would find out I was his mate so I could stop lying to him.

When we reached his house, I was reluctant to step through the glass double doors lined in what looked like gold.

"Tristan, what happened?" The last person I expected to see was Christophe's right hand-man, Seth. But before I could heave Tristan up the stairs, Seth had opened the door and was now staring at us.

Unlike Christophe, Seth's features were softer somehow. His light hair was cut short, and his green eyes made up most of his face.

"Nothing out of the ordinary." Tristan gave him a conspiratorial glance, and before I knew it, Seth was wrapping Tristan's arm around his neck. I almost moaned from the loss of his body heat against my side.

"I'm sure you know Seth," Tristan told me, regaining his footing, "my older brother."

I blinked. "Your brother?"

Tristan stared at him. "You told me you knew Kanji?"

It was the first time he'd said my name, and hearing it pass his lips did things to me I wasn't proud of.

Seth rolled his eyes and reminded me of my place. "He's a Kuro and doesn't need to know all about our private life. Let me help you inside. I was worried about you."

"I'm fine," Tristan breathed before directing his gaze back at me. "Are you coming inside?"

"I don't think that's a good idea." Seth had a warning tone to his voice as he eyed me. Seth was known for giving younger Kuro lesser punishments, but there was something hard in his eyes I hadn't seen before. The death of his older brother must've made him hate us.

"He's right." I held up my hands and slowly backed away. Being surrounded by the glamour of their house was too much for me. "Oh wait, I'll go back and get the leaves you wanted."

Tristan narrowed his eyes and firmly pushed away from his brother in an attempt to come after me, but I was already too far. "There's really no—"

"We went to all that trouble. I'll be right back with them." Then before he could stop me, I was racing down the paved streets back to the woods.

Seth and Tristan were brothers, and Christophe was his childhood friend? There was still so much about Tristan I had yet to learn, and not knowing caused an intense loneliness to creep deep into my chest. Not knowing about him was unacceptable.

But now that he mentioned it, Seth did have similar green eyes, although they were nowhere as intense as Tristan's.

After escaping to the cover of the trees, I risked a glance behind me to see if I'd been followed, but I was still alone. In Tristan's state, there was no way he could've come after me anyway. I took a deep breath and regathered the leaves, stuffing them into my sweater pockets.

I felt useless, and it wasn't just because Tristan was sick. I knew that if a Sidhee had attacked us, I wouldn't have been much good to him. Maybe I could act as a shield if he pushed me in front of the Sidhee and ran, but I knew he would rather stay and fight to the death.

There was the snapping of a branch behind me, but my reactions were too delayed, and when I spun around, a hand was wrapped around my throat. Adjusting my eyes to the darkening sky, I saw Christophe standing there with an infuriated expression.

"Let me go," I choked out, raking in what air I could.

He was wearing a short-sleeve shirt that showed his flexed muscles and a pair of shorts. There was the rough feel of bandages against the tender skin of my throat and his sword sheathed at his side. So he'd been training.

"Christophe," I pleaded, "let me go." I wouldn't give him the satisfaction of tugging at his hand because I knew I'd never be able to overpower him. Instead, I maintained eye contact with him until his grip loosened enough for me to wriggle free.

"You are ill-prepared." He sounded disgusted. "What if I had been a Sidhee?"

"But you weren't." I massaged my throat. "That really hurt."

Christophe narrowed his eyes. If he came any closer, he was going to push me into the riverbank. "Why are you here?"

"Prince Tristan wasn't feeling well. I came back to get the leaves—"

"No, why did you come back here, alone?"

"Should I have stayed with the prince? I'm sorry—"

"That's not what I'm talking about." Christophe took me by the shoulders and shook me. "It's dangerous to be out here."

"I patrol the forest all the time, and we're not far from the road. What's wrong with you today? Did something happen?"

The flicker of emotion in his eyes was all I needed to answer my questions. Oh shit…. Tristan thought Christophe was after some human guy, but what if I was the one he wanted?

After tugging the leaves from my pockets, he pressed them into the tiny confines of his short pockets. Without them, I felt exposed and cut off from Tristan.

"Go home, Kanji," Christophe told me. "Tomorrow bring your healer."

"I have to go to Pasky first."

"No need, I already made sure to include your kind in our training regimen."

The bandages clinging to his hands looked like they were what held his hands to his arms. Bright blisters poked angrily through the bandages, smears of crimson clinging to the outdated sword. "What?"

"Attend to your kind, but you'll find there's no need for you to train with them tonight. Not that they could go any longer."

"What did you do?" I demanded, seething rage rocking my body.

"You should be thanking me." He smirked before turning his back to me. "After I'm done with them, your kind will have a fighting chance. Go home."

I was too shocked to argue.

CHAPTER NINE

"WHAT THE hell…."

Whatever I'd been expecting, it wasn't this. I could tell most of the Kuro had already gone home, but the ones that remained looked downright exhausted. Zain had greeted me at the front gate silently and walked with me to our meeting spot beside the water.

No Kuro was standing; rather they were splayed on the ground like they wouldn't be able to get up. I noticed the same bright blisters on their hands, but unlike Christophe, they weren't covered.

I located Joel and Chiaki handing out bottles of water and granola bars, but it was a wonder they could keep themselves upright.

"What did he do to you?" I managed to whisper, turning away so our conversation could be concealed.

Zain deeply inhaled, his eyes focused on the water. His black hair, still streaked in bright purple, was plastered to the side of his head and when a chill went by, I saw him shiver.

"Here." I shrugged out of my coat and offered it to him.

His eyes flashed, and he took a step back as though I'd handed him a loaded gun. "No, put your coat back on, Kanji. I'm fine."

I knew he wouldn't take my coat, so instead of pestering him, I hugged the fabric close to my chest to suck what little warmth I could. "Why didn't you contact me?"

"Other than the fact Captain Christophe watched me like a hawk?" Zain muttered humorlessly. "You were guarding the bratty prince today, right? You couldn't just leave."

"The prince isn't bratty." I sounded too defensive and toned it down. "He would've understood."

Zain looked like I'd slapped him. "A Dryma have sympathy? Hard to believe."

"He really would've."

"What's wrong with you, Kanji? Why are you defending a Dryma? Look around at what they're going to put us through."

"We were the ones that started it," I reminded him quietly.

"Yeah? Well, if they hadn't taken our freedom, then we wouldn't have done this. The Dryma are the ones at fault, not us."

"What are they planning on using us for?" I asked hesitantly, diverting the subject before I let something about Tristan slip.

Zain sighed, and when he looked at me again, I saw my best friend looking back at me. His eyes were rimmed in dark shadows, and his upper lip was bleeding, but the fight was still there. "Captain Christophe has reason to believe the Sidhee will come here. I assume to claim the youngest prince, although he didn't specifically say. When they come, we have to guard the trees while the Dryma fight on the offense near the Sidhee entry to our world. But come on, we both know the Sidhee are cunning and will attack the trees."

"Not only will the Dryma die, but so will we."

Zain held up his hands. "It's a win-win situation for the Sidhee."

I stole a glance behind me and saw my kind had seen me and were struggling to stand. Joel gave me a halfhearted wave before offering a water bottle to Lyon.

"This can't happen, Kanji."

"I know," I whispered. The water had been so beautiful when I'd been beside Tristan, but now the ripples looked like muddy tire tracks. The smell of the earth was like overripe, putrid fruit.

"If we plan on fighting, we might as well have a party and spike all the Kool-Aid with arsenic because we're going to die anyway."

"So not funny, Zain."

He shrugged his heavy shoulders. "Sorry. Still true." Zain took a step toward me. "Not to be weird or anything, but I really need to...."

"What? Oh...." An unmated Kuro experienced a kind of loneliness only understood after finding a mate. Being near another Kuro was a way of numbing the pain. Our foreheads touched ever so gently, our breathing ragged. Zain wasn't one to show weakness so whatever Christophe had put him through must've been hell.

"You smell different," he remarked.

"Do I?"

"Little bit."

"New soap, I guess."

"We have to find our wings." Zain abruptly pulled away and straightened the buttons of his ranger jacket. "Before we have no more time."

"What do you suggest? Seducing Christophe?"

He ignored me. "You guard the prince... figure something out."

"I already told you what he said. Only Christophe knows."

Zain glared. "I don't believe that. Not for a second."

Unfortunately, neither did I.

POOR CHIAKI was so nervous, he had a hard time walking without stumbling. "Are you sure this is okay?" He gestured to his plain black pants and dark hoodie. They weren't well-worn and probably the best clothes he owned.

"You're fine." I parked the car on the curb outside of the royal mansion. Unlike the day before, the male with the toy soldiers was gone and there were no picnickers. Hopefully, they had finally gotten the memo there was going to be a war and decided to become useful.

Chiaki stared out the window at the house, his eyes wide. "I'll have to tell Aiden about this place."

"He wasn't happy, was he?" I guessed.

"Um, no. He wanted to come too, but I told him I'd be fine."

"You will," I assured him. "We're just picking roots and such. He's going to teach you how to become a healer using natural remedies and whatnot."

"Think I can do it?" Chiaki asked earnestly, turning his blue eyes on me.

"Definitely. Ready?" I'd been apart from Tristan for less than twenty-four hours, but the time had passed agonizingly slow. Eventually, the time I could be away from him would become shorter and shorter until I was consumed.

"Ready as I'll ever be."

This time, I completely bypassed the front door and went to the greenhouse. I heard Chiaki complimenting the flowers and sharing their names, but he wasn't expecting a reply.

"Kanji, is that you?"

"Yes," I called as I rounded the curve and saw Tristan immersed with his work. A sturdy-looking wooden table had been set up just outside of the greenhouse and was plastered with the leaves we'd collected. There were small vials containing what I assumed was rainwater. "This is Chiaki."

Chiaki stopped as far away as possible while still being able to see Tristan and bowed stiffly. "Nice to meet you."

"My brother will be along any minute, but in the meantime, why don't you look around inside? Be careful to not touch anything." Tristan lifted a vial from its setting and swished the liquid inside.

Chiaki shot me a glance before disappearing into the greenhouse. I knew he'd be enamored with the floating flowers just as I was and wouldn't come out until we called him.

Slinking across the stone steps, I moved as close to Tristan as I could without touching him. Once again, there was the stabbing pain I'd been found out, but he didn't even look at me. "I assume you told him what the hovering flowers are for?"

"Yes, on the way here."

Chiaki had been very silent as he mulled over the possibilities of what those flowers could achieve, a delighted smile on his face.

"Excellent. Wouldn't want him to get frightened and run away."

Tristan was wearing a loose cotton shirt and dark shorts that would've been better suited to fashion week. His blond curls were tucked behind his ear, daring to spring out at the slightest provocation.

"I'm glad you're feeling better," I whispered as I admired the tiny pink drops he was adding to the vials. The substance turned the color of honeysuckles as the color dissolved.

"For now."

His scent was intoxicating. As he moved, I noticed a large bandage wound tightly around his arm. "What happened?"

"Oh this?" Tristan beamed a radiant smile. "Christophe and I were practicing. Normally I'm more careful, but I allowed myself to be distracted."

"By what?"

"My mate."

There was no one around… I could reveal myself. All I would need to do was douse myself with the hose lying on the ground like a coiled snake and he would know. But even though I hated myself for being the source of his sadness, I couldn't.

Instead, I said, "You must miss them terribly."

Tristan licked his full lips, and I wished they would consume my mouth. "More than words can explain."

I nearly fell over.

"Kanji?"

"Yes."

"I don't mind that you're standing so close to me, especially after you helped me yesterday. But my brother might."

"Sorry." It took a lot of effort for me to move. "I'm going to go and collect Chiaki."

Stupid, stupid, stupid....

Chiaki was staring at the flowers intently, just like I thought he might. "What do you think?" I asked.

He jumped, startled. "Beautiful. It's amazing what he's proposing to do, if you think about it. He must be very intelligent to engineer this."

I remained silent. "We should get going."

"Okay." He was reluctant to leave the flowers, but did so at my command.

Seth was talking quietly to his brother when we got out. He gave me a disinterested stare, but was taken aback by Chiaki. I knew exactly why.

Chiaki's blond hair wasn't the only characteristic that made him look like an outsider amongst the Kuro. Having naturally large eyes was part of being a Kuro, but because his face was small, he had a cartoony feel about him.

"This is Chiaki," I told Seth quickly, wishing he'd stop staring.

"Hello." Chiaki's voice was small at my side.

"Christophe said he was going to let him choose who the healer was," Seth remarked to Tristan who was still fiddling with the vials. "But he probably should've chosen himself. This kid is supposed to learn how to heal the Kuro? As if."

"Be kind," Tristan said patiently, wiping his hands on a tea towel. "I don't look like much either."

A noise escaped my lips, but I managed to cover it with a cough. "Chiaki can do what's necessary."

Seth nodded and shoved his hands into his pockets. At least he didn't have his whip hanging from his belt as a constant reminder of his power over us. I could only imagine what that would've done to Chiaki's nerves.

The next few hours were spent plucking greenery and explaining their uses to Chiaki. Seth was constantly surprising me because I had thought he was accompanying us out of a sense of duty, but he was actually the other Dryma healer. The way Tristan and he discussed healing techniques made me jealous because they talked in a language foreign to me.

Becoming a healer wasn't like studying to gain knowledge. It was a deeply rooted desire to heal that not everyone was born with.

Clearly, Seth was warming up to Chiaki despite his attempt to keep up the cold façade. Easily they talked about everything, and at one point, Tristan wandered over to where I was feeding ducks scraps of a roll I wasn't hungry enough to eat.

"Aren't you hungry?" he asked, squatting down beside me so our eyes were level.

"Not really." If this kept up, I was going to be reduced to skin and bones.

"Seth has this under control for now." He motioned behind us where Chiaki was inspecting a speckled flower. The color was stunning, but that's where the appeal ended. "Come with me. I need help getting some more of the flowers I missed yesterday."

"Won't your brother worry?"

"I told him."

Dutifully, I followed Tristan through the bramble, each step bringing us farther from Seth and Chiaki until we were completely hidden. "Isn't the water over—"

My words died in my throat as I was pushed against the trunk of a willow tree. Tristan had my chin cupped in his hand, and before I could speak, he pressed his lips to mine. The kiss started off slow and sensual, but soon, he was daring to drag out the very air concealed in my lungs. My legs went limp, and I would've fallen if his strong arm hadn't been wrapped around my waist.

Tristan released his grip on my chin so he could entwine his fingers with mine at our sides. After being denied for so long, his kiss felt surreal. The careful construction I had built to hide my feelings for him gave way and emotions flooded my senses.

"Wait—" I managed to turn my head to the side, breaking off our kiss.

"Please." Tristan's voice was hoarse as he leaned his forehead against my chest. My heart was thumping madly, and he was going to hear every beat. "Just let me hold you. This isn't fair to you, but you remind me of my mate. And the sadness is consuming. For a little bit, just let me hold you."

Tears of glass cut through my eyes and poured down my cheeks. With my body caught between the massive tree and Tristan's body, I was powerless to wipe them away. This was all I had wanted, so why could I only think of how I was betraying him? Betraying Zain and the others?

Was I ever going to be able to do anything right?

Just let me hold you. He'd said it twice, his grip tightening around my body as his breathing heaved out of him. If he had any desire to cry, I didn't hear or see it. Tears were like tiny bugs you can't see but are always there, following and waiting until you let your guard down. I hated crying and was ashamed of myself.

"Am I cruel?" Tristan buried his fingers in the strands of my hair. "I know what they've done, and still… I want them."

I couldn't bring myself to answer, because any words I had would've been a lie. If he were cruel, then I was the worst of all. Because even though I knew I had to fight for my kind, there was nothing more precious than my mate. His pain was like a knife through my heart and damn the consequences, I was going to find a time when I could reveal myself to him.

His knee parted my legs, my cock jerking to life. If he noticed, he didn't say anything, just straightened slightly and held me closer to him. I felt like a lifeless doll, but while in his grasp anything he wanted was what I was going to deliver.

I tugged on his loose cotton shirt, wanting him to be closer. I meant to offer him words of comfort, but before I could find my words, he had released me and stepped away. "We should go and find my brother."

"Probably."

"Kanji, please…."

"I won't tell anyone," I promised. "Everyone has moments of weakness."

And just like that, he was back to being the strong, muscular Dryma who could destroy me in moments if he desired. I would keep true to my promise not to tell, but not replaying the memory over and over like a broken record was another story.

CHAPTER TEN

A WEEK ticked by, slowly bringing October weather. Joel and I had cleared out the local thrift store when we'd gone to gather warm coats and gloves for our kind. While we waited for the cashier to ring up our purchases, I saw a romance novel tucked into the pocket closest to Joel's heart. His blistered hands had healed and hardened over to form calluses.

Despite my attempts to train with the other Kuro, Christophe had told me there was no need. My only purpose in life had become to watch over my kind and to protect Prince Tristan.

Finally, I'd had enough and forced Joel to divulge what they were learning. It was all very basic sword fighting and how to kill a Sidhee, but no matter how many times I ran through the thoughts in his mind, it wasn't the same as if I'd had a weapon in my hands.

"So the Dryma are just going to give you a sword before the battle?" Mari asked humorlessly as she flipped the remote controller from hand to hand nervously. "How can they be so sure when the army is coming and then have enough time to pass out weapons?"

We were finally watching the movie we'd planned on seeing in theaters, or at least trying to.

"Christophe is having swords created for our kind and will have them early next week. He's putting some sort of tracking device on the weapons to ensure they have to stay in the woods."

"There's still the problem of us all not being there at the same time."

The "us" didn't escape my notice. "He may be many things, but dumb isn't one of them. He will be prepared for the Sidhee and will let us know. Without us in the woods, they are as good as dead. That, if anything, should lessen your fears about him abandoning us."

Mari snorted and settled on a comedy, something I knew she wasn't going to enjoy. Her dark hair was in a single braid down her back like a tousled spine. "I don't like it."

"Neither do I."

My aunt had gone out with some of the older female Kuros to a local diner. I wanted to be happy she was out, but wondered if she wasn't just trying to give Mari and I time alone together. Her sideways glances and attempts to have us eat dinner together by candlelight hadn't gone by unnoticed.

"Thank you for taking care of my aunt these past few weeks," I told her. Mari was wearing a loose T-shirt and skirt, but I was absolutely freezing. My jeans, wool socks, and long-sleeve sweater were hardly keeping me warm.

"No problem." She seemed embarrassed by my thanks, a dust of pink rising on her cheeks. "That's what friends are for."

The word hovered between us… friends. She had her hand palm up on the couch between us, as if begging me to take it and secure our bond. Blue nails and soft skin goaded me into making me feel obligated to take her hand, but I couldn't.

"I'm gay."

I was experiencing pressure from Christophe, from myself, and from Zain and the others. The part of my brain that could compartmentalize my feelings gave way, and I broke.

Mari cleared her throat. "What did you say?"

"I like guys," I told her.

"I know what you said." Her voice was clouded in disbelief. "But how can you say that?"

"Because it's true."

"No, I won't accept you're gay and neither will our clan," she whispered venomously as she plucked my hand from my lap like a discarded flower. "Maybe you don't act like it, but you're our prince, and you can't be with a guy. You need to have a female mate, you need to have children, you need…."

"Mari, enough." I firmly wrenched my hand from her grasp. "We've been friends forever… I hoped you would've understood."

"Humans can be gay," Mari countered, jumping up so she towered above my sitting form. "Kuro can't be."

"What about Chiaki and Aiden?" Standing up would've only provoked her further, so I remained seated.

Mari blanched. "An anomaly. Besides, they aren't princes, they don't need to have children."

"Mari—"

"Did you mate to a guy?"

I took a shuddering breath. "No."

Smiling triumphantly, she placed her hands on her slender hips and trained her large eyes on me. "Then there's no proof you're gay. Sure, maybe right now you like guys, but after you mate, that will be a thing of your past."

She was trying to grasp on to whatever she could. I understood her anger and yet, I couldn't feel sympathetic.

"If I ever meet my mate, I won't deny him if he accepts me."

We were caught in a standstill where words evaded me. Luckily, my phone began to buzz in my pocket, giving me an excuse to look away from her.

"Hello?"

"Hey, Prince Kanji. I didn't mean to interrupt you or anything."

I licked my lips. "Don't worry. What's up?"

"Well…." Chiaki hesitated, his voice low. "Joel has been gone for a long time and he didn't have protection duty or anything so I'm really worried about him."

"Where did he go?" Joel loved being at home, so for him to be gone a long time wasn't like him.

"He didn't say, but someone called him and he left right away. Sometimes he goes out, but never like this."

"How long has he been gone?"

Mari was staring at me intently, her rage dissipating as she realized something was wrong.

"Since this morning." Chiaki took a breath. "I'm not sure, but I was in the same room when he took the call, and I thought the voice sounded like Seth's."

My heart skipped a beat. "The Dryma who has been teaching you about healing? What makes you think so?"

"Well, his voice sounded similar from what I could tell. And Seth always asks me about Joel when he's teaching me."

I hadn't even realized because I'd been too absorbed with Tristan and helping him gather plants. After Chiaki had gotten used to Seth, they had pretty much been left alone while I was with Tristan. I had no reason to believe Seth would harm Chiaki because he'd always been kind to younger Kuro, but it dawned on me I had no idea what they discussed.

"He asks about Joel?"

"Yes. Like how he's doing and if he has enough money. Stuff like that...."

Oh shit... how had I not seen it? All of the Kuro Seth had taken pity on lived or had lived with Joel. Zain had told me Joel was gay so I wouldn't be surprised if he had a secret boyfriend, but Seth? I thought back on the times we'd gone to the Crystal Cove and tried to imagine Joel's face when Seth was there. Sad was the only word that sprang to mind.

"Just stay at home and call me if Joel contacts you, okay? I'll go look for him."

"I will. Please find him."

Without Joel to take care of the young Kuro who lived with him, the teens would've been separated and shipped off to whoever could afford them in our community. I'd always respected Joel, and he was an old friend, but this went beyond respect. I owed it to Chiaki and the others to find Joel.

I dialed Zain.

"Kanji, what's wrong?" Over the rush of the wind, I could hardly hear Zain. He was at Pasky with Lyon and a few others on guard duty.

"I was just wondering if you've seen Joel. Chiaki says he he's been gone since this morning." I tactfully kept the part about Seth out. If Zain found out, he would've abandoned his post and marched straight to the gated community to confront him.

"Not around here. Sure he's not just not having a little fun?"

"I don't think so," I told him, maneuvering my phone so I could pull out of my drive and still talk. Mari had a displeased expression on her face as she watched me from the front door, but I knew it was because she wanted to go with me. "I'll look for his thoughts."

"Let me know if you find him." A fit of coughing took over, and when he continued, his voice was hoarse. "And make sure to punch him for having us worry."

"Find Joel, make sure he's safe, punch him," I rattled as I blasted the heat in my car. This was the first day I wouldn't see Tristan since starting guard duty, and even though it was supposed to be my day off, I couldn't have been more miserable. My ribs were sticking out like bony fish skeletons. "Do you want anything when I swing by later?"

Zain coughed again. "Something warm to drink. I didn't think it was supposed to be this cold. Shit."

"You're with Lyon, Xavier, Micky, and Shinji today, right?"

"Yep. They could use something too."

"Of course. See you later."

"Bye."

Without Zain's voice on the other end, I felt isolated. I had half a mind to drive by Tristan's house in an attempt to catch sight of him, but of course Christophe would be lurking around and notice me.

There were few places Joel actually went, apart from the bar down the street where we sometimes drank until we couldn't see. I doubted he'd go alone, but maybe he'd asked Seth to meet him there?

The Crystal Cove instantly jumped to mind, but instantly disappeared. If Joel and Seth were in a relationship, I doubted they'd be so stupid as to be anywhere near Christophe.

Meeting in the woods was an equally plausible suggestion, but then again, Kuro rangers were all over Pasky.

My concern over my relationship with Tristan had made me selfish. How was it I hadn't known about Joel and Seth? I felt sick.

Once I reached the edge of the woods near the campgrounds, I parked my car and opened my mind. *Joel. Where are you?*

Despite the cold, the campground was rather busy. Last minute campers and hikers who wanted one more hurrah before the weather froze them out were crowded at their cars, loading up on their gear. Amongst the heavy backpacked humans, a few stared at me. A teenage girl with braces and long blonde hair almost to her knees watched me from across the parking lot. She definitely didn't look happy to be there.

Joel, come on. Are you out there?

Stepping over a low branch, I was careful to not make eye contact with any of the humans lest they want to make conversation. After years of working as a ranger, I knew the type.

I was starting to think I'd misjudged where Joel could go when a sudden thumping deep in my chest knocked me to the ground. Human words wandered through the dense trees, but their eyes didn't see me. Gathering a fistful of earth in my hands, I tried to ground myself. Closing my eyes, I also closed my mind and slowly, the crushing weight was lifted.

"Joel," I whispered. "What happened to you?"

A Kuro prince's duty was to ensure his flock was able to function properly. Part of that meant leading the other Kuro on the migration pattern, but since we couldn't fly, I had never done that. When I was thirteen, I'd been able to speak to other Kuro in my mind and by age fifteen, I could also read their thoughts. My uncle had warned me to be careful because there were instances when I would be able to feel immense emotions as well as thoughts.

After he'd died, I'd felt my own sadness but not my aunt Catarina's so I'd assumed the talent wasn't something I possessed. But now I wasn't so sure.

Was this Joel's pain I was feeling? Was this his way of calling out to me because he needed me there to stabilize him?

On shaking legs, I forced myself to keep going. The dim light of the sun was little more than a sporadic burst between the cover of the trees, but I didn't need to see to know where to go. The leaves beneath my feet crunched in protest, and the air whipping my hair against my face tried to delay me. I knew I was close.

As I sprinted, I couldn't help but wonder if I ran for my friend or for myself. The wound inside my heart had been stitched up over and over without scarring. Each time I thought of Tristan, the stitches tore. I needed him. The gut-wrenching pain I felt told me Joel needed Seth, something I could relate to.

Out of breath and exhausted, I burst into an abandoned campground site. Plastic bottles and brightly colored snack wrappings lined the otherwise flawless ground. A bottle cap spun in circles within the current of the river. I stepped around the makeshift fire with tiny embers dancing like ballerinas.

"Joel. What happened?"

He was on his knees facing the water, his face buried in his hands. The gut-wrenching sobs were what I heard first, and then he attempted to clear his throat. "Kanji, what are you doing here?"

"I should be asking you the same thing." I nudged a candy wrapper away with my foot. The dirt was wet, and I felt the cold seeping into the knees of my jeans, but the expression on Joel's face was enough to make me forget about my discomfort. "Chiaki was worried about you."

"Chiaki?" His voice sounded foggy, and I wasn't surprised. Judging by his red-rimmed eyes, I assumed he'd been sobbing for a while. "How long have I been gone?"

"All day from what he said."

"Oh."

"What are you doing out here?"

"Read my thoughts," he sniffled. His usually neat hair was a disaster, sticking up every which way. Joel must've left his house in a hurry because he was wearing a thin shirt and no sweater.

"You sure?" Unless I had to, I tried to respect their privacy, and I wasn't sure I wanted to see what had transpired between Joel and Seth.

"Just do it."

Taking a breath, I prepared myself for the mental anguish I knew I was going to feel from prying open Joel's mind. Like a movie replaying itself, the images of the day poured into my mind. I saw Joel answer his phone and tell Seth he was on his way. I could feel the excitement he'd felt at being summoned by Seth, but also the anxiety because this wasn't how they met.

Their meetings were always well thought-out, planned down to the last minute they would spend together. The call had worried Joel, but still he'd come.

Without speaking, Seth had taken Joel into his arms and enveloped him in a searing kiss that left them both breathless. Then the words had come. "It's over."

Joel's overwhelming pain was too much for me to handle, so I closed my mind and refocused on the present. "Why?"

"Didn't you see?"

"It was too much."

Joel nodded. "He told me we couldn't keep doing this. He said it's wrong of us."

"Was he your mate?" I focused on the bottle cap still twirling in the water, caught within the ripples.

"No." Joel laughed, a harsh sound. "Kuro and Dryma can't become mates. It's impossible. But he was the only one I've ever loved."

Impossible? Then how did you explain Tristan and I? "How long was it going on?"

"Three years."

I blanched. "Three years? How come I didn't know anything?"

"We were careful to hide our emotions," he explained. "I bet you're angry with me."

"No." I wrapped my arm around his shoulders and drew his shuddering frame close to mine. From afar, I was sure we looked like two starved teenagers with an unnatural growth spurt. "We all deserve love, Joel. And in this world where we have nothing, if he made you happy, then I'm okay with it."

"He was everything to me."

"I'm sorry…." Was this what I had coming to me? This heart-ripping emptiness I couldn't evade? "Really, Joel, you don't know how sorry I am."

"When does Zain get off?" he asked suddenly.

"An hour or two. Why?"

"I was just thinking I'd really like a drink, and he tends to act really stupid when he's drunk."

I smiled. "I'll call him up and tell him to meet us there, but Tomas will probably show up too."

Joel sighed patronizingly and stood up, helping me to my feet. "Well, that's okay as long as he doesn't take all the shots again."

"You should probably call Chiaki too and let him know you're all right."

The old Joel appeared, and his face was wracked with guilt. "I can't believe I've been gone all day. Maybe I should just go home and make sure they're okay."

"Don't worry about Chiaki and the others. They're tough. Let them know you'll be home soon, and let's go get those drinks."

Joel smiled, but somehow his expression was just as hollow as when he'd been crying.

CHAPTER ELEVEN

"CAN YOU help me?"

"Whatever you need," I told Tristan. The night before, I'd drunk too much with Joel, Zain, and Tomas, and now I was paying dearly. It felt like there was a sledgehammer pounding the inside of my skull.

Tristan eyed me but didn't say anything. In the weeks I had been by his side, we'd fallen into this unspoken agreement where he knew I cared for him, but never explicitly pointed it out. Because we never spoke about it, I was sure he thought I was only interested in him because he was the Prince of the Dryma. He had no idea I was his mate because of the soap Chiaki had made me, and he had no desire to make me his.

Each time he spoke of his unwavering devotion to his mate, I felt a pang of love deep in my chest but always had to hide my reaction.

I'd longed for his touch, even if he was substituting me for "Mason," but he hadn't given in to his desire.

"Here, hold this." He handed me the beginning of a pink measuring tape and then walked the circumference of the tree until our hands grazed. He made note of the measurement and then jotted something down in a small notebook.

"Are we doing this for your flower experiment?" I asked as I gathered the measuring tape he'd discarded.

"Precisely."

Which explained why we were in Pasky. I'd contacted the protectors through my mind and told them Tristan and I would be here. Confusion and anxiety ran through their minds, but my command was enough to keep them away from where Tristan was measuring.

"Why aren't we measuring the royal trees?"

The weather was uncommonly beautiful today, the sun daring the clouds to try and take over. Tristan wore shorts and a skintight shirt that made me drool with lust. His muscles were perfectly on display, but he wasn't the kind to preen. He'd come here to collect data, and that was all that filled his mind.

I admired his tenacity—one of the main reasons I loved him.

"Christophe volunteered to let us use his tree. Without knowing completely what will happen, he thought it was better I didn't experiment on my family's."

I checked for any worry for his friend but didn't see any. His face was a mask of indifference. There was a shuffling behind me, and then Tristan's arms wrapped around my body. Unable to move against the crushing strength, I gave in.

His breath was hot in my ear and smelled of his greenhouse. "Kanji, I—"

Whatever he was going to say was erased by the harsh warning cutting through the forest like a battle-ax. "Wait, something's wrong."

His hands fell away, but my mind wasn't with Tristan. I scoured the trees, darting through the eyes of the Kuro on the nature reserve. My mind landed on Micky's.

Sidhee approaching.

"There are Sidhee here," I told Tristan as I grabbed for his hand and took off toward Micky's voice. "I'm going to take you to the cliffs, and then you can fly home. The Sidhee won't be able to come after you."

Tristan maneuvered our bodies so he was the one leading me. "And what about you?" His bag thumped against his side, the sweet scent of flowers overwhelming.

"I have to go help my kind," I told him. The thought of having to leave him killed me, but I couldn't abandon Micky. "Some of them are still children."

"I understand." Tristan stopped and turned around so I could see the hard set of his jaw, the determination in his eyes. "I will fight with you."

"What? No!" I cried. "You're crazy if you think I'm going to let you stay here. My job is to protect you, and I will do just that."

Tristan's voice was kind. "By now you have to know your purpose wasn't to protect me. It was to keep you out of the action."

I was so startled I forgot we had to keep running. "What did you say?"

"You're a prince, a Kuro, but a prince all the same. Your position might not be comparable to mine, but you are still important."

"Do you honestly expect me to not fight with my friends? With Kuro who are little more than teenagers?" Even though I had suspected as much, I couldn't contain the anger I felt at being elevated from the rest of my kind. Zain, Joel, and even Tomas were all important to my clan too.

"Now isn't the time to fight with me." Tristan tightened his grip on my hand. "We need to contact Christophe and tell him there are Sidhee here. Has anything else happened?"

I drove through the minds of the rangers, but other than fear, I couldn't feel or see anything else. "Micky already called Christophe and told him. The guard should be on their way."

"Good. What is your plan?"

"None of the rangers have any weapons apart from guns," I said hastily, allowing him to pull me through the trees and closer to the cliffs. "Guns are useless against the Sidhee, which is why we've been waiting on those swords Christophe promised us."

I couldn't see Tristan's face as we marched through the woods, our pace slowing to a crawl so we could hear the sounds of the woods and be prepared if anything jumped out.

What's happening? Are you okay? I asked Micky, before sending the same message to the other rangers.

His voice was quiet and concerned. *I'm all right. I saw a Sidhee, but after I doubled back to stand guard over the tree, he was gone.*

Micky was the only one who'd seen a Sidhee, but the other Kuro had felt the presence of a lurking demon.

"Everything seems to be okay," I told Tristan as we broke through the woods. There were brightly painted signs to warn hikers of the approaching drop off into the ocean. Pasky was full of small rivers and lakes, but along the south border, there were steep cliffs dropping off into the ocean. "But I still want you to go."

Tristan released my hand and approached the side of the cliff, his toes just about dangling off the edge. I expected him to tear his shirt from his body dramatically like I'd seen Christophe do and soar into the air, but he was nothing like the captain of the guard.

Patiently, Tristan stared into the bowels of the ocean.

"If we're not in danger, then I see no reason why I should leave."

I checked and rechecked, but there had been no further sightings of the Sidhee amongst the Kuro protectors. Had Micky somehow been wrong about seeing one of the demons? Was it possible he had succumbed to his exhaustion?

"Just to be on the safe side, I want you to go back to your house. Christophe will probably intercept you and guard you the rest of the way."

The gap between us widened as my heart sank like quicksand. No matter what, I couldn't allow him to see my eyes. Couldn't let him see how much this hurt me.

"Kanji," he murmured, his voice melting with the water until I couldn't tell the difference between his voice and the rocking of the ocean. "You're shaking."

"I'm not," I lied.

"You look like you're going to cry."

"I'm not," I said defiantly. "Why would I cry? It isn't me who is being pursued by the Sidhee."

"The Prince of the Sidhee could've had me." Tristan didn't miss a beat. Like he knew we would have this conversation all along. "But he betrayed me and then the Dryma as a whole by killing my brother. Any relationship I have with him is over."

"Christophe said you were friends with Calhoun. Said you knew him as a child."

"And this bothers you, why?"

"I want you to be happy." The words tumbled from my lips like yarn from a wicker basket. Once they started, the endless color couldn't be regathered. "All this time, you've talked about your mate and about it being impossible, but I want you to be with them. I want you to feel contentment."

Tristan held me like a suit of armor, tight and unrelenting. "Calhoun isn't my mate, if you were insinuating so."

"No, but by the way you speak, your mate must be someone the Dryma dictate you can't have." Please, for the love of God, realize it's me so I don't have to feel this anymore.

"Prince Tristan." The voice belonged to a mammoth of a Sidhee with worn skin and sunken red eyes. I didn't recognize him as one of the guards I had seen with Calhoun, but it had been dark and my focus had been on the prince. "Don't attempt to fight. I'm only here at my prince's command. He wishes for me to escort you back to our world."

Before Tristan could speak, I protectively stepped in front of him. I was aware that my spindly, lanky frame wasn't much, but there was fight in me if the life of my mate depended on it. The Sidhee stared at me with amusement before barking out.

"And who is this? Your puppy?"

At least I knew he hadn't been with Calhoun that night because he would've remembered the degraded way he had treated the "fallen prince."

Tristan's hand was firm on my shoulder, my eyes falling to the sword in the Sidhee's hand. His eyes were glazed over, his mouth slightly parted like a madman awaiting final judgment.

"Go, Christophe will be here soon," I told Tristan, taking a step backward so he had no choice but to as well. Any more and I would've pushed him clean off the cliff.

"Not without you."

"I can't leave," I whispered vehemently. I didn't doubt Tristan could carry me, but if we left, who was to say the Sidhee wouldn't settle for attacking my kind? Or attacking the trees?

In the split-second it took me to assess my surroundings, the Sidhee had gathered his sword in his two gnarly hands and lunged at me. Bracing myself for the feel of his cold blade, I felt the blow but not from the direction I was expecting.

My knees collided with the ground and could taste bile. I wiped at my mouth while rolling to my stomach. Tristan had pushed me out of the way and now had both his hands in a struggle for the sword. True to his word, the Sidhee didn't seem interested in killing Tristan, which gave me small hope my mate would be able to overpower him.

In my attempt to stand, my foot slipped over the wet grass, and I lost sensation in my fingers as I tumbled from the cliff. The ground dropped out from beneath me, the air bursting from my lungs. Scrambling for anything to hold onto, I raked my nails across the roots clinging to the side of the cliff. But it was no good.

My feet dangled beneath me, heavy as stones. Tristan screamed my name, but my fear burned my ears and I could only see the red hatred of blood smearing my vision. Mustering all the strength in my arms, I attempted to raise myself, but my muscles were weak from how little I'd been able to ingest.

The ocean roared beneath me like a monster waiting to swallow me whole. The sheer drop was frightful, but if I could hold my breath long enough to reach the surface, I could swim to the shore.

"Kanji, take my hand." Tristan's face was smeared with dirt and red with effort. His green eyes were smoldering with anger as he stretched out his hand. What he didn't see was the frame of the Sidhee behind him. The time it would take for Tristan to grab me was all the time the Sidhee would need.

I let go.

Colliding with the water, I inhaled the scent of salt just before a wave toppled over my head, blinding me. Kicking viciously, I managed to break the surface, but the sheer intensity of the waves took me by surprise. I was nowhere near prepared for the presence of the ocean to be so strong.

I was angry with myself for even letting the thought of failure slink into my mind. Tristan was fighting a Sidhee on his own, and my drop into the ocean was meant to give him enough time to fight and be free. I wasn't meant to die.

The thought of giving in enticed me more than I was willing to admit.

No. I was a Kuro at heart even if I couldn't fly. Water ran through my veins, and I couldn't let it defeat me because I was trapped in a human form. Paddling through the waves, I once again broke the surface and raked in oxygen until I thought I might pass out. The cold water made my hair stick to my face like seaweed, and my clothes were as tight as a seal's skin.

The beating of wings sounded above me, but it was different than what I was used to. The wings were heavy, and when I looked up, they were dark. I noticed the line of the dark feathers glittering like tiny diamonds. Feathers?

Tristan's hands were cold and sweaty as he swooped down to take me into his arms. I caught the scent of his wings, the smell of earth and home, nothing like the other fairies. More exhausted than I realized, I struggled to maintain consciousness. It was a losing battle, and I felt my eyes sink into the back of my skull as I was lifted gracefully into the air.

How long had it been since I'd been able to fly? Even though I wasn't the one with the wings, a part of the wall I'd built around my heart came crashing down. The air slapped my face, and I didn't mind the rough feeling of my cheeks afterward.

"Tristan," I murmured, inhaling the earthen scent of his bare chest. Reaching for his feathery wings, I expected him to slap my hands away. But he didn't. After I touched the silky feathers, I knew for certain. "You're a Kuro."

Tristan's handsome face outlined by the sun was befitting of a Greek god. Then one word shattered the last of my illusions. "Yes."

DROPLETS OF water streamed from my mouth, and there was a choking sound I wanted to silence. After a few more minutes of the persistent coughing, I realized the noise was coming from me.

Soft blankets greeted my searching fingers as I tried to find something to hold. There was a flickering light, and when I managed to lift my heavy eyelids, I saw a floating lantern like the ones that had been at the masquerade ball. The dark purple curtains were drawn, refusing any lingering light of the sun.

"Where am I?" I croaked, my tongue thick, rough like sandpaper in my mouth. The scent of flowers was wrong. I wasn't in a Kuro's home… I was somewhere else entirely.

With a jolt, I remembered my fall from the cliff and into the ocean. The feathery dark wings belonging to Tristan—the youngest Dryma prince. As my eyes adjusted, I realized I was in a large room with a high ceiling. There was a settee and oversized chair near a set of french doors. The bed, the dresser, the desk and matching chair… everything was pale white; the innocent color of water lilies.

"My bedroom," Tristan murmured. A warm rag was pressed to my forehead in an attempt to dry my skin. "Are you feeling better?"

Better? How could I not be better now that I was in Tristan's room? Everything smelled of him, the delicate but persistent scent of earth.

"Yes." I accepted a flute glass he offered me and drained the sweet-tasting liquid in a few gulps. "What is that?"

"Rice milk tea infused with jasmine to calm you."

I wiped my mouth and forced myself into a sitting position. "I'm calm."

Tristan had changed into a pair of loose pants the color of the ocean, but my eyes settled on the rise and fall of his bare chest. His eyes narrowed at my expression, the ultimate sign of his guilt.

"You're a Kuro," I said lifelessly.

I expected him to fight me or claim I was mistaken, but he simply sighed. "Yes."

For a long moment, the weight of his secret crushed down on me. "Who else knows?"

"My family and Christophe are the only ones."

"But how?"

"My father had a momentarily lapse of judgment with a Kuro female. I never met her, so I don't have more details to offer."

Who could've possibly been his mother? I liked to think I knew all the Kuro in my clan, but how many females had died in the twenty-four years Tristan had been alive?

"She was no one of importance or so my Dryma mother says. She died shortly after giving birth to me." His voice was void of emotion even though I could tell by the slump of his shoulders divulging his well-kept secret was difficult.

Suddenly, my body was enflamed in remorse. "Tell me one thing. Did you not want to fly away because you were worried about me finding out? Or were you actually worried about my safety?"

"How can you even ask such a thing?" With fluttering, Dryma hands, he pushed his hair from his face. The bed dipped down as he placed his legs on either side of mine, trapping me beneath him. His hand was warm as he held my chin and captivated my lips.

After waiting for so long, I could hardly believe he was kissing me again. His mouth wasn't gentle as he took over my body, demanding I yield to his control. Over and over, the sick truth of reality reminded me he was half Kuro. The gap between us had softened ever so slightly, but there was the new danger of our relationship being discovered. If his family had gone to such lengths to keep his true nature a secret, there was no telling what they would do to keep him away from me.

Joel had been right; only Kuro can mate with other Kuro.

If anyone found out, then Tristan's secret would be revealed.

"No, stop." I turned my head to the side, but Tristan kissed my eyelids and my cheeks instead. "We can't." My hand collided with his toned, golden chest.

With his other hand, he ghosted his fingers along my hipbone and up along the curve of my spine. "I'm sorry for lying to you. There shouldn't be secrets between us."

"It doesn't matter."

His kisses were driving away the last of my resolve.

"I won't tell anyone," I promised. "Not even my own kind. You don't owe me anything. I'm not your mate."

Abruptly, Tristan pulled away so he could stare into my eyes. "Now who's lying?"

Shock reverberated through my body, and as I inhaled at the skin at my wrist, I already knew there would be no lingering traces of Chiaki's soap.

"Water washes away everything, even lies." Tristan licked a line from the corner of my mouth to my collarbone, forcing my back to arch to his will. "After the ball, I thought I might never see you again. Knowing that was enough to drive me insane."

"How long have you known?" My voice was little more than a whisper, and I knew I didn't have long before I completely succumbed.

"I've had my suspicions it was you since the first day at the greenhouse." He removed my shirt and traced each of my ribs. "I might not have seen your face, but I could hardly forget your body. The curve of your back, your long legs, the silky hair touching your shoulders…. And your eyes… the most radiant blue I've ever seen. Do you know how stunning you are?"

I scoffed, "Bony you mean?"

"Swans are meant to be graceful and thin."

Tristan's hands were at my belt, undoing the buckle, but there was more I had to say.

"I didn't mean to lie to you. Or for your brother to die."

"I know," Tristan hushed me. "Are you working for the Sidhee?"

"Never. I was at the ball because…."

"The Sidhee changed their mind about joining us and you decided to come in their place? After being our prisoners for so long, I can hardly blame you."

He was wrong. We had set out to destroy the Dryma, but now I wanted nothing more than to save him. "That was before I knew you. If there is anything I could do for you to make you happy, I would do it without hesitation."

Then he was lifting me from the bed so he could pull down my pants and briefs, easing them down. "I believe you. No more talking. These past few weeks have been hell. I just want to openly admit my love to you and make you mine. Please… let me?"

I tightened my hold around his neck. "Whatever you want is yours. I already gave you myself once, so you don't have to ask."

"So you haven't changed your mind now you know I'm half Kuro?"

"Not a chance."

But there were words circling my head like mothballs. Words I couldn't say aloud, like how concerned I was we would be found out and he would lose everything.

My doubts died in my throat as he flattened me onto my back and sidled his way down the bed. Hoisting my legs over his shoulders, he kissed the inside of my thigh, slowly working his way toward my erect member.

With expert hands, he wrapped his fist around my shaft and applied just the right amount of pressure to elicit a deep throaty moan from with me. His eyes gleamed with desire, and then his mouth replaced his hand. The sensations as he licked the length of my shaft, darting his tongue into my slit and increasing suction was too much. My hands wrapped into his golden curls, and I lost the will to be gentle. I needed him with a fervor that broke apart everything inside of me until I wasn't sure where I ended and Tristan began.

My breathing hitched as he took me into the back of his throat. The last time we'd had sex had been rushed and secretive, but this time I could tell Tristan wanted to take his time with me. He wanted me to writhe beneath him, to scream and beg and plead. All things I would do if he asked me to.

My cock slid from his mouth with a wet popping sound as he slipped his fingers into his mouth and prodded my entrance. He pushed past the tight ring of muscle, my body clenching in an effort to keep him within me. If it had been possible, I would've wanted him to take hold of my heart in his beautiful hands.

"Oh...." I whimpered, my head lolling back as he kissed the tip of my throbbing cock.

"Are you enjoying this?" His voice was deep and strained with the effort of denying his own release. But he was patient and wanted to ensure my pleasure was just as good as his, if not better. "Everything I do... your eyes tell me it's not enough. That you want more."

"I do," I assured him, tugging his hair with a newfound confidence.

In his dimly lit bedroom, our positions were irrelevant. Who was a Dryma? A Kuro? A Sidhee? None of those labels mattered. "Tristan, I love you. It won't be enough until you're inside of me."

His eyes flashed, but instead of preparing to enter me, he once again lowered his head and swallowed me whole. Gasping, I muttered a string of syllables resembling his name as my legs tightened with pleasure and my stomach pooled with heat. I was so close I ached with unadulterated need.

Slapping my hands over my mouth so as to stifle my scream, I arched my back as my orgasm tore through me. His mouth around my cock and his fingers at my entrance combined with his eyes trained on me was enough to make me pass out.

Gently, he gripped my wrist with the fingers not buried inside me and entwined our hands. Taking the gesture to mean he wanted to hear my voice, I gave him exactly what he wanted.

Slowly, he let my cock slip from his mouth, but only after he'd extracted every drop I thought was within me.

His body was enflamed as I ran my hands over every scrap of flesh visible. Eyeing his swollen, thick cock, I started to slide down the bed so I could take him into my mouth, but his hand on my hip stopped me.

"You don't need to," he whispered, nuzzling my neck with the tip of his nose.

"I want to repay you for the favor."

"There is nothing to repay. Everything that I want to give you, I will. I don't want to be like this, not with you. We don't need to worry about getting even. If you have all the pleasure, I wouldn't be troubled."

His selfless words caused burning tears to spring to my eyes. "Do you honestly think that is enough for me?"

Tristan beamed as he reached over to his nightstand and withdrew a bottle of lubricant. He generously coated his length and positioned himself at my entrance. I braced myself for the pain I knew came before the pleasure, but he paused.

When I looked up, I couldn't contain the surprised noise crawling from my throat. His eyes, those bright emerald precious stone eyes, were staring at me. The desire to crawl inside his head and see through his eyes was unrelenting. I wanted to see what he saw in me that made him have such an expression.

"Your desire for me is what makes me want you more than you can imagine. You aren't a weakling who takes anything I say as law. You fight me. Challenge me. Kanji, believe me when I tell you everything about you is important to me."

I choked on my words. Nodding, I secured my arms around his neck as he pushed his length inside of me. The pain burst into my body but rapidly spread into pleasure. I couldn't imagine better sex in my life, but it was my partner who was responsible.

Knowing my mate, the Dryma prince I'd lusted after for weeks, was holding me tightly against his skin made the pleasure overwhelming.

"Your body is amazing," he panted, his hands flying over me as though I were a musical instrument. "So tight and warm and perfect."

"I'm glad my body can give you pleasure," I murmured into the crook of his neck. He tasted like the salt of the ocean.

"And do I give you pleasure?" Tristan's voice was low, teasing me as he rocked so deep inside of me I could feel him in my stomach. My legs were weak and useless beneath him, the strength of his arms the only reason I could move at all.

"Do you ever need to ask?" I repeated his earlier words as my inside channels squeezed around him.

"I always thought I had everything, but I couldn't have been more wrong. This is what I was missing. This is what I wanted to feel."

"Sex is pretty great."

Tristan nibbled on my earlobe, and from his labored breathing, I knew he was close to finding his release. "No, not sex. Love. I love you."

Unable to contain myself, I scraped my fingers over the broad expanse of his back and coaxed him deep into me. Tristan cried out my name, and I held on to his shuddering frame as he emptied his seed inside of me. The feeling of his slickness jolted me into a frenzied state of pleasure where my muscles tightened and contracted in an attempt to keep him within me.

My vision clouded over, my fingers going numb from exertion.

"Is it safe to stay here like this?" I asked, kissing the muscles of Tristan's arm. I paused to lick the crook of his elbow, pressing small kisses to his tanned flesh.

He was staring at me with a hungry expression, his cock jerking to life inside me. "No, but I think we can spare a few minutes."

The words were left unspoken but were just as crushing. In his bedroom, where we were alone, we were lovers and mates. But once we abandoned the safety of his bed, our positions would once again separate us.

Clinging to Tristan with every ounce of strength I had left, I only prayed I wouldn't experience what Joel was going through. The better part of my brain told me to not get my hopes up.

CHAPTER TWELVE

"WHERE IS everyone?" My voice was still hoarse, but I blamed my moaning rather than the drop off the cliff.

I had no idea how many rooms there were in Tristan's mansion, but I estimated close to twenty, the size of a small hotel. The rugs were of an exquisite material. Intricate designs detailing the Dryma histories were woven into tapestries hung on the walls. I wished the Kuro had something half as grand to show for our long existence, anything that put us on the same level as the Dryma and the Sidhee.

"My parents were evacuated, somewhere in the States. My older brothers have joined Christophe in their desire to protect our kind, so they aren't here right now either." Tristan's voice was heavy with a desperate sadness I wanted to fill.

Pausing in front of a large painting, I found nine sets of green eyes staring down at me. I recognized Seth and Tristan, although they were little more than teenagers. I raised my hand with the intention of touching the handsome face of my mate, but stopped before my skin could collide with the painting.

When all was said and done, this painting could be the only thing left of Tristan and his great family. My concern for my kind had made me completely overlook Tristan's grief.

"I need to contact Zain," I told Tristan as I turned away from the painting and finished my trek down the long hallway to the door leading to the garden. "I need to make sure every Kuro is okay."

Tristan followed me, his steps silent in comparison to my thunderous ones. "I already contacted Christophe," he said quietly. "There was no damage done to your kind or to mine. As we speak, he is passing out weapons."

"Will they be kept in the woods?" I asked. There was a twinge in my shoulder where I must've twisted my arm during my fall, and now that the high of our lovemaking had gone down, I was in a lot of pain. "Something tells me the Sidhee are no longer going to be satisfied running through the woods. They are going to remember the Kuro's role in serving you and come after us."

Tristan's hand grounded me as he wrapped his strong fingers around my wrist. "I won't let anything happen to you."

"I'm not worried about myself." I couldn't look into Tristan's eyes because I knew the moment I did, I'd want him to take me back to his room and ravish me until I couldn't walk. "I'm worried about my friends."

"Christophe isn't going to let anything happen to them."

It wasn't until I'd entered the garden and saw the dark sky that I realized how much time had passed since the fight with the Sidhee on the cliff. The garden was picture perfect, with lanterns covered in colorful cloth on either side of the stone path. They looked like tiny stone animals with fire in their bellies.

"Where exactly are you going?"

"To the greenhouse, obviously."

"Yes, but why?" Tristan sounded highly amused.

I paused at the glass door and turned to look at Tristan, losing my breath in the process. He had put a shirt on and a tailored jacket I was sure was designer. His blond curls hung limply around his face, the very top of his head a slightly darker color because that part was still damp.

There was no denying he was perfect, like a marbled sculpture artists would die to sketch, but the way he looked at me was what turned my bones to jelly. The raw need in his eyes told me he would do whatever necessary to keep me safe. If he could look only at me forever.

"I want to be near the flowers. They make me feel safe," I admitted, turning away so he wouldn't see my cheeks redden.

"What you're failing to realize is that you don't need them." Tristan stepped closer to me, the lanterns casting him in a surreal glow. "Because you have me. I can protect you. I can keep you safe."

"It's not your job to protect me."

"I didn't say I had to," Tristan amended thoughtfully. "I meant I'm here to back you up. I know you're strong. The strongest male I know actually."

I smiled. "Except for Christophe of course."

"I think it depends of what kind of strength we're talking about. He has a certain physical strength hard to rival, I admit, but when it comes to inner strength... you have me beat."

"I want to kiss you."

"What's stopping you?" Tristan challenged. I expected him to move closer, but he stayed in the same spot beside a birdbath trickling with water. He was challenging me to take what I wanted.

"Anxiety? Worry? Approaching war? Take your pick."

"Right now there's only us."

His words undid me.

Hesitantly, I crossed the garden path to him, my heart thumping against my ribs. I moved slowly because I wanted to take in his appearance and commit every detail of his face to my mind. If I hadn't taken my time, I wouldn't have seen the shadowy figure taking shape near the back door.

Tristan must've seen my look of alarm, because he spun around, situating me securely behind him. It wasn't until Christophe stepped out of the shadows that Tristan relaxed his stance.

"Christophe. Why didn't you announce yourself?" Tristan fumed, his voice low and throaty. How much had the captain heard?

"My apologies, Tristan. I didn't know you were doing anything that would make you blind to my presence." Christophe looked anything but sorry. In fact, the sallow look in his eyes made me want to run. His belt was loaded with so many weapons he could've passed for a medieval Batman.

"I was attacked by a Sidhee earlier," Tristan said curtly. I saw the reluctance in his movements as he abandoned my side, but all the same, it would've been suspicious if he had stayed so close. "Surely you can imagine why I might be on edge."

"Surely," Christophe repeated. There was dirt caked in his bright red hair and grass stains on his starched white pants. "The area has been made secure. The Sidhee you dealt with could offer no useful information before he died. I passed out the weapons to the Kuro as promised and came to take Kanji back to his home."

"He should stay here," Tristan said firmly. "He is the Kuro prince and needs more protection."

His words took me by surprise. If he wasn't careful, the captain was going to know something was awry.

"I posted him as your protector because it seemed like a good idea." Christophe's voice was dark. "But now I see the toll it has taken on your health, my prince. It is my job alone to protect Kanji, and I will do so. No harm will come to the Prince of the Kuro. So unless you have any objections why I should not take him home where he has been safe all this time, I will escort him now. Besides, your brothers have gathered in the meeting hall and want to speak with you about the approaching war."

I saw the struggle running through Tristan's mind. On one hand, letting his mate leave his side was tearing him apart piece by piece. But if he put up a fight, Christophe would demand to know why.

Before Tristan could protest, I stepped forward and gave Christophe a slight bow of my head, a sign of respect. "I would like to return home as soon as possible. I'd like to touch base with my kind and make sure they are prepared to fight."

Tristan turned his head to the side so neither Christophe nor I could see his expression, although I could guess.

Christophe didn't hide his greedy smile, and I wished I had the nerve to slap his high cheekbones. "I saw your car parked out front. I will follow you to your home and give you further instructions."

What could I say? Nodding once, I tried to give Tristan a reassuring smile, but he remained rigid near the entrance of the greenhouse and refused to make eye contact with me. The sinking hole in my chest I'd been working on closing burst wide open.

I DROVE as quickly as I could, hoping that at the next turn, Christophe would drop out of view and give up on following me. No such luck.

Once I pulled into my driveway, I knew whatever Christophe had to say wasn't going to be good. He slammed his door with more force than needed and practically leapt at me. His hands were tight on my shoulders as he slammed me into my car, his eyes burning into mine.

"What were you two doing?" he snarled, his face red.

I had to be careful because even though Tristan was my mate and a Dryma prince, it was Christophe who held most of the power. He was the one holding on to our freedom, treating us as though we were little more than marionettes.

"It's the middle of the night," I protested, wriggling slightly so his grip wasn't quite so tight on my arms. The damage was already done, though. When I woke up the next morning, my arms would be dotted with purplish bruises everywhere his fingers had dug into my pale flesh. "You don't have to shout."

Christophe blinked and loosened his grip slightly.

"We weren't doing anything. He saved my life, that's all."

Christophe leaned in so close, I thought he was going to kiss me. His anger I could take. His demeaning of my kind I could take. But forcing himself onto me after I'd finally gotten my mate... there was no way I could submit so easily.

"Don't forget our agreement," Christophe hissed, his voice full of ice. "After we fight the Sidhee, I will give you the key to your kind's wings. But you will forever be mine."

Tersely, he released me and stormed back to the expensive car worth more than my house without waiting for my reply. Apparently, whatever I said didn't matter to him, and why should it? No matter how hard I tried to disillusion myself, he was right.

I was the key to our wings. All I had to do was sacrifice myself.

"Tristan, I'm sorry," I whispered, knowing he was too far to hear, but foolishly hoping he would.

OTHER THAN being exhausted and weighed down by heavy swords, the Kuro swans appeared to be all right. As many as could fit had gathered in my house even though it was the middle of the night. Those that couldn't fit in my tiny house had poured into the backyard, some of them with their female mates.

Zain took one look at me before bellowing for a path to be made so I could go to my room. If I were any sort of prince, I should've grabbed a glass of whatever Chiaki had made and helped him pass it out.

But their eyes devoured me like a swarm of great white sharks. Mari was standing amongst the other females, a sword in her hands although I couldn't see who she'd taken it from. I knew I had to act quickly because when Zain followed me to my bedroom, I saw his blue eyes had darkened to the color of swamp rock.

"I'm working on it," I reassured him as I squeezed his shoulder. "I promise, I'm trying."

"I've never doubted you, and I'm not starting now" was Zain's solid reply. "All I'm asking is that you try faster. We can't win against the Sidhee...."

I believed he didn't doubt me, but his lower lip was bleeding where he'd been gnawing at the tender flesh, and I knew time was running out. The Kuro had nothing, which meant there was nothing to lose.

"Kanji?"

My phone buzzed in my pocket, and when I saw Tristan's name, I was brought back to the present. "Thinking. Sorry."

Zain stared at me before heading back downstairs to continue the training Christophe had left for them. I wanted to go with them, but before I could, Tristan's number appeared on my phone.

WHEN TRISTAN had contacted me the night before and told me to come to his house, I thought Christophe would be there to protest, but he'd been shockingly absent.

"What are you thinking about?"

We were situated in front of a Dryma tree with a wicker basket between us, one of Tristan's hovering flowers situated inside. Even in the sunlight, the flower was more radiant by contrast, gently pulsing with life.

"Nothing important," I muttered, not wanting to share the murderous intentions of my kind with Tristan. "I'm surprised, though. The last time I saw you, I was under the impression Christophe wasn't going to let me come near you—"

My words died in my throat as he wrapped his arms around my chest, cradling my head on his shoulder. I couldn't see him because he'd seized me from behind, but I could feel his heart beating in my eardrums.

"I convinced him the safest place for you to be was with me. And when he couldn't give my brothers an explanation why not, he gave in. Besides, I know how much you love these flowers, and I wanted you to be here."

Always so considerate. He gave me a chaste kiss on my earlobe before releasing me.

"So, is your body all right?"

"What?"

Tristan cleared his throat as he detangled a chain of flowers I didn't recognize laced around a dark black cord. "The other night, I wanted you so badly I wasn't able to hold back. But what I wanted was to give you pleasure you wouldn't easily forget."

"I didn't," I assured him. "And I'm fine. I wasn't a virgin or anything."

Tristan's head snapped up, his green eyes sifting through the confines of my soul. "It might be selfish of me, but from now on, I want to be your only."

"How is that selfish?" I whispered, as I gathered the untangled flower chain in my hands and spread it out around the tree. "When I want you all to myself too?"

We met at the center of the tree, each holding the long thread of fragile petals. "What are we going to do?"

"Run away," I suggested. "Or I could kidnap you, and then they'll be so busy coming after us, the Sidhee and the Dryma will forget all about having a war."

Tristan kissed my nose, but I didn't find the gesture condescending. "Right, because kidnapping me would go over so well."

"Prince Calhoun seems to have the same idea."

My statement was meant to be comic relief, but Tristan's jaw locked and he stepped past to me to go loop the chain around the tree again. I waited for him to circle his way back to me.

"You were friends with him," I stated.

Tristan sighed as he fastened the edge of his cord into the chain clinging to the tree. The cold weather actually seemed to be affecting him because he wore slacks and a sweater. I was bundled in a long-sleeve T-shirt, heavy jacket, and a knit cap.

"You've brought up my being friends with him before. I have to assume you aren't going to let this go? Why does it mean so much to you?"

Then I realized Tristan and I never talked about our families or friends. Other than his brother and my uncle, both of whom were dead, we knew next to nothing. Being ignorant of each other's personal lives made it easier. Without being completely immersed in one another's world, we hadn't crossed the last of the boundaries between us.

My heart sank.

"Kanji." Tristan's voice was concerned at my ear as he stroked my long hair from the root to tip. "I didn't mean to upset you. Of course I will tell you everything you want to know."

"The Sidhee betrayed the Kuro," I said, taking his hand into mine and inhaling the addictive scent of his palm. "And you're a Kuro. Why would you befriend a Sidhee knowing what you do?"

"For a long time, I think the Dryma have been trying to find a way to disconnect from the Earth. Knowing what we do about the Sidhee, I think it was my father's intention to make use of me by having me get close to Calhoun. The end goal was to have us move into their world. We were both children. How was I supposed to know what his plan was?"

Tristan was irresistible, and I felt bad for doubting him. I giggled in spite of myself.

"What's so funny?"

"Imagining you as a child. I bet you were so pretty."

The slightest of blushes colored Tristan's cheeks. "Not as cute as you."

I shrugged. "So if that was the plan all along, then what happened?" I knew already that Calhoun hadn't come because of what I'd done, but if they had been friends, surely he would've tried to come and talk to Tristan just to make certain the deal was really off.

"We were friends when we were young, but we stopped talking after I became a teenager."

"Why?"

Tristan refocused his attention on the flowers, and I knew by his expression I didn't have a lot of time before he'd become completely absorbed. "Something my father said about fairies having limited time in the human world. I eventually put two and two together and focused my attention on the study of genetics."

"I don't want you to not be a part of my world."

He gave me an unfathomable expression. "Being away from you isn't even an option anymore. Hence the flowers." Tristan's voice was thoughtful as he gently picked up the flower the way he would a baby. "The flowers will save us. They have to work."

"And us?" I whispered, fresh pangs of guilt stabbing the space between my ribs.

"I've already promised to release the Kuro."

But that's not what I meant by "us." I'd been speaking of my relationship with Tristan.

There was a lost look in his eyes, and I knew anything I said would be dissected and weighed for value. His focus was upon the breathing flower in his hands, and I found I even loved his isolated stare.

"I have one more question," I asked, tentatively moving to where he was standing beside the tree trunk. "If you don't mind?"

Tristan's head snapped up, his eyes clouding. "Whatever did I do to give you the impression you would be a bother to me?"

I shrugged. "Just wanted to make sure I wasn't interrupting any complex thought processes or anything."

Tristan crossed the last of the distance between us and leaned his forehead against mine. His earthen smell sent waves of need straight to my groin. When he spoke, his voice was deep and throaty. "You talk about me like I'm a genius."

"Aren't you?" I teased.

We weren't touching anymore, but being this close to him was enough to drive me insane. How much more could I possibly come to love him?

"What is it you wanted to ask me?" He diverted the subject as he glanced at the sky. Assessing how much time we had left to complete our experiment before the time ebbed away.

"Why do you still have your wings?"

He gave me a confused expression. "I'm also a Dryma."

"I may have been half unconscious, but I remember what your wings looked like. They were stunningly beautiful and feathery. Kuro wings."

"I'm not sure," Tristan admitted as his hands fluttered along the petals of the flower. "Christophe is the only one who knows how your wings are contained. My father made me swear to never fly in public so questions wouldn't be asked."

"You must've been lonely."

I could feel what he had. The aching pain between the shoulder blades and knowing something was lacking, but never being able to find a replacement. Worst of all was the restlessness branching out in your body like a weed. "Not being able to fly is like being an outside prisoner. You can go anywhere you want, but you only want to get into the prison."

"I was lonely?" Tristan echoed in disbelief. "Not anything like what you must've felt."

"Yes, but it got better after I found you."

My words lingered between us until I did the only thing that made sense. Our feet were barely touching, my side pressed against his and our hands on the flower. The closeness was enough.

"So what are you going to do?"

"Do you see these green leaves embedded into the wires?"

"Yes."

"They are actually weeds," he explained proudly. He lifted the five-pointed flowers, but I found myself staring at his long fingers. "They are called cinquefoils, and they have five clefts and five bractlets so they appear to be ten cleft. Each corolla, the flowery thing, has five separate petals."

"Okay," I breathed. "I may be a forest ranger, but I know next to nothing it would seem."

Tristan humored me. "Cinquefoils tend to grow in dry fields or old meadows, so I had them sent to me from dryer climates. They have a narcotic type of effect, so the hope is they will be able to numb the life inside of the tree."

"I know this one is Canada thistle. What is the point of using those?"

"Canada thistle is very hard to get rid of. They are known as creeping roots so if a little piece manages to get away when trying to extract them, others bloom in its place. I thought this would help with the transfer of life."

My mouth dropped. "Brilliant."

"Me or the flower cocktail?" Tristan laughed.

"Both."

"If this works, then you can tell me I'm brilliant."

"And then I kidnap you."

"No." He kissed my cheek. "You've got it all wrong. I'm the one who will be kidnapping you, and when we're far away, I'll take you into my bed and never let you escape."

Before I could think of a reply, Tristan dug in his pocket for his cell phone and hit a button. Together, we managed to keep the flower intact long enough for him to tuck the phone into the crook of his shoulder and neck.

Because I was so close to him, I could hear Christophe's urgent voice on the other end. "Is everything all right?"

"Yes." Tristan wouldn't meet my eyes, and I couldn't determine if it was because he was focusing or because he was remembering the night Christophe had taken me home. "I am ready to start the experiment."

There was a pause. "So you want to know the results?"

"Yes, and I wanted to warn you in case you were training."

"I'm not at the moment."

But even through the phone, my heightened hearing could pick up the beating of wings. Were the Dryma flying with their tailored swords while they watched my kind clumsily fight with heavy weapons better suited to a museum? The thought made me sick, but Tristan distracted me as he placed the phone on the ground with the speakers on.

"Ready?"

I wanted this to work, wanted to taste the airy sweetness of freedom. More than freedom, I found myself wanting the experiment to work because Tristan longed for it.

"Yes."

I closed my eyes for a brief moment as our grips loosened. The shallow vase filled with water was beneath our cupped hands, tiny bugs and twigs caught within the small ripples. Slowly, we pried our fingers from the flower and the connecting weed-threaded wire until there was only the slightest of contact.

Exchanging a look, I expected there to be cameras on us, documenting this irreplaceable moment. Of course most of the Dryma and Kuro didn't even know we were here, and those who did were being tight-lipped.

Since learning Tristan was also half Kuro, I'd been getting better at dissecting his emotions. He was nervous of failing, and I could hardly blame him considering what was at stake.

My palms itched nervously and my knees knocked together as we let the last of our contact with the flower slip away.

At the very least, the orb-flower continued to hover above the water rather than sinking to the ground. Tristan took a vial out of his pocket, the one part of the experiment that was based in old Dryma magic.

Sprinkling the area in a fine mist, Tristan stalked the tree as if in a trance.

The petals were alight with what looked like blue fire, the core of the orb as bright as neon lights. All at once, the weeded cord grew alight, shooting from the flower end all the way around the base of the tree where we'd wound it.

Satisfied, Tristan located his phone and approached the tree before taking a switchblade from his pocket. The silvery blade reflected the light of the flowers, a brilliant shade of blue.

"Ready?" Tristan's voice was excited as he spoke into the phone. "Stay where you are, Kanji."

The knife was meant to cause harm, not to kill Christophe. There was no reason for me to be worried about the captain, but the anxiety slithered up my legs and nestled into the base of my spine.

Tristan shot me another glance, seemingly worried about my safety before he plunged the knife into the thick calloused bark of the tree. The cut was deeper than a bird would've succeeded in doing, but not by much.

The lack of response from Christophe made Tristan gutsy, and before I could weave through the entanglement of roots, he had struck into the tree again. The sound of the blade sliding into the tree eerily sounding like a knife sliding into flesh.

That was when Christophe hissed, a stream of obscenities cascading from his mouth. Tristan stood completely still, his broad shoulders straight so his back was pulled taut. I took the phone from him, not daring to take the knife from the tree.

"Are you okay?" I asked Christophe.

There was another hiss, and then, "Fine. I just have a bloody wound in my arm I have to take care of now."

His arm... it could've been worse. "I'm sorry. Tristan was trying to be gentle."

"Where is he? Why are you the one talking?"

I took a breath, prepared to answer, but Tristan silently held his hand out for the phone. I gave it to him and then proceeded to take the knife out.

"Sorry, Christophe. I thought it had worked. Something went wrong with the wavelengths."

I couldn't hear what the captain said because I was too focused on the blade. Clinging to the silvery metal were bright red droplets the color of fire ants. Trees didn't bleed, but Dryma did.

Constantly, the trees were being subjected to harsh weather, people pissing on them, and animals. But this was different. Tristan had attacked with the intention of causing harm, and the stripping of the bark reflected it.

After he hung up and slid the phone into his pocket, Tristan refused to look up from his shoes. My heart slid into my throat, and I could taste coppery blood on the tip of my tongue.

"Tristan?" I asked hesitantly, taking a step toward my paralyzed mate.

"It was supposed to work." His voice was shell-shocked, his fingers twitching at his sides. "I don't understand. I needed this to work. For the Dryma and for you...."

"This was the first try." I circled around until I was in front of him. The flower was still hovering over the shallow basin but was no longer glowing. "Like I've said, I don't know a whole lot about flowers, but I would say you did great. It just needs tweaking."

Tristan's eye twitched. "But how much time do we have?"

There was a dull look in his eyes that told me he wasn't going to be able to listen to anything I said. Quietly, I fell to my knees in front of him and lifted his sweater so I could kiss the space just below his navel where there were blond curls.

He jolted in surprise. "What are you doing?"

Kuro swans, aided by magical pheromones, were supposed to be seductive, especially the males. I'd never really been one to make girls or guys drop their pants, but I tried my best to appear desirable as I looked up at my mate through my long eyelashes and longer hair.

Something he saw in my face must've pleased him because his breathing hitched and his eyes darkened as he wrapped a fist into my tangled hair.

"Will we be seen?" I asked softly, unbuttoning his pants and easing them down his tanned thighs. "I want to have time to please you."

Tristan's voice was commanding and dripping with need. "The guard is on the north side still and so are your Kuro swans."

I could've changed my mind about pleasuring him, and Tristan wouldn't have forced me to. He was the kind of Dryma who wanted me to be the center of our pleasure... always. Yet deep inside myself, I knew what he needed wasn't to talk; it was to see me on my knees, ready to do whatever necessary to please him.

We'd been outside for hours, so the scent of river clung to his skin as I licked my way downward. All the while, I kept my hand on his thick, swollen cock, determined to please him while still tasting his skin.

Then he made a guttural, impatient sound, and I knew I'd tortured him enough. Opening my mouth, I took him as far down my throat as I could manage, using my hand to stroke the rest of his shaft. Even though he hadn't been naked in the woods, his cock had the same earthen taste I couldn't get enough of.

"Kanji," he moaned, thrusting gently into my mouth. "Your mouth is amazing. So soft and wet...."

Aiming to please, I increased suction, pressing my tongue into his slit and pushing on the underside of the shaft. For several moments, there wasn't a war approaching. There weren't three different magical species waiting to rip each other's throats out. And there was nothing saying I couldn't be with my mate.

"Touch yourself," Tristan commanded, his hand tightening in my hair so he could assert dominance.

Instantly, I obeyed. Unlike his skin, mine was cold, and I shuddered at the sudden change of temperature as I wrapped the hand not clinging to Tristan's cock around my own.

"Now look at me."

Again, I obeyed. The moment my eyes collided with his, a jolt of electricity shot through my body. He hardened, completely filling my mouth with his length.

"Are you close?" Tristan asked softly, stroking my cheek.

I nodded, already feeling pleasure just from having him stare at me.

"Come first, so I can watch you."

It was a simple enough request, but the moment the words had left his lips, I was a trembling, shaking mess. His eyes on me, his cock in my mouth, and my hand stroking myself were too much, and I couldn't contain my orgasm. Ripples of pleasure washed through me, most of the sensations brought on just by knowing Tristan was staring at me like I was one of his precious flowers.

Seconds later, he jerked in my mouth, and I could taste his hot seed trickling down my throat. Determined to not let a drop go to waste, I held on so he had no choice but to ride his orgasm to completion.

"Kanji, dammit, so amazing."

In my presence, he'd never sworn before, but I found I liked the deviant side of him. After I let him slip from my mouth, he remained still while I pulled up his pants and fumbled with the buttons. Before I could stand, he had collapsed in front of me, his hands woven around my body like an intricate tapestry.

"Never, I'll never let you go," he vowed as I buried my face into the crook of his neck. "I love you too much to lose you."

I managed to turn my head to the side and instantly wished I hadn't. Lying on the ground like a discarded condom was the floating flower.

CHAPTER THIRTEEN

TO A human who didn't know us, our appearances might've made us look like a violent gang with our dark long hair and dark clothes. In reality, we were all just exhausted, and the latest news Zain had brought me only pushed my anxiety through the roof.

Zain had been dying his hair different vibrant colors for as long as I could remember; yet now his hair was the same dark shade as mine. He didn't so much as have a streak of color. Joel's coat was an extralarge, and I wondered if he hadn't done that on purpose so he could stash his romance novels in the pockets. Out of the four of us, Tomas still looked the same with bleached hair and multiple piercings.

Normally, younger Kuro wouldn't be present at our private meetings, but Micky and Chiaki were already so involved it really didn't matter.

My aunt was inside cooking a large Crock-Pot of food, and from the kitchen window, I could see Mari staring at us.

"Time out," I said, trying to make sense of Joel's words. "Seth said what?"

True to my word, I hadn't said anything about Seth and Joel's relationship, but Seth coming to his house in the middle of the night to talk wasn't something we could hide.

Joel was in bad shape. I was starting to lose track of time, especially now I didn't have ranger shifts, but I figured it had been almost a week or maybe two since Seth had broken off their relationship. Instead of getting better, Joel looked worse.

"Seth told me to be careful and to prepare for the worst." He wrung his hands together, the skin of his knuckles calloused. "He said there's been further development with the Sidhee's plan. Their goal isn't to kill the Dryma, but rather take prisoners. We used to serve them, so Christophe is going to offer us back up as slaves."

My mind was reeling. "But why? Besides, the Sidhee didn't even want us anymore, so why would they now?"

Tomas was gnawing at his bottom lip ring. "Yeah, that doesn't make sense. Those bastards want us back? Why?"

Joel shook his head, concern flooding his eyes as he looked at Chiaki and Micky, who had remained mostly silent throughout the meeting. "I think they've run into problems when they want to come to this world. The Sidhee only have to steal souls if they leave their world and want to get back in. Seth said they've wanted to come here more and more often."

"So they intend to ride us like horses," Zain said flatly.

"Seth wasn't clear. He only told me because…."

"Because of what?" Tomas pressed.

But I knew why. Seth was bound by duty to serve the Dryma, and he was one of the princes, so he had double duty to also protect his family. He'd taken a great risk to tell Joel anything at all, which had to mean on some level he still cared.

"Because he's kind," I interjected. Joel shot me a grateful look. "Tomas, stay here with Micky and Chiaki. Joel and Zain, come with me."

"Where are you going?" Micky asked, breaking his silence. I wished he hadn't because when he spoke, I had no choice but to look at him. If he went to public school, social services would've been called because the darkened skin surrounding his eyes made him look like a zombie.

"The Crystal Cove."

"I want to go with you," Tomas protested, pulling his wool cap low so his eyes were mostly covered.

"I need you here."

Something in my tone of voice must've sounded final, because he backed off. I searched Joel and Zain's faces for arguments but couldn't find any. Quickly, we made a break for Zain's jeep so Mari couldn't see us.

When would this stop? This running? The betrayal we all were a part of and couldn't admit, even to ourselves?

Zain and Tomas had been at my house all day, detailing the training they'd experienced at Christophe's hands. When Joel had come over unexpectedly, Chiaki and Micky at his heels, he'd been out of breath and frantic. Seth had confided in him the night before, but he'd been so tired and had accidentally fallen asleep. All I had to do was look at Joel's rugged form to know he was suffering without the added guilt of being a delayed news bringer.

Due to our hasty getaway from my house, we were dressed in casual clothes. Zain wasn't even wearing his coat, which he'd left on my couch. Beneath his thin cotton long-sleeved shirt, I could see goose bumps.

"What I can't understand," Zain started as he swatted at the steering wheel like he would a fly, "is why Seth would tell you anything? One, why would he bother? Two, what did he expect you to do with that information?"

Joel's hand thumped against his thigh nervously. "I don't know."

The words were as true as they could be. Truthfully, I was as confused as Joel because I couldn't figure out why Seth would betray his captain and friend when the news was only bound to hurt Joel more. Had he secretly hoped Joel would forget about his wings and flee?

If that was the case, then Seth didn't know the first thing about Joel and his unwavering loyalty to not only me, but the children he'd saved.

The Crystal Cove was so staggeringly normal I almost burst into laughter. The Kuro world as we knew it was rapidly falling into chaos, so to see one aspect of our lives completely the same was both shocking and frustrating. Out of everything in our lives, why was the club the one place that remained unchanged?

Zain started to park in the usual spot far away from the club so human customers could have the spots closer to the club's entrance.

"Park up front," I told him before he could navigate his jeep into the dirt parking space near the grass.

"What?" He seemed confused but did as I asked.

"If they are going to damn us," I said softly as I unbuckled myself and slid from the heat of the car into the cold October air, "then we might as well break all the rules too."

"They still have our wings," Joel said, the voice of reason reminding us why we were here at all. "We have to play by their rules."

He was right of course. Except for the fact that Christophe had promised he would free them in exchange for my life. I would give him enough time to explain himself, because for all I knew, Seth had been lying to Joel in the hopes he wouldn't fight.

"Hello, can I help—What are you doing here?" Marvin was once again permitting entry to the gleaming floors of the Crystal Cove. I'd lost track of time, but judging by the throngs of humans, it was a weekend. In three seconds, his face had gone from friendly to red with anger. "I wasn't aware Christophe had a meeting with you."

"He doesn't," I said tersely, finally conceding to run my fingers through my hair in an attempt to look more presentable. "Please let him know we have arrived."

"I will do nothing of the sort." Marvin looked past me to a group that had just entered, bringing the chill with them. "If he didn't call you here, then you can wait outside, and he'll get to you when he's free."

If this had been before the Sidhee attacks, I would've nodded and backed off. I would've forced Zain and Joel to stand outside with me until our toes turned blue and we couldn't feel our feet in our shoes. I would've bowed to Christophe formally and expected no apology. Something in me snapped, and I just couldn't do it.

"Where are you going? Hey, wait!"

Normally Marvin would've had the advantage against our wiry, slender frames, but his bulky build hindered him as he tried to reach us. He got caught up in the clusters of humans, and realizing he would have to harm them in an attempt to get us, settled for picking up a phone.

It didn't matter either way; Christophe was going to realize we were here.

"Should we have done that?" Joel whispered urgently as he followed me up the stairs, Zain in the lead so he could get rid of any further obstacles.

"Joel, I'm sorry." I stopped outside the large conference room where we usually met Christophe. "I shouldn't have asked you to come with me. If you want to leave, I won't hold that against you."

Joel stiffened, his dark blue eyes flashing defiantly as he stared at me. "I will never leave your side, Kanji."

A surge of pride flooded into me. I moved forward with the intention of opening the door, but Ivan beat me to it. He stood rigid at the entrance with his short hair perfectly slicked back.

"Let them pass, Ivan."

Ivan was reluctant to follow Christophe's command, but eventually gave in and stepped to the side. Seth was standing like a jaded soldier, with his arms pressed firmly to his sides and his eyes downcast.

"To what do I owe this pleasure?" Christophe was wearing an immaculate black suit and a loose tie that made him look like he belonged on the cover of *GQ* magazine. He surveyed us just long enough to know who we were before turning away to pour himself a drink. The blinds were drawn, and the chairs were neatly stacked along the wall. The only glass in the room was the one in his hand.

"Is it true?" I asked, directing my question at Seth rather than Christophe. "Is it true you plan to sacrifice us if necessary?"

I expected Christophe to refute my accusation or to at least feign ignorance, but he didn't even turn around.

"Christophe… is it true?" I tried again.

At my side, Joel was shaking so hard it was a wonder he hadn't collapsed. I risked a glance at Seth and saw his honey-colored eyes water with pain.

"Where would you have heard such a rumor?"

I stared at Seth pointedly but before I could speak, he did. "I told Joel with the intention of—"

"I know what your intention was." Christophe's voice was dangerously low as he calmly set the glass down and turned to Seth, still ignoring me. "How could you? How could you betray your own kind for a filthy Kuro?"

Seth bit down on his lower lip, looking to Ivan for help. Unfortunately, his so-called friend was preoccupied with a paint chip on the wall. "I had to."

Zain grew restless, clearly confused over what was happening. With a sick realization, he stared at Joel like he'd sprouted another head. Before he could demand an explanation, Christophe backhanded Seth, the sound reverberating around the empty room.

"If you weren't a Dryma Prince…."

Seth straightened, and I had to admit I admired his strength after being humiliated. "But as it stands, I am. And I decided they had the right to know."

"Right to know what?" Zain practically screamed. "Just spit it out."

Christophe narrowed his eyes before speaking in words far too tame for the present situation. "Should our fighting prove to be futile,

I plan on handing over your wings to the Sidhee. It is true you were betrayed and the Dryma now have power over you, but Prince Calhoun can see the benefit of having Kuro at his command."

"So you would sacrifice us to save yourselves?" I whispered bitterly, wondering why I hadn't seen it before. The proof of what Christophe was had always been in front of me, but I had clung to any shred of humanity I could find in him for my kind's sake.

And then he shrugged as if we were little more than the dirt Tristan used to nurture his plants. My mind disconnected from my body, and I must've lunged at him because Zain and Joel each took hold of an arm and held me back.

I struggled, flinging words and accusations at Christophe I wasn't sure were even in the English language. At some point, I regained control. "I'm fine now, guys. Let me go."

Zain and Joel did as I asked, but hovered close by, clearly waiting to see if I was going to fly off the handle again.

Christophe nodded to Seth and Ivan. "Wait outside. I want to speak to Kanji alone."

"The hell you will." Zain tried to step in front of me, but I held out my arm and shook my head.

"I'll call you if I need you. Just go."

Zain's plain dark hair was covering his face, but I could feel the reluctance to leave my side. I pressed my hand to his bicep and repeated, "Go."

Once the door closed behind their retreating figures, I whispered, "Why? You promised me you would free my kind. Am I not worth enough now?"

The captain's eyebrows disappeared into his hair. "Not once did I say you weren't enough for the freedom of your kind."

"Then why?"

"I'm not going to give *you* up, Kanji," Christophe said, as if his betrayal meant any less now. "And giving the Sidhee your wings is my last resort. I do not plan on failing, so your worries are pointless."

"Where are our wings? How are you confining them?"

He looked startled by my direct question, but quickly recovered. "When the Kuro were initially betrayed by the Sidhee, your wings were simply a part of the power asserted over you. It was then transferred into a tangible object. A stone."

"A stone?" I asked blankly. "Our once lustrous, sought after wings are contained in a stone? Where?"

The glass clinked against the tray as he set it down and approached me. I hated Christophe and hated myself for thinking he was beautiful. "Do you remember when we first met?"

"We are talking about the stone, not how we met."

"Do you remember?" he insisted, a hint of urgency creeping into his voice.

Either he was mentally ill or knew exactly how to curve the conversation in his favor. "We were very young. My mother and father took me to meet you and told me to not upset you. They committed suicide later that week."

There was almost a hint of pity in his eyes. "And then when did we unofficially meet?"

"I can't remember. Why?"

Ever so gently, Christophe brushed my hair from my face and whispered into my ear. "Those flowers Tristan is cultivating are a waste of time and so are his efforts to capture you. I suggest you forget about him the same way I am ignoring his pitiful attempt at freeing our kind from the Earth."

Anger overwhelmed me. "Do you have any idea how brilliant he is? How amazing of a plan he has concocted?"

With Christophe so close to me, I could hardly breathe. "No, and I don't care. If the Sidhee defeat us, then your kind is finished. Besides, even if Tristan was able to connect our lives to flowers, how would that help us fight the Sidhee?"

"You could run with the flowers and who knows, the Sidhee might just give up when they realize they can't threaten the trees. When they realize you are free."

Christophe contemplated my words. "The whole reason Tristan was supposed to be given to the Sidhee was because we were going to go live in their world and cut off our ties with the human world and the trees. If I had any faith in the flowers working, then we wouldn't have even bothered with this plan. The Sidhee will come for us long before we have time to worry about a bunch of stupid flowers."

I was floored. "Why would you want to live in the Sidhee world rather than work with what you have here?"

"There is no point in continuing to live in the human world. As our presence blends further into the humans', there are little traces of the life we used to have."

"But the Sidhee can come here at will but can't return without a soul that willingly agrees to go with them. How would you be able to come here when the darkness of the Sidhee world was too much?"

This was the first I'd heard of this plan, and I realized the impracticalness of living in the Sidhee world. How my ancestors had managed was beyond me, but at the same time, they'd been able to come and go as they pleased.

"Kuro swans could be the way to pass through this world and theirs. Which is why I know they will take your kind rather than kill the Dryma."

"If you think we will fail, then give me our wings so we can flee."

"You can't be serious."

"Then let me fight with my friends."

Instantly, his hands were around my neck, preventing any sound from my throat. "There is no need for you to fight. I will keep you safe."

"Why?" I gasped, clawing at his hands. "I… can't… breathe…."

Releasing me, Christophe backed away to the wall and threw open a window. Before I could call out to him, he was gone in a flurry of diamond dragon wings and fiery red hair, and I was left with a swollen throat.

Why had he bothered to ask me if I remembered when we met if he wasn't going to tell me in the end? Had Christophe finally lost his mind, or was he reminiscing about our past because he knew he'd have to give up the power of our wings?

"Where is Christophe?" Ivan demanded, pushing past me once I opened the door. He took one look at the open window and said, "I suggest you leave immediately."

"You don't have to tell us twice," Zain muttered.

Seth had his body pressed to the wall like a chameleon to a tree, easily overlooked. The hope Joel felt was cresting off his body in waves, but Seth didn't so much as blink.

As we made our way downstairs and out of the club, I caught Marvin glaring at us, along with other Dryma dressed in clothes more expensive than anything I'd ever even tried on. Watches gleamed from their wrists as they silently counted down the time until we were gone from sight.

"Joel," Zain started as he unlocked his jeep.

"I know, I know." Joel's voice was heartbroken. "What was I thinking, right?" The weight of Seth's indifference was so great, Joel broke down in the parking lot, squatting beside the jeep and wrapping his arms around his body. "I'm sorry, so sorry."

Zain crouched beside Joel, his face one of despair. Joel's love for Seth was undeniable, and even though he apologized to me, he wasn't apologizing for feeling the way he did. His words let me have vain hope Tristan and I could one day be accepted. "Sorry, Joel, I should've known he was your lover."

CHIAKI, MICKY, and Tomas were clustered around the table playing a card game with Mari, but none of them seemed invested. The moment we walked in, they were on their feet, alarm in their eyes.

"Well?" Tomas demanded. "What's happening?"

"The bitchy fairy flew away," Zain said before I could say anything. "But his plan is to sacrifice us if things go bad."

Chiaki slumped back into his chair, pulling out his phone presumably so he could contact Aiden and hear his mate's voice. I longed for the same and wondered what was stopping me. The way I saw things, I'd already broken all the rules.

"I'll be right back," I told them as I slipped from the kitchen and up the stairs to my room. The door wasn't even closed fully before I had Tristan on the phone, listening to the monotone rings as I waited.

"Hello?"

I instantly moaned, relief flooding my body.

"Kanji, are you okay? What's wrong?"

"Hearing your voice sounds so good."

Tristan made a noise in the back of his throat, and I could feel his comforting smile spread out over his lips. "What's wrong, honey?"

Honey? He'd never called me anything other than Kanji and "Mason," so to hear him use a pet name exposed his worry. "Please, help me." I cradled the phone in my hands as if I would be able to crawl through the metal and into his arms.

"Help you?"

"Christophe promised to give us our freedom after the fight, just as you did. But he lied. He plans on letting us all become massacred."

Tristan inhaled sharply. "And what did he say would happen to you?"

I opened my mouth to tell him I would become his slave, but stopped myself. The last thing I needed was Tristan seeking out Christophe and starting a fight when they needed to be on familiar terms for the sake of my mate's safety. "He didn't tell me anything."

"I will help you," Tristan promised. "Isn't that what I've been saying?"

I hated having to doubt him. "With the flowers, I know. But Christophe doesn't believe in their power, and my kind has no idea what's being done with them either. They need something to believe in. Please, I'll do anything."

This was the conversation I should've had with Christophe before letting him fly away. I should've collapsed on my knees, gripped his leg, and begged for dear life. But even in the swarming chaos circling me, my pride held me back.

"The flowers will work, and then at least you'll be free, and the Dryma can run from the Sidhee."

I loved Tristan, more than I'd ever loved anyone or anything. There was no denying he was irresistible and intelligent, but was he simply clinging to this hope because it was all he had?

Guilt ate away at my insides. "And if they don't?"

There was a pause and then words heavy as stones. "Trust me. I love you."

"I love you too."

"I'm going to come over to your house later tonight. Wait for me."

Even after he'd hung up, I held the phone as if it were his hand. My hair had all but fallen out of my ponytail, so I thought the shadow in the corner of my eye was just my dark locks. But when the shadow moved, I realized Mari was standing in the doorway.

Her face was expressionless as she stared at me, her hair falling in waves around her shoulders. "Your aunt saved you some food. Come and eat."

My heart clenched like a fist and I waited for her to ask me about the phone call, but she simply turned away.

How much had she heard? I'd rather she screamed or interrogated me, anything other than acting completely calm as she descended the stairs as though it was the most natural thing to do.

Chapter Fourteen

In the hopes of creating an illusion of normalcy, I ate two full plates of food and continued with the card game. Tomas was practically peeling his lips from his face, and Zain's leg looked like it was attached to a vibrator. Chiaki seemed to understand what I was doing and jumped into the game with more force than necessary.

Eventually, they went home to sleep before the next day's patrol, and Mari offered to take my aunt home with her.

"Why?" I asked although I wasn't one to argue. My aunt Catarina looked perfectly content to go home with Mari.

"My mom called and asked her to. You weren't here for that. My mom really needs the company," she told me, shrugging into her heavy winter coat. Her words cut me deep, and I realized how right she was. I was constantly concerned for my kind, but between the Kuro and Tristan, I'd spared no time for my aunt.

I pulled her into a tight hug, my aunt sighing in surprise. "What's with you, Kanji? I swear, I haven't hugged you since you were twelve."

"Has it been so long?" I joked, releasing her as Mari pretended to focus on a tree outside. "Guess I didn't realize."

"Get some sleep." She rested her hand on my cheek, and for the faintest moment, I wondered what she was seeing in me that made her remain so loyal and concerned when I'd been unable to save her mate. "Mari, feel free to stay here as well."

"Maybe I'll come back later." Mari stared at me like the only thing she wanted was to tear my clothes from my body. "We still have to talk about something."

I'd gone so far as to admit to being gay, but she was too far-gone in the idea of becoming my mate to listen. Maybe that was why I finally broke. "We have nothing to discuss."

My bedroom flooded with light from a car outside, and I checked my phone to see if Tristan had called me, but I didn't have any missed calls.

There was the sound of footsteps on my tiny concrete porch, but then I heard Mari's voice floating up through the floorboards and realized with a desperate sigh it wasn't Tristan at all.

"Mari, I thought I told you we had nothing to discuss," I called as I pulled a hoodie over my bare chest and went down the stairs to locate her. "Besides, it's like four in the morning. Couldn't you have—" My words died in my throat as I saw Mari standing in the middle of my living room, a scarf loosely looped around her slender neck. Since my uncle's passing, her presence had been a constant in my house, so it wasn't seeing her that shocked me. It was the Dryma.

"Christophe?" I asked in disbelief, switching on the dining room light to make sure the darkness wasn't deceiving me. "What are you doing here?"

The real question I should've asked was why they were together. Christophe's eyes narrowed, and he was wearing the same outfit I'd seen him in at the Crystal Cove. "Were you expecting someone else?"

I shook my head, praying Tristan wouldn't suddenly show up. "I forgot. I was going to go check on the protection duty."

"He's not coming," Mari said flatly.

"What?" I lowered my phone. "Who isn't?"

"Your lover, the youngest Prince of the Dryma."

If I hadn't just seen her mouth move and heard the words in her voice, I would've been in complete denial.

"He's not my lover." I focused on not stuttering. Please, Tristan, don't show up now. "I've only been guarding him."

"Chiaki tells it differently. He said you needed to make a soap to mask your scent and then Micky told me about seeing you kiss in the woods." Mari had no expression in her face apart from seething rage.

Looking at them side by side, I mentally kicked myself for not realizing how similar Mari and Christophe were. From the beginning, they had both made their intent of having me known, and at every turn, they had refused to believe any other possibility.

My voice trembled, and I had to stuff my hands into my sweater pockets to keep them from becoming numb. "And your first thought was to tell Christophe, the Captain of the Dryma Guard?"

She flinched as if I'd slapped her. "So it's true."

"And if it is?" I whispered, the weight of my secrets slowly lifting as I spoke the truth.

Mari opened her mouth but never got a chance to speak.

"Absolutely unacceptable. I could punish you for this. I should tie you to a pole and flog you until your legs give out. I should—" Christophe ranted.

"Then do it," I interrupted quietly.

I'd been dreading this moment for so long, I realized I'd been prepared for a long time. The only thing I could feel was Tristan's lips on my skin, his strong tan hands entwined with mine and his emerald eyes burning into my mind. "Mating isn't something you can control. Do you really think I would've chosen him otherwise?"

But the answer was yes, I would've, because Tristan was the kind of mate I had lain awake at night thinking about. The mate I thought I'd never have.

"Impossible," Mari stuttered, her hands clenched into fists at her side. "I absolutely won't accept that he's your mate. He's a fairy for crying out loud and a guy!"

"How did you get Chiaki and Micky to tell you anything?" I ignored her outburst, desperate to know why two of my most loyal followers had betrayed me. Now that I knew Micky had seen Tristan and I kiss, it made sense why he'd been acting so quiet and nervous earlier.

Mari smirked. "I just used Aiden as leverage. Who would miss one Kuro after all?"

Up until this point, I'd been seeing the tired expressions of my kind, the deterioration of their health as they struggled to maintain their lives. Joel and the others may have looked half dead, but they were the ones who were fighting. Mari was a lot weaker than I gave her credit for, and now I saw exactly what our imprisonment had done.

"I'm sorry. I never meant for this to happen. If I had taken you as my mate, maybe you wouldn't be so full of hate."

My apology was not what she needed to hear. Before she could attack at me, Christophe barred her movement with one arm and reminded me of his presence.

"Why did you tell Christophe?" I repeated.

"To make you come to your senses," Mari screamed, spittle flying from her mouth. "I thought if I revealed your relationship to him, he would prevent you from making a mistake by becoming a slave to that prince."

Laughter erupted from inside of me; I just couldn't stop. "You do realize Prince Tristan isn't the one looking to enslave me, right?"

Mari's eyes grew so large, I thought they might burst from her tiny skull.

"Thank you for offering proof of what I had suspected all this time." Christophe cleared his throat and effortlessly swept Mari to the side as though she was a pile of dirt. "I will ensure your prince is not allowed to see Tristan again."

"What are you talking about?"

He was standing in front of the living room door, but if I was quick, I could make it to the back door. And then what? Driving away in my car was only going to hinder him for mere moments.

"No more waiting." Christophe reached into his pocket and withdrew a small plastic bottle full of liquid that bubbled like Coca-Cola. "You're mine now."

"What? Don't touch him," Mari roared as she flung her entire body at the captain. In her defense, I could still see the lingering traces of the old, caring Mari in her eyes. "I swear I didn't know he was after you."

What kind of male, much less a prince, runs when a female is in trouble? I leapt forward, prying Christophe's hands from around her neck before he could snap the delicate bones. Then his arm wrapped around my neck and he forced the liquid down my throat with his other hand. It burned and tasted of copper mixed with rotten vegetation.

I could hear Mari screaming, but her words made me feel like I was underwater. Clawing at Christophe's arms, I attempted to spit out the liquid but knew he wasn't going to let me go like the other times.

The ground slipped out from beneath me, the chill air slapping at my exposed skin like a succession of tiny needles. In the last moments of my clarity, I saw Mari racing like a gazelle down the highway toward the other homes. I tried to piece together why she would be running and why her dark-headed figure kept getting smaller and smaller, but calculating the answer proved too complicated, and I gave up.

"Just relax," Christophe whispered, his voice rough like a demon's. "I won't let you fall."

His hands felt like napalm on my flesh, and even if it meant my death, all I wanted was for him to release me.

I WAS seized by an uncontrollable cough that felt like pine needles scraping at my throat. Forcing my eyes to open, I expected to see my fresh blood on the floor where I'd coughed, but there was only water.

My body was propped up in a bed with a quilt softer than anything I'd ever felt and the walls were the plainest white. I'd never been to a hospital because human remedies would've been useless, but I imagined this was exactly what one of the rooms would look like. Between the lack of furniture, the oversized bed, and windowless walls, no wonder humans feared hospitals.

Sitting up, I had to put my head between my knees to keep the room from spinning. Then the weight of what had happened pummeled back into me. Mari betraying me to Christophe, who took me to this abandoned room. Tristan had never come for me, so when he showed up at my house, would Christophe be there waiting for him?

"Are you fully conscious now?"

The door and only exit opened, admitting Christophe. He no longer had his shimmery dragon-scale wings on display, but he had taken off his shirt so he'd have easier access to flying if need be.

"Where are we?"

"Do you know why Castle De Mar was named that?"

It didn't escape my notice Christophe didn't move from in front of the door. The way my legs felt, he could've stood on the opposite end of the room and still reached me before I could make an escape.

"No." My mouth was dry from my retching, and I could taste saltwater like I'd been plunged into an ocean headfirst. "Why?"

"Mar means 'sea' in French. The castle is large on its own, but there is an underwater portion only known to a few individuals. The king and myself to be exact."

My jaw dropped. There was no way we were underwater. I pressed my hand to the white wall above my head and closed my eyes. The waves were faint, but they were there, the humming of the lake vibrating through the walls.

"We're under the lake?" I repeated incredulously.

Christophe crossed his arms over his chest, and I realized I'd never seen him shirtless before. The muscles in his chest and abdomen were impressive, but knowing his personality soured his appearance. "This is where I kept your wings."

I meant to charge him, but my pounding headache and jellylike legs held me back. Instead, I discarded the warm quilt and placed my feet on the floor. "And where are they now?"

"Gone." He brushed a red lock from his forehead. "For a very long time actually. I've had them in safe-keeping elsewhere until such a time when the Dryma would have use of them."

"Did you bring me here to gloat?" I narrowed my eyes and rubbed my arms vigorously in an attempt to get some warmth into them.

Christophe narrowed his eyes in concern. "Are you cold? I can get another blanket for you."

"Why are you being nice to me? Aren't you the one who kidnapped me?"

He abruptly stopped. "I brought you here to keep you away from the war."

"You mean to keep me here while my kind fights for you?"

Christophe looked at me like I was idiot for not realizing it sooner. "I will do whatever is necessary to keep you safe."

"Tristan is going to find me," I challenged.

But in my haste to get back at him, I hadn't even realized Christophe's mood. For a second, I thought he was going to slap me, but he let his arms fall loosely to his sides, a dumbstruck look on his face.

"The entrance to the underwater caverns is hidden and yet completely visible if you know what you're looking for. Tristan and your friends won't be able to find you, even if you use your telepathy."

To hell with my limbs feeling loose, I couldn't sit any longer and let him talk down to me. "And you think taking me from the prince, from my tribe was the best thing to do? When they realize what you've done, they won't fight for you."

Christophe shook his head and whispered, "Actually, my plan is perfect. The one enviable trait Kuro swans have is their loyalty to their prince. Right now, they are being told you will be returned after they fight."

"But that won't matter," I exploded. "You already betrayed us, and the Kuro know it."

"Even so, they will fight for your safe return, even if it means they will then be imprisoned elsewhere."

I fumbled for an answer but couldn't come up with one because he was right. If I knew anything about Zain and the others, it was that they would lay down their lives before letting me come to harm.

My only choice was to beg. "For some strange reason, you have this obsession with me. I'll give you anything you want, anything at all, just don't give the Kuro to the Sidhee."

Christophe blinked, obviously taken by surprise at my pleading. It was clear he had expected a more physical altercation. "What's done is done. My only priority is you."

"I don't understand. Do you hate Tristan that much? I thought he was your friend."

"Tristan was only a means to an end," he roared, the walls shaking. "Ever since that time, I have only wanted you. Tristan is the one who betrayed *me* by taking you when he knew how I felt."

My head swam in confusion. "I don't—"

"You saved my life. Don't you remember?"

Now I was the one with the dumbstruck expression. "I've never saved your life."

Christophe slammed his fist against the wall so hard I waited for the water to flood in from the hole his hand had made. When he removed his fist, bits of the plaster crumbled to the floor. "That day was the most important day in my life. The day you saved mine and Tristan's life, and you still can't remember? Did you hit your head that hard?"

I disentangled my legs from the sheets and stared at him, trying to determine whether or not he was messing with me. But he looked dead serious. Then it hit me.

"Tristan told me a human saved you from drowning when you were children. Are you confusing me with him?"

Christophe was under a lot of stress, which must've been why he was confusing me with a stranger from years ago. "No human saved us. It was you."

I was thrown into a fit of coughing, tasting the bitter liquid he'd fed me to make me sleep. "Stop joking around. Don't you think I'd remember something like that?"

"We weren't careful back then because we thought we were invincible. We hadn't even noticed the riptide in the water and would've drowned if you hadn't been there."

I held up my hand to stop him, but he ignored me.

"We were saying good-bye to Calhoun and the main portal from their world to ours is through the lake. But Tristan and I hadn't realized the aftermath of the portal closing." He took a breath. "When I realized you were a Kuro, I was angry and ashamed. Up to that point, we'd been taught your kind was worthless and dirty, but you were the most beautiful creature I'd ever met. I was so confused."

"I don't remember—"

"I was angry and told you to get lost. In your haste to get away from me, you stumbled down a hill and lost consciousness, and apparently, you never recovered your memories. I thought you just didn't want to talk about that day."

That fall had been the worst I'd ever been injured. My aunt Catarina had hardly left my side even though I couldn't move for nearly two weeks. The shock of his words was too much for me to handle. "If you've liked me all this time, why did you make my life hell? Why did you punish me?"

"You left me no choice," Christophe said simply. "Those scars on your back from my whip were from when you tried to escape."

I could still feel the sting when I moved my shoulders together, but the shame I'd felt that day was tenfold. "I was just a child."

"Which is why I had to make sure you never left again. Never left me."

"You're crazy." I edged toward the door, all the while knowing I wouldn't make it in time. His honey eyes were alight with a dead fire that twisted my insides. Like hell he was going to let me go, but all the same, I had to try to get back to Tristan. "If you were in love with me all this time, you should've said so."

Before I could react, he had both of my hands above my head, my back pressed against the wall. Leaning in so I could see every freckle on his cheeks, he whispered, "If I had told you, would you have stayed?"

I swallowed my pride. "Maybe."

"Liar. You would've run like you are trying to right now."

"Christophe." I stopped twisting in his grip and stared into his eyes. "Let me go. You're hurting me."

He only moved closer, his lips inches from mine. I turned my head to the side, but he was still the one in control. "I won't give you to Tristan."

"It's not his fault. Mating isn't something you can control," I told him, trying to stay calm, although his fingers felt like spades locking me into place. "He didn't set out to hurt you. Just like I didn't want to hurt Mari."

At her name, Christophe flinched and his jaw locked. "I won't release you."

In the split-second his hands weren't on my wrists, I ducked down and bolted for the door. His hand wrapped around my arm and yanked me back. Luckily I collided with the bed, and the only bruises were butterfly-like shadows on my calves where I tripped into the bedframe.

My fear ticked away inside me like a clock constantly rewinding itself. Just before disappearing into the hallway where the only sound was that of rushing water, Christophe called back to me, every bit the composed captain I'd known over the years. "I have a war to fight, but I will be back to claim you when I'm done. Don't forget your promise."

"My promise? What about yours?"

But he had already abandoned me.

CHAPTER FIFTEEN

I USED to think being trapped in a human form and unable to fly was the worst kind of torture. After being locked away in the whitewashed room with the sound of the waves crashing at me from all sides, I realized how wrong I'd been.

Worst of all was hearing my kind's thoughts and knowing they couldn't hear mine. Whatever was keeping the rooms beneath Castle De Mar so secure was hindering my thought waves.

But I could feel one thought coming from them: determination. They wanted me returned and were willing to fight, but all I wanted was for them to leave me behind. The cold room reeking of feigned innocence was where my betrayal had gotten me.

Abandonment was what I deserved.

My knuckles were bloodied from where I'd beaten on the door in an attempt to force it open. If they ever wanted to put someone else in the room, Christophe would have to replace the door because my dried blood was never going to come off.

After about an hour of screaming, I stopped. Either no one could hear me or no one cared to.

At some point, I fell into a deep sleep where I could smell Tristan's scent lingering on the pillow. But when I woke up, his scent was gone, and in its place was a rancid odor like rotten vegetation.

Time stood still in my prison, but I was sure at least two days had passed. Tucked into the corner inside a wicker basket was bread, peanut butter, and bottled water so at least Christophe hadn't wanted me to starve to death. Somehow, the thought wasn't very comforting.

"Figures," I said, draining the last of my third water bottle. Just because he said he'd come back didn't mean he actually would. "I hate peanut butter."

Realizing how crazy I was starting to sound, I splashed some of my precious water onto my face and vigorously rubbed until my skin felt raw. I hadn't tried to contact Zain or the others since my first day of imprisonment, but I didn't need to hear their thoughts to know the war had begun.

My hands trembled violently, and I felt so sick it was a wonder I could keep from vomiting. And I was experiencing a whole new level of heat deprivation that made me wonder if I were dead.

I needed to find Tristan, and we needed to find Zain, and then... then what?

My thoughts jumbled together until I couldn't remember what my plan was. I could feel the beating of the Kuro's hearts as they fought with their meager weapons against the Sidhee. From what I could tell, Prince Calhoun wasn't there, but I was only able to see through the eyes of the Kuro, so for all I knew, he was locked in a battle with a Dryma. Or... had he succeeded in taking Tristan?

The amount of rage I felt at having my mate taken baffled me.

The Sidhee were attacking the trees rather than the Kuro, treating my kind as little more than annoying insects. With the Dryma circling the trees and adding double protection, the fight seemed to consist of beating wings and swords clashing. What was the aim of the Sidhee? Did they really just want to take Tristan and leave?

More likely, the Sidhee wanted to assert their dominance over the Kuro and Dryma, which explained why their fighting seemed half-hearted. They would kill a few of the Kuro, a few of the Dryma, take Tristan, and have power over us forever.

Through Chiaki's eyes, I saw that he rushed from Kuro to Kuro, offering assistance in the form of herbs and potions to promote strength and healing. Then Zain's battle cry roared through my ears as he saw Christophe and the monstrous Prince Calhoun locked into conversation across the battlefield.

As my friend charged them, they were gone before he even got within earshot.

Chiaki, Lyon, and Aiden were amongst the youngest fighting, and I knew Micky was there, but I couldn't seem to locate him amidst the chaos. The Sidhee were better prepared for fighting, wearing steel armor and carrying swords that didn't look like they had been cheaply made.

Chiaki and Aiden's heartbeats were joined together as they were pushed toward the mouth of a lake by foreboding Sidhee who had covered their faces. I assumed they had done so to appear more menacing and even though I could not see them for myself, a shiver raked through my body at the thought of having to face them.

Aiden's eyes were wide as he glanced at his mate before his foot slipped into the murky water and the lake swirled around his ankle as if daring to drown him. I clenched my fists tightly and tried to breathe through the pain I felt at being rendered so utterly helpless.

The Sidhee moved closer, raising their swords with a deafening clash that would've been enough to startle the fiercest of wildlife.

In an instant, time seemed to stand still as Chiaki and Aiden exchanged a look I would be able to recognize anywhere. How many times had Tristan looked at me the very same? The look of pure trust and resilience?

Aiden and Chiaki backed into the lake together, the Sidhee charging them at full speed. But I realized what the young Kuro mates were doing. When the Sidhee had collided with the dark water, they lost their footing. The heavy weapons they wielded were no longer an accessory, but an accomplice in their downfall.

Turning at the same time, Aiden and Chiaki spun away from each other, and I could feel the pain within their bodies at having to do so.

But the movement was necessary because they managed to get behind the Sidhee and now had the advantage. I marveled at their quick thinking and watched as their basic Kuro instincts took over.

Acting as a swan would, they defended each other by using the water to their fighting advantage. Attacking the Sidhee from behind, they pushed down on the heavily armored backs of the steely eyed demons, and when they tumbled to the lake bed, Chiaki and Aiden used their own dime-store swords to keep them down.

I had watched swans defend their mates by attempting to drown other swans who endangered their well-being. But to see the bravery scrawled across Aiden and Chiaki's faces as they enacted the most basic of survival instincts, warmth flooded through my body.

There was so much movement within the woods, and I was torn from their minds and reeled through the minds of the other Kuro.

Even though some of the Kuro were also acting on the most primal of instinct, with a heavy heart, I realized there was little to be done about the endless waves of Sidhee coming from the water.

The very same water that had saved Chiaki and Aiden from destruction was also the main portal from the Sidhee world to the human world. The lake water was neutral, shifting to aid whoever claimed its powers.

But I knew there was no stopping the waves of militarized Sidhee, and when I tried to locate Chiaki and Aiden again, I couldn't. Faintly, I could hear Aiden's muffled thoughts as though he were underwater, but I prayed viciously that he hadn't been forced beneath the waves by the Sidhee pouring into our world.

I managed to locate Christophe and saw he was standing in the one still part of the forest where there didn't appear to be a battle. When I saw he was talking to Prince Calhoun, my pulse raced, and I didn't need to hear their exchange to know he was talking about Tristan.

If I wanted to save my mate, I could no longer be a weak spectator. I needed to break free of the walls surrounding me and find my mate and aid my kind in whatever way I could.

Zain, come find me. Tristan's flowers can save everyone. They can preserve the souls of the trees.

I repeated the lines over and over until I could see my thoughts scrawled on the walls. If Calhoun really only wanted Tristan and Christophe only wanted me, then everything that had transpired was my fault. There was no way I could imagine beautiful, intelligent Tristan being the slave to the hideous Calhoun.

This entire war had been started with the intention of creating a union between the Dryma and Sidhee, but finally I understood what Tristan had been trying to do. He had wanted to create a new alliance by alleviating the need for the Kuro to be servants. If his flowers worked, then there was no reason why Kuro and Dryma couldn't be friends and push the Sidhee back into the darkness.

That was what my mate and lover wanted, but it was too late to have faith in flimsy flowers, no matter how fragrant and eye-catching they were.

There were voices outside the door, and then the sound of a key in a lock. I couldn't deny I looked terrible, but what did Christophe expect after leaving me caged like an animal?

"What are you doing back here?" I growled, using the bedpost as support so I could keep from falling. "Is the war over?"

"No."

Seeing Tristan dissolved the last of the strength from my legs, and I would've crumpled like a quilt if I hadn't been gripping the bed for dear life.

"Kanji, I'm sorry I couldn't find you sooner." Tristan crossed the room and pulled me into his arms. He carried the scent of fire and blood in his arms, but I couldn't have cared less. "Christophe told me he took you but refused to tell me where. I finally figured it out and had to have Seth tell me where the key was."

"Seth helped you?"

Tristan held me at arm's length so his precious stone eyes could rake over my body. "He still loves Joel, even if he can't admit it. After leading me here, he went back to protect your friend."

"Take me there. I need to fight with them." Pushing him away was the hardest thing I'd ever done, but I couldn't think until there was some space between us. When he was so close to me, I felt like I was underwater.

"I knew you would want to fight." Tristan's golden hair was tangled, and his jacket was torn at the sleeves exposing the coppery skin of his shoulder. "First, come with me for one last experiment."

I closed my eyes. "There isn't time. I have to go and fight. Zain saw Christophe and Calhoun talking, so—"

"They were talking about me." Tristan's eyes sparkled as he stared at me. "By now I'm sure you've realized Christophe wants you and so the obvious solution is to give me to Calhoun. He gets rids of me and doesn't have to sacrifice your kind. Win-win situation for him."

"I won't lose you. I love you."

Tristan's hands were warm on my face as he cupped my chin and hesitantly kissed me, his tongue darted into my mouth as he took possession of my lips. "For now, everything is fine. Calhoun has called off the fighting while they try and locate me. Don't worry about your friends or your family because in this moment, everything is okay."

"Once Christophe sees me with you, he's going to attack. We have to get away."

"You're the only one who believes like I do. Please, just one more attempt?"

How could I think of denying him when he stared at me with such raw possession and trust? "Where do you want to go?"

"To a royal tree."

Then I was scooped into his arms, and we fled from the room. The hallway was narrow and just as white as the room I'd been entombed in.

The swishing of water was louder and assaulted my ears. Tristan held me tightly against his body, and I could hear his pulse racing as we fled through the hallway and into the open space of the castle. Before I had the chance to take in my surroundings, Tristan spread his dark feathery wings and we were lifted into the air.

The Castle de Mar transformed into a tiny shack as we gained height and were overtaken by fierce gusts of wind trying to hold us back. Not knowing when I'd have another chance, I wound my fingers into Tristan's hair and kissed the nape of his neck. He inhaled sharply and tightened his grip on me.

"So easily you can unarm me. Even when there is so much else to take in, all I can ever see is you," Tristan whispered as he bent his head so he could take the brunt of the wind. I saw his bag strapped across his side and a single flower threaded with weeded cords peeking out.

"Whose tree?" I asked as we started to descend into the thicket.

We'd landed on a small island no larger than my house with a thin thread of water on one side and a waterfall cascading off the side of the cliff. Across the ribbons of water, I could see the south shore and some of the trees we'd been destined to protect.

"I don't remember having to protect any of the trees on this island," I informed Tristan, thinking he'd made a mistake.

Tristan had his back to me as he stared at the ocean, the unruly wind tousling his hair and clothes. "This is the right place."

"Are you sure you didn't mean across the lake on the mainland? There are Dryma trees over there."

"No." His voice was low and husky, sending ripples of need down my spine. "I didn't make a mistake. It's just… this tree isn't as important as the others."

"How can that be?"

A colossal weeping willow stood imposingly in the center of the island, and I wondered how I could've missed it. The trunk looked like it was made of intricate rope woven together to form the cherry-brown bark. Some of the leaves clung to the summer by refusing to let go of the vibrant green color, while also admitting defeat and accepting yellows and oranges. Octopus-like branches danced intricately, weaving together like DNA strands. Half of the tree appeared to be hanging from the cliff, but I saw the roots firmly fixed in the rough dirt of the island.

"This tree isn't as important as the others." Tristan pressed his palm flat against a knob in the trunk and stared at the pebbles clustered around the base. "Since it belongs to me."

"How can you say this tree isn't important? Are you seeing what I am? This tree is remarkable... like you."

Tristan gave me a look that suggested he couldn't fathom what I saw in the magnificent tree.

I turned away, letting my hair cover my facial expression so he wouldn't see the tears clinging to my eyes. All this time, how had I not noticed the beauty lying in the trees? The absolute fragility clinging to the branches and the immense strength surging upward from their trunks?

"Look at me," Tristan pleaded, letting his hand fall to his side.

"No."

"Why not?"

"I'm embarrassed."

"Of crying? That only shows you're compassionate. Let me see you."

"No."

"Please let me see your face. I want to imprint your features into my mind."

Slowly, I looked up at him, wiping my eyes with the back of my hand. "Don't experiment on your tree. There is still time for you to run. I will stay and guard your tree for the rest of my life."

Tristan pressed his lips together in a thin line, and I could tell he was barely keeping it together. "Do you know why the Sidhee betrayed your kind?"

I shook my head, confused by the sudden change of subject.

"This is something I should have told you long ago, but I was afraid of you hating me. You know how my mother was a Kuro and that she died shortly after giving birth to me?"

"Yes."

"There is more to that story, and I purposely concealed it." Tristan stared at the tree like this was his last opportunity. "The King of the Sidhee, Calhoun's father, was in love with my mother. Your father agreed to give her to him as a farewell present, and then your kind would've been free to fly where you wish. But my mother instead fell in love with the Dryma king and conceived me. As punishment for not fulfilling the Kuro's end of the bargain, the Sidhee king killed my mother and cursed her child, me. He took away the Kuro's freedom because he felt betrayed.

Of course, this wasn't your father's fault, but all the same, Calhoun's father blamed him."

"What did he do to curse you?" I was rooted to my spot, just like the trees, when all I wanted was to pull him against me.

"That day you saved Christophe and me from drowning, I bonded to you."

"That's not possible. I bonded to you first." I remembered the tears he'd given me, the ones I'd infused into my soap.

"If you had bonded to me first, you might've been able to hide it. But it was me who was hiding from you."

I remembered what Chiaki had said about keeping his mating a secret from Aiden. But if it had been Aiden who was primary, he would've had to accept him before Chiaki would've realized.

The primary mate was the stronger one and had to accept before the ritual was complete.

My throat felt dry. "I don't see how there is a connection between our bonding and the Sidhee stealing the Kuro's wings."

"Ever since you saved our lives, I've loved you all this time. I thought I was strong enough to keep you from ever finding out, but when I saw you in the Crystal Cove, my resolve broke. Even if our time together was short, at least I got to experience true happiness with you."

"Why are you talking like this? Where do you think you're going?" I stammered, moving closer to him. If I could just get him to hold on to me, maybe I could talk some sense into him.

"I love you, and I'll do anything for you. So you need to kill me, and then you'll be free."

"You aren't making any sense. And I would rather die than harm you."

"Don't you understand? The curse the Sidhee put on me. The reason it would've been better for you to hate me… it's because I am the key to your freedom. All you have to do is kill me, and your wings will be released."

"You're the stone Christophe was talking about?"

Tristan nodded solemnly.

"There has to be another way of restoring our wings without harming you."

Tristan sighed, a heavy sound that swarmed like thousands of bees around my head. "There is no other way. There is nothing left in this world for you. A dead end. Kill me, take your wings, and fly away."

"But the flowers? What was the point in you studying genetics, in growing them if they won't work?"

"I wanted them to work so desperately because it meant I could've been with you." Tristan scooped the flower from his bag and cradled the tender petals. "I know you told the Sidhee we didn't want to complete the contract."

My jaw dropped. "Then this is my fault. Everything. You're not to blame. I am."

"Even so."

Tristan reached into his pants pocket and withdrew a knife. As he unsheathed it, I saw a gaping hole in the tree where the bark had been scraped away. A stab to the exposed flesh of the trunk would result in more than a flesh wound. He would die.

"At the time, you hadn't recognized me as your mate, but I was grateful you saved me from a loveless marriage to Calhoun. I had no way of knowing whether or not you would accept me after we met at the Crystal Cove, so I prepared myself for an attack at the ball. But to my surprise, you had already accepted me as your mate."

"You expected me to kill you?" I whispered.

"For the sake of your freedom, yes."

"Haven't you been listening when I tell you how much I love you?" Even if I did manage to get close enough, I wasn't strong enough to wrestle the knife away. "I refuse to harm you."

"Then I'll do it myself."

"Wait!" I screamed, my arm outstretched as if I could will the knife into my own flesh. "You say you love me. Show me... one last time."

For the longest moment, I waited to see if Tristan would strike the tree. Ever so slowly, he lowered the knife until the blade clattered on top of the rocks. "Christophe and Calhoun are looking for me, and time is short. But when you plead with me to take you, how can I refuse?"

I released a breath I didn't realize I'd been holding. Pulling my shirt off, I felt the cold air slap my already tender skin. Tristan watched as I shucked off my pants and briefs, my body naked and ready for the taking.

"I won't be gentle," Tristan whispered as he slid his jacket from his shoulders and reached into his pants for a condom. "Luckily I have this to use as lubricant, but I'm still going to take you hard. So you'll remember."

I bit back my tears and let him push me face first into the bark of the tree. The usual scent of smoke, dirt, and insects was absent. Instead, the only scent I caught was Tristan's. I heard him discard his pants and then the sound of foil being ripped. His fingers were at my entrance, prodding deep inside so he could stretch me.

He gained possession of my neck, biting and kissing with such intensity, I knew I'd have purplish bruise marks for weeks to come. My plea had been a way of giving me time to think of a plan, but my reasoning was rendered incapable.

"Are you ready?" Tristan breathed into my ear, parting my hair with one hand while his other hand dug into the flesh of my hip. "My intention is for you to remember what it feels like to have me buried inside of you, but I don't want to harm you."

"You won't," I assured him, clinging to the tree. I felt the harsh bark beneath my nails as he impaled me in one swift thrust.

Gasping, I pressed my forehead to the tree to stabilize myself. The sticky heat of his cock entering me over and over drove me into a lust-filled frenzy. No matter what I did, I couldn't get him close enough.

"How can you even think this is enough?" I gasped through pain liquefying into pleasure. "I'll never accept this. I'll never let you die."

Tristan stopped his movements inside me so he could press a hand to my forehead, gently easing my skin away from the trunk of the tree. His other hand wrapped around my body and gently stroked my hardened length.

"No more talking."

His voice was soft, but I relented because he was right. If I managed to stop Tristan from killing his tree, he could easily turn around and destroy himself another way. I refused to believe he would be gone from my life, but his will was stronger than mine.

He was the primary mate, the one who dictated who could bring me to my knees with simple words.

Over and over, he thrust inside of me while he whispered words of love into my ear. Like a knife, he cut deep into the core of my being, forcing me to relent and accept his love while at the same time, knowing there was little time left.

"Come for me, Kanji," he ordered as his thrust lifted me from my feet.

My legs tightened and my head grew fuzzy with warmth. "No, I'm not ready to let you go."

But his hand on my shaft forced me into a breathtaking climax where my eyes rolled into the back of my head and an aching moan forced its way from deep within my stomach. Tristan emptied himself into me, panting and moaning my name with such fervor he made "Kanji" sound like an absolution rather than a name.

After easing out of me, he helped me back into my pants, pressing kisses up my thighs and stomach.

In the moment it took me to slip back into my shirt so I didn't freeze to death, he had put his pants back on and had the knife once again in his hand.

"I'm begging you," I put my hand on his to steady him. "Don't."

"Kanji, kiss me."

He had my back pressed up against the tree, the gaping hole exposed just to the right of me. With his free hand, he cupped my chin and enveloped me in a scorching kiss I thought would burst my heart.

I wrapped my arms around him as if my meager strength was enough to keep him there with me. The tears bursting from my eyes were like shattered glass, and I did nothing to stop them. His lips stayed firmly pressed to mine, and I ran through every possibility I could in order to save him. Every option I hadn't exhausted.

He had the single flower discarded at the base of the trunk and maybe, just maybe, this time the transfer of energy would work.

There was a cord wound around the tree where it had connected to the tree, so maybe his experiment was to knife the tree without dying. I convinced myself he wasn't really going to die and that he was simply putting on a show for me to prove human science and our ancient magic could be united to create peace.

The last scent of flowers swarmed around me as Tristan raised his arm and buried the knife into the base of the tree.

I expected him to scream or cry out, but there was only silence. Using the tree as leverage, I held him as he slumped onto me. His eyes were glossed over, the bright green color fading like the leaves of his tree.

"Please," I sobbed. "Please stay with me. I don't care about my wings. I don't care about my freedom. Make me your slave for life if that's what you want. Just don't die."

His eyes locked onto mine, and he moved his lips, but no sound came out. I felt the familiar twinge in my shoulder blades, but I could feel the wings beating faintly inside.

"No, I won't let you die." I eased him to the ground and reached for his flower.

My uncle had said I would find a mate who would save my tribe, who would save me, but I refused to believe this was what he meant. Without my mate, I was as good as dead.

"Come on, flower, work dammit." I fidgeted with the weeded cord around the tree and placed the flower on top of Tristan's chest. His breathing was slow and labored, a crimson stain of blood pooling across his chest like a butterfly. "This flower, it can still work. Put what's left of your life into here, and then we'll both be free. Please, Tristan, please."

His eyes closed, and his head sagged to the side like a stuffed doll. How was it, I couldn't even save my mate, yet my kind believed me to be a revered prince?

"Why am I so weak?" I sobbed, clinging to the threads of Tristan's jacket for dear life. "Why?"

As Tristan's breathing slowed, I could feel the increased pressure of my wings as they dared to tear apart my skin. I saw the seal the Dryma had placed on my inner wrist fading. I barely had enough time to discard my shirt before I felt the sting of my wings protruding from my tender skin. The silky feathers fluttered against my arms and shot surges of relief through my body.

Dropping to my knees, I cradled Tristan in my arms and swatted at his cheeks in an effort to wake him. When he didn't stir, I pushed the flower into the bag and strung the strap onto my shoulder. "I'm going to save you. The Dryma in you may have died, but the Kuro in you belongs to me."

I could hear screams coming from the reserve where the fighting had started again. Two sets of arms gripped my arms from behind and when I managed to turn my head, I saw Zain and Tomas with their inky wings.

"Take him out of here before Christophe comes back," Seth told them as he knelt beside Tristan and pressed a hand to his fallen prince's chest. "I'll do what I can."

Whatever had transpired between Zain, Tomas, and Seth had occurred while I was unable to see their thoughts, but they had somehow united.

"Let me go," I screamed, violently thrashing against their grips. "I have to save him. I have to do something."

"It's too late." Zain's voice was quiet as he pulled me into a viselike grip. "We have to get you out of here."

"That's my mate." I reached for Tristan, my fingers just out of reach of his skin. "No! Let me go. I'm your prince."

"Which is why we have to save you," Tomas whispered. "Come on."

My wings, what I'd wanted for so long, were like heavy bindings clinging to my back. My friends tore me from Tristan's bleeding form and spiraled up into the air. Seth closed his eyes as he crouched dutifully over my mate's form, but it should've been me down there with him.

"Stop, I need to be with him."

They were silent. I could feel the sadness leaking from them as they tore me farther and farther from Tristan until all I could make out were the fading branches of his beloved tree.

His flower broke loose from my bag and whirled to the lake below. I tore from their iron grips and dove down with both arms outstretched. When the silky petals touched my skin once more, I could feel the faintest pulsing of life. My feet skimmed the top of the water, my heavy wings beating behind me like the crescendo of my heart.

The weight of Tristan's love plowed into me. All this time, he'd loved me and had been waiting for a time when I would destroy him for the sake of my freedom. And even though he'd expected me to betray him, he'd also been hoping I wouldn't.

My mate had truly believed in the flowers saving both the Dryma and the Kuro. And so did I. Even if it was a vain, foolish thought, I would never let go of what he'd believed in.

I refused to believe the pulsing of Tristan's flower in my hand was just a coincidence.

Other Kuro had joined Zain and Tomas, but although they were fast, they could not keep up with me. I dove back down to the island and gathered Tristan's body. Before Seth could stop me, I was in the air with my mate locked within my arms.

I would never let him go.

ANA RAINE writes because she loves to believe in magic, dragons, and that there is more to life than what human eyes can see. Ana lives in Michigan where, when it's not snowy and wet, there are beautiful state parks and lakes to visit. When she was eighteen, she married her best friend and they live with their two cats, Mason and Misaki. Ana has celiac disease, but that hasn't stopped her from learning how to cook and bake so she can eat tasty treats. Fudge, enchiladas, and anything involving yucca/cassava are her absolute favorite.

Ana has studied in Osaka, Japan where she learned about theater and drama. She would love to go back after she is sure her Japanese is efficient enough. Ana loves anything to do with foxes, especially Arctic foxes. One day, Ana will find a way to incorporate her love of foxes into a novel, but until then, she'll stay focused on fairies, shape shifters, and mythology.

Feel free to stop by her blog for tasty recipes, freebies, and more.
Blog: anarainebooks.blogspot.com
Twitter: @AuthorAnaRaine
E-mail: anaraine@rocketmail.com

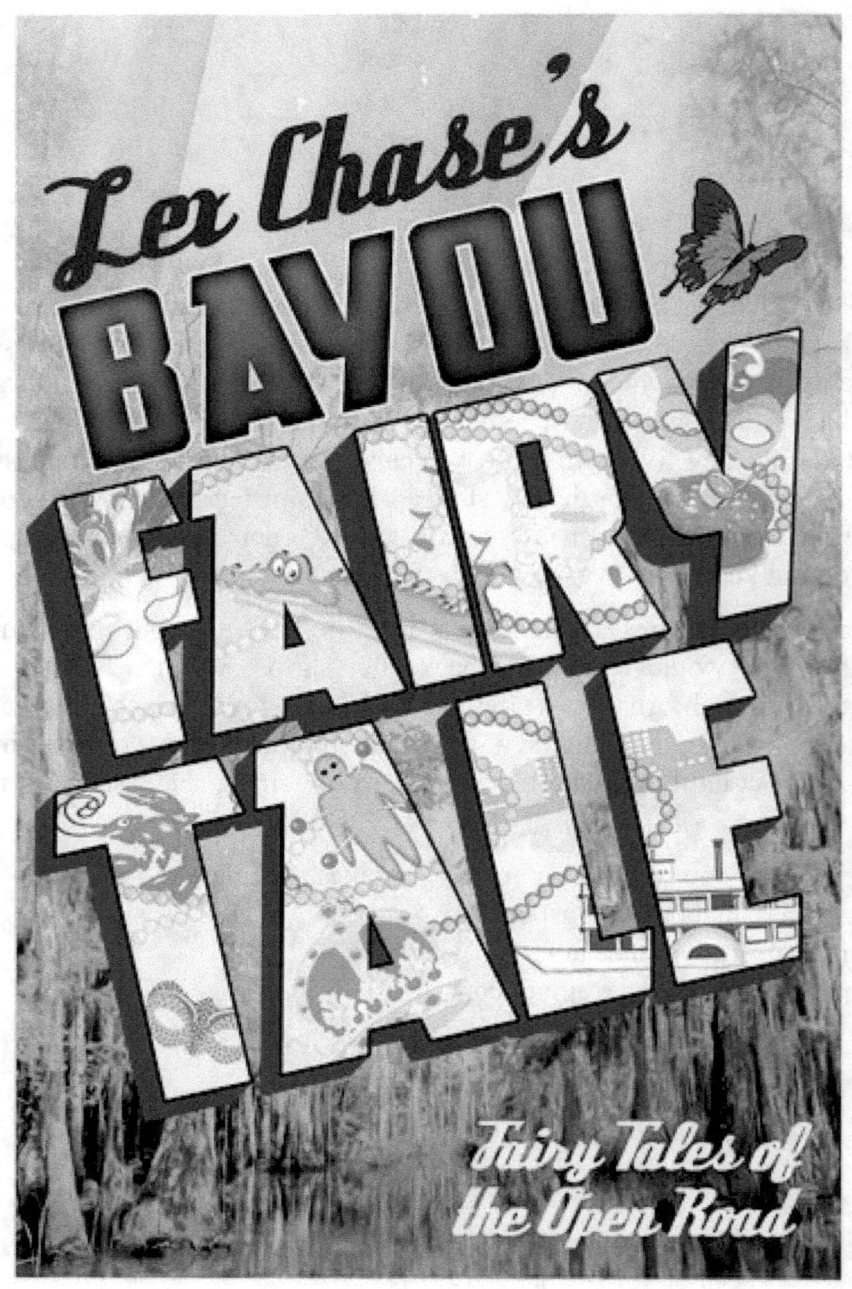

Betrothed
A FAERY TALE

THERESE WOODSON

www.dreamspinnerpress.com

Cardinal Sins

LISSA KASEY

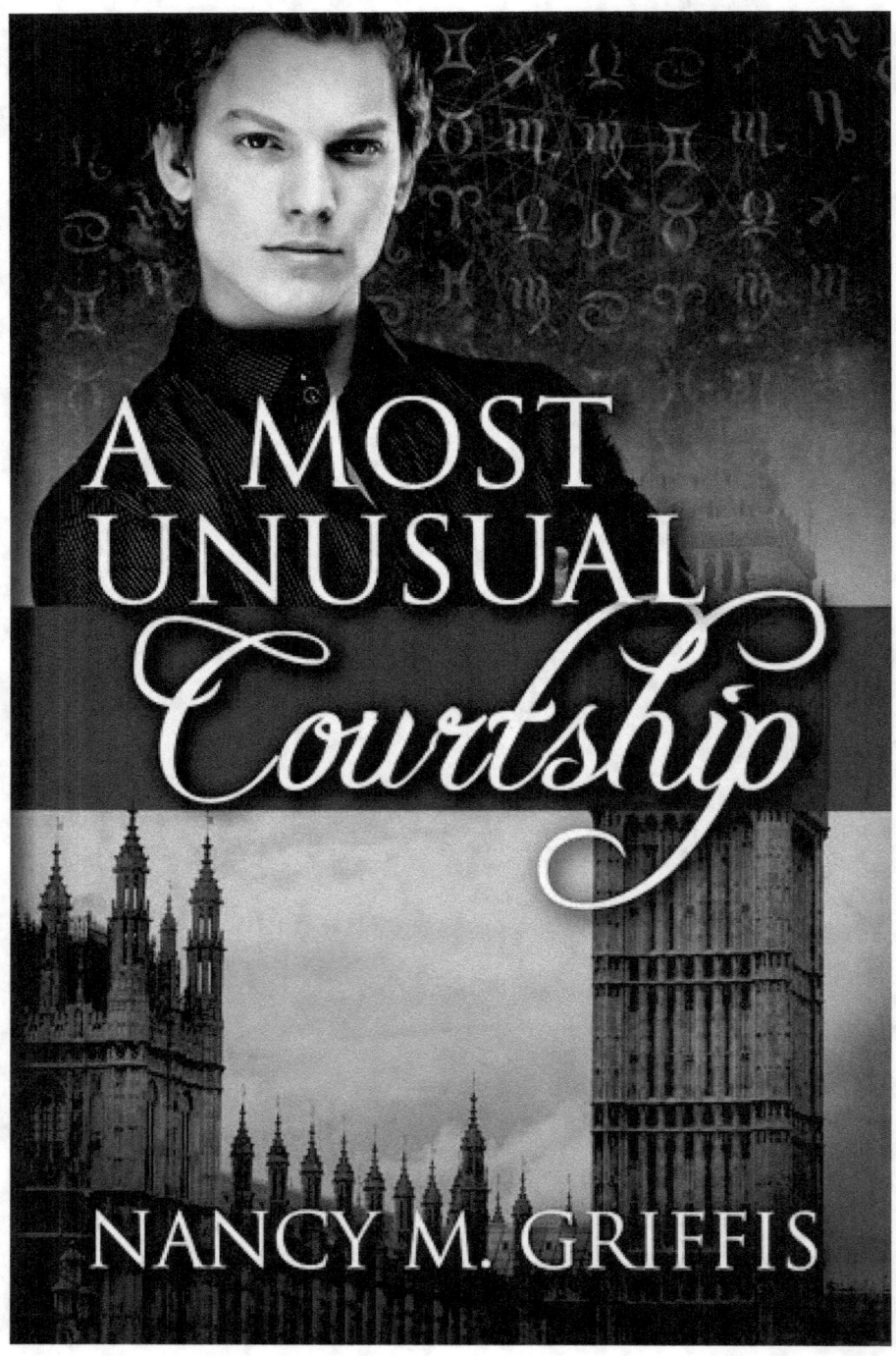

A MOST UNUSUAL Courtship

NANCY M. GRIFFIS

www.dreamspinnerpress.com

www.ingramcontent.com/pod-product-compliance
Lightning Source LLC
Chambersburg PA
CBHW070122260626
47160CB00004B/1578